IT TAKES A KILLER

J.S.GIBBS

SHEDLOAD BOOKS

BERKSHIRE ENGLAND

ALSO BY J.S. GIBBS:

Beyond Understanding

Lost Souls and Favourite Places.

CHAPTER 1

"Arch, Arch, get your shoes on and we'll go for a bike ride to see the horses."

For the umpteenth time John Krill silently tutted, his lips barely moving as he mouthed 'Arch'. What sort of a name was that to be called, poor kid? The three year old had no doubt been officially registered as Archie rather than the more outmoded Archibald, but even this diminutive was seldom used by either of the boy's parents, who lived next door.

"Honey, can you help Arch put his shoes on and find his helmet?"

Honey? For some reason Krill also found the use of that word annoying. Was it jealousy? He'd been called honey himself a few times, or 'hon', but not recently, probably not for several years, and definitely never by either of his wives! Nor had he been anyone's sweetheart for some considerable time; so yes there was without doubt an element of resentment.

Krill had learned quite a lot about his neighbours since they'd moved in; he'd put up with twenty months of daily, sometimes hourly, disturbance of his peace and quiet. The level of disruption had really taken off when they'd placed a piano adjacent to the party wall, which was next to the dining room where he did all his writing, or at least it was where he was attempting to write his memoirs. Unfortunately for his neighbours, their predecessors had been an extremely quiet and soft spoken middle-aged couple, who seldom had visitors, and like him, both relished and preserved the serenity which village life had to offer.

He hadn't used his undoubted professional expertise to investigate 'The Honeys', as he called them, or snooped, or deliberately eavesdropped, but he'd picked up lots of snippets about their complicated lives, mainly from the numerous phone conversations held in their garden, where he could even hear the loudspeaker responses of Ma or Pa or Lysander or Georgina or whichever friend or relative they were constantly chatting to! Thank God they were only renting, which gave him hope that they might soon move.

"Let's go Arch."

Arch - umpteenth plus one! Strangest of all had been the recent conversation between Mrs Honey and a friend or relation about what they should call their rather fractious six month old, who thus far had been consistently referred to as 'William'. It went something like: 'We haven't registered his birth yet because of Covid, so we could change it. I do like William, and even Will at a pinch, but now I'm worried that he might end up being called Willie, and that would be just too awful!'

How ridiculous, thought Krill; evidently 'Arch' was OK, but Willie wasn't! At least it was a recognisable name and not an architectural feature or a prefix. After hearing the conversation, he tried to recall some famous Willie's or Willy's and didn't get very far: Willie Thorne the snooker player, and Willie Whitelaw the politician. He didn't think 'Boxcar Willie' would count. Her husband was Richard to other adults, but not he assumed 'Rick' or 'Ricky', and definitely never - perish the thought - Dick!

Yes, they could certainly mentor people in the art of how to annoy your neighbour. A bike ride meant half an hour to an hour of relative peace and quiet; a chance to snooze, recumbent on his deckchair in the hot Berkshire sunshine; or read undisturbed, provided 'Mr Honey' stopped William from yelling too loudly in his cot and did not put him outside in his pram!

Grumpiness, or possibly even being a curmudgeon, seemed to have come upon Krill quite suddenly. He didn't have a decent excuse - he was very fit for his sixty eight years, and had no serious aches or pains - no gout, rheumatism, sore knees, or bad back, which might justify his increasing irritability. Would he have become thinner skinned with age even without months of provocation? He would argue that it was a temporary bout of impatience, which would be resolved the instant his neighbours moved, or were evicted. Of the two, he had to admit that he favoured the latter, which probably added a generous dose of vindictiveness to the melting pot of uncharitable thoughts.

7

Certain words heard over the high hedge made his ears prick up. Obviously, even the slightest hint of dissatisfaction with where they were living and the possibility of renting somewhere cheaper, but also any mention of a holiday, or even a day on the parental boat. His hopes had risen when there'd been talk of them going away in August to visit a sister in the north of England, but they'd been subsequently dashed by distraught comments by Mrs Honey that they couldn't really afford a holiday this year. And how could he arrange any short or longer jaunt of his own without knowing whether it would clash with a lengthy absence of the Honeys? That would be the ultimate miscalculation - to be away from his precious cottage when the longed for peace finally descended.

He'd just found his way back into the intricacies of a Booker Prize winning novel when there was a cough at the gate. He looked up, both surprised and slightly alarmed.

"Inspector Krill?"

He hadn't been called that for a while, and anyway it was Chief Inspector. He inwardly groaned. Was it a budding novelist wanting to pick his brains about police methods? A journalist trying to investigate an old case - he'd had his fair share of those over the years. A relative of a failed victim or of someone he'd arrested, still seeking justice or retribution? How had this woman found out where he lived, and how did she have the audacity to come to his cottage!

The sun disappeared behind a cloud and he got a better look at her. Mmmm he thought, very attractive, especially the free flowing dark hair; late forties or fifties, well dressed, around five six in height. Was there an accent? The way she'd said 'Inspector' had sounded slightly foreign. He rubbed his cheek; fortunately he'd already shaved, and his tee shirt was fairly fresh. He stood up.

"Can I help you?" he asked.

"You are Inspector Krill?"

Definitely an accent, maybe East European.

"Yes, well I'm retired now; have been for some time."

"Can I come in?"

By 'in' he assumed she meant through the gate and into his garden.

"Let me get that," he said, "the latch is a little rusty."

He held it open and she came down the two small steps. As she squeezed past him he revised his earlier estimates and updated his assessment: five seven, maybe a well preserved mid fifties, very nice legs and bum, expensive perfume.

She automatically held out her hand and then sheepishly withdrew it. It was one of the few he might have been tempted to take in his own since it had become more or less proscribed due to Covid.

"I am Malgorzata Worciecawoska," she announced.

He hoped that she wasn't expecting him to spell it or even repeat it accurately! So, probably Polish then. He rather liked her accent. Her voice was a little deeper than average, which to him equated with sensuousness.

9

She continued: "I have seen you in the village. Once I think, when I am with Graham. Graham, he points you out and says that it is the famous police inspector who caught the serial killer. Another time we come down this lane and he tells me this is the house of Inspector Krill."

"Graham?" he enquired.

"Yes, Graham Standish. Maybe you have met him? He is sometimes going to the public house by the river, and he is, sorry was, on the parish council."

Krill nodded. "Yes, I have heard his name mentioned by a few people. Are you two friends?"

"We were to be married in Warsaw this autumn," she explained.

He smiled, still very confused about her visit. Had this Graham Standish sent her, and if so why? He looked at her expectantly.

"You see Inspector, I believe that my Graham has been murdered!"

CHAPTER 2

Krill was still processing her rather alarming statement, when there was the clinking sound of next door's double gates being swung open. Not a long cycle ride then for Archie.

"You'd better come inside, Malg…"

"Margaret is the English for my name. Graham found that easier too."

They both ducked their heads as they went in, him more so than her. His small cottage was perfect for one, an intimate two at a pinch, but was not ideal for guests. He suggested that she sat on the well-worn sofa, and quickly removed the as yet unread Sunday paper from it. It wasn't until she was seated, that he realised she was the first person to enter his domain for many weeks. Too late now to worry about viruses, he thought.

"Can I get you some tea, or a coffee, Margaret? I have quite a good machine for coffee, and could even manage a cappuccino."

"Yes, thank you Inspector, a cappuccino would be very nice."

"Please, no more 'Inspector'. John; could you perhaps call me John?"

She smiled. "OK, John."

Lovely smile. Had he not been definitely dead, and possibly murdered, Krill would have considered Graham to be a very fortunate man. But then he'd probably been like so many in the village - financially 'comfortable' or wealthy, and therefore a 'catch'; whereas his own assets and his police pension had been severely drained by the divorce settlements. He was lucky to have been able to buy a property in the Royal Borough at all, never mind one described as having character, and with a garden and parking to boot!

As he was whisking the warmed milk, the ivory plonks of a Beachboy's melody erupted through the wall. He used to like 'Wouldn't it be nice?' but hearing it fifty times in just a few days would cause even the most avid Beach Boys fan to waiver. So his response to the question posed was without doubt a resounding 'NO!', it's not nice at all, not one little bit, and especially not when I have a guest!

He placed the cappuccino on the low table at her feet and closed the dining room door.

"Does your wife play the piano?"

"My wife? No, I'm not married."

Margaret looked quite confused.

"Oh the piano? It's being played next door. So, Margaret, tell me about Graham."

She took a tissue from the small handbag on her lap and wiped her eyes.

"It is still so difficult to speak about. He was a very nice man, a true gentleman: kind, amusing, thoughtful. Always wanting to buy me a gift, always planning to take me somewhere - Ascot, Henley Regatta, Wimbledon. And holidays too - Rome, Paris, Barcelona." She glanced away and sighed, lost briefly in her memories "We were together for almost three years. It is perhaps the happiest time of my life since I leave Poland more than thirty years ago."

"And you were to be married?" he asked.

"Yes. I am divorced and he is a widower. My house in North London is being sold, and I was coming to live with him here." Margaret frowned quite severely as she reached the crux of the matter that was troubling her. "But his son is the very big problem - always difficult, always trying to make trouble; more and more since he knows that his father wants to marry me. I met him only once and he was the opposite of his father. Graham apologised and said it was nothing to do with me, with who I am, that his son had been the same with other people. 'Offhand' is the word he used; very rude and impolite is how I would describe it!"

He knew a little about second marriages.

"It's not easy for children if their parents remarry, even though they may want them to be happy. My father married for a second time in his sixties, after my mother died, and it made things awkward, for both myself and my brother."

"Yes, I understand this, but you or your brother did not kill your father to stop him, did you?"

"No," he said smiling, "that wouldn't have gone down at all well with my colleagues." Besides which, he thought,

13

given the difficult choice, he would have much preferred the removal of his would-be stepmother! But what if the relationship between father and son was poor? Might a child in those circumstances see the elimination of their parent as a means of avoiding all future problems, and also a way to profit immediately? Could an engagement act as a 'wake up call'? It still seemed very unlikely to Krill, even if there was no love lost between father and son.

"Why do you believe that Graham was murdered, I assume by his son?"

"Oh it is so obvious! It is so convenient for his son to stop him from marrying me. He will inherit a fortune, so his motive is very big. Graham had talked about changing his will, and maybe he spoke of it to his son and this was the katalizator, the catalyst. Now I do not even know what was in his will." She paused. "But please do not think that I wished to marry him for his money. I may not be as rich as Graham, but I have my own house and no mortgage, and I have an income from paying guests." She had a further thought: "And I have been a British Citizen for many years because my husband was English. I wanted to marry Graham because he makes me happy, and now I want justice for him!"

"What evidence do you have, Margaret? His son may have been upset at the idea of him marrying you, and he probably worried about how it would affect his inheritance - those feelings would be quite normal - however, to commit murder, now that's another matter entirely. I'm sure it happens, but very very rarely in my experience. It's much more likely to be a plot in a crime novel than in real life. I can't think of any murders which I investigated, or those dealt with by my colleagues, where a father planning to remarry was the cause."

"But you will agree that it is a possible motive?" She was almost pleading with him to see that she was right.

He wasn't convinced. "Yes of course it's possible, but as I say, based on the evidence, it's most unlikely."

"How can you be so certain when you have not yet heard all the evidence!"

"No, you're right." Was he humouring her because she was so attractive? Probably. "How did Graham die?"

"How he died and how they say he died are two separate things. They say he got the virus, but I do not believe that, because he was a very healthy man for his age, and he took great care not to catch it."

"How old was Graham?" he asked.

A sad shadow crossed her face. "He was only sixty five, and very fit, very active."

Active? Krill wondered what that meant? That he played golf, cycled, walked for miles, or something else? He pictured for a moment Graham being highly active with her. It was a bittersweet image.

"There would have been a death certificate, Margaret, and the person signing it would have to be satisfied that it was due to natural causes."

"Yes, this is true, I know this, but the son is a very clever man, he would have found a way. Maybe he is calling Graham's doctor and saying that his father has the virus, then he says he is worse, then he says that he is dead. Did the doctor even come to see the body? Maybe, maybe not. But what can he see if he does come? Just my Graham cold and lifeless in bed. Do you not think, Inspector, that now would be a very good time to commit a murder because of so many deaths that are occurring, especially if you were a cunning selfish person who thought his inheritance was going to be stolen? What is one more elderly person dying amongst so many? He would think he could slip it through the net."

Krill hadn't really thought about it but had to admit that there was some logic to her argument. In all probability, not every death was being examined as thoroughly as it would have been prior to the pandemic. Maybe people in authority made assumptions and cut corners because they had no time to do otherwise?

So far Margaret had made the case for a motive and a possible opportunity, but what about means? He asked her to explain how she thought Graham's son might have committed the crime.

"That is so easy - poison!" She said it with some venom of her own. "His son is a chemist so he knows about such things. He waits until I am away visiting my mother. Perhaps Graham tells him that I will be in Warsaw for several weeks, and he seizes the opportunity. He visits Graham and puts something in a drink or in his food. He even takes his phone and sends me a message to say he is feeling ill and he hopes it isn't the virus. But I know this message is not really from Graham because of what it says."

"But if he was feeling unwell when he sent it, then it could account for it being different. Do you still have the message?"

"Of course. But the problem for the son, his big mistake, is that Graham would never send this message to me if he was ill; never. And for two reasons: first he would not wish me to worry, so he would wait until he was better and then possibly tell me; and second, he was a very proud man who would not want to show any signs of weakness, or growing older, or admit that he was in any way vulnerable. It is because I am a young woman and he sometimes worries that I am maybe too young for him, so he hides anything which makes him appear older. He loses weight, he changes the way he dresses, his hairstyle, how he spends his leisure time, and it is all because he meets me. He tells me this, and how I have made him a young man again."

Krill couldn't stop himself from holding in his stomach and smoothing down his short sparse hair. He'd been worried about going bald ever since he'd been at university and a disgruntled barber, with an axe to grind, had complained about all the lazy longhaired students on the streets of Birmingham. He had then tapped the back of Krill's head with a comb, and said that he would soon lose his own hair if he didn't have it cut more regularly. That curse had come true a few years later, when he'd spotted a pink patch in the mirror; this had spread, and even worse, he had started to go thinner on top. Finding a stylist who could put off the inevitable without resorting to a combover had been a priority for several decades, but when all the hairdressers had closed he had been forced to cut it himself using a long discarded beard trimmer. He hoped that his grey buzzcut made him look a little like a retired astronaut rather than just a bald old codger!

"You see, Graham always wanted to be there to care for me, to look after me, and not the other way around; so this message that I received from him was totally out of character. When I try to speak to Graham on the phone there is no reply - nothing. Then, by the time I come home the funeral is over, and now I see there is already a For Sale sign in the garden. Why would the son be so quick with all these things unless he has something terrible to hide?"

"How did you find out that he'd died?" he asked.

"Not from his son, no! It is from a friend in the village, who we sometimes meet in the pub, and once he invited her and her husband to dinner. She sent me a message saying what a dreadful thing to have happened, and how she is so sorry, and what a wonderful person he was. At first I wonder what she is talking about, and who is this wonderful person? So I ask her, and she is so shocked that I do not know about my own fiancé!"

"Did you try talking to his son?"

"Yes, of course, but he ignores my messages and does not return my calls. I am hoping that you will find out what happened, and whether there is any proof of foul play."

What could he do? Not very much. He could probably see the Death Certificate and make some enquiries about Graham's son. He knew that he would only be able to obtain a copy of the will before probate was granted, if the executors agreed, which was very unlikely; and anyway, how would that help? If Graham had been in the process of drawing up an alternative will then seeing it might be of some relevance, but client confidentiality did not usually end when a person died, so a solicitor would be unlikely to tell him about its contents, even if there was one in existence.

"Was Graham cremated?" It seemed a little harsh even as he said it, just blurting out a query regarding the disposal of a loved one's remains, but it was important information.

"Yes, I think so, although I believe that he wanted to be buried. He did not say this to me in so many words, but we would often walk through the churchyard here and he would smile and say how peaceful it was." Another tear ran down her cheek which she quickly wiped away. "I do not even know what has happened to his ashes. Perhaps his son has not bothered to collect them? Do you not think that it is very horrible for me to be treated this way?"

So, he thought, any evidence of poisoning would have literally gone up in smoke. Krill knew that it was impossible to find even the slightest traces of DNA after cremation.

"Let me write down a few details about Graham, what you know about his son, and how I can contact you again. I think you shouldn't expect me to be able to find out anything useful, any significant evidence of a crime, if one was committed, but I will do what I can."

"Thank you Inspector. At least I will know that we have tried to get justice for him."

"You haven't approached the police about this?" he asked.

"No, do you think I should?"

"No, not at this stage; let's keep it between ourselves. I don't think you should mention your concerns to anyone else." He worried that if she started telling other people that Graham's son was a murderer, then she might end up in court herself. "Best not to forewarn him, if a crime has been committed. Better to let him continue to think that he's got away with it."

"Yes, you are right! And I knew that it was the right thing to do, to come to see you. I believe it was not just a coincidence that Graham tells me about you and even shows me where I can find you. Maybe he has a premonition that one day this could happen to him!"

CHAPTER 3

A few days later Krill and Margaret were having lunch in the garden of a gastropub located in a nearby town, which was famed for its many antique shops. Before the virus changed everything, he hadn't even known that it had an outdoor area; he now felt that he'd somehow missed out on a treat by not bothering to see what was hidden behind the eighteenth century building. He'd eaten there several times in different seasons, sometimes in the dining room next to a roaring log fire, but mostly in the crowded bar; he remembered that they prided themselves on having a very wide selection of gins.

He was feeling rather euphoric, because Margaret had seemed quite eager to see him again when he'd phoned her, and, as an added bonus, his neighbours were definitely away! He didn't know for how long, but he hoped it would be for several days or even for a week or two. It was like living in a different cottage when 'the Honeys' were away. That morning, as he'd sat outside the front porch holding his mug of black coffee, he'd marvelled at the mostly natural sounds of the pigeons flapping past and calling out, of insects buzzing busily around him, and the occasional short hum of a solitary plane in the sky or of a car travelling down a nearby road. No phones, no piano, no loud chatter, no screaming baby! It had all seemed very peaceful, and definitely not the kind of place where coldblooded patricide could be committed!

"You said on the telephone that you had news?"

"Yes, but it might not be what you were hoping for, Margaret."

"So, what is it that you have found Inspect... John?"

"Well, I managed to speak to Graham's doctor, who owed me a favour because I helped his son a few years ago; he was happy to tell me off the record what he knew, which wasn't much. What he did say was that he was entirely satisfied that his death was from natural causes."

She didn't seem impressed. "He would say that, wouldn't he, or he would be in big trouble."

"Yes, that's true," he admitted. "His GP was a little surprised that Graham had succumbed to the virus, because he was still quite young and as far as he knew there were no underlying serious health conditions."

"I tell you that Graham was a very fit man."

Krill tried not to regurgitate his earlier jealous thoughts about Graham's fitness 'activities'.

"But he and his colleagues had seen other similar cases, and some which involved even younger patients who'd caught it and died, so it didn't start any alarm bells ringing."

"Was Graham taken to hospital?" she asked.

"No, and again that is a little unusual but not unique. Sometimes the deterioration is rapid, and if someone lives on their own then maybe there's no one around to spot the warning signs in time. Again, there's been a few people who have not been found for several days, so in a way Graham was fortunate that his neighbour was worried and called his son. He was dead when his son arrived. At least that's the story."

"Pah! And do you believe this cock and balls story?"

Krill raised his eyebrows and was tempted to correct her use of the idiom, but didn't; he found her mistake rather amusing, and besides he didn't want to be distracted by an explanation as to why two farm animals were somehow linked to lies and falsehoods, not that he knew the answer to that riddle without looking it up. He'd certainly heard many a 'cock and bull' story during his time at the Met, but not previously stopped to think about its origins.

"And what of this message to me; I still do not believe that Graham sent it."

"When did you receive it Margaret?"

She looked at her phone and showed it to him. "The eighteenth."

"He died around the twenty third. I spoke briefly to his neighbour, the one who raised the alarm, just to say how sorry I was to hear of Graham's death, and she was still quite shocked by it. She'd been away for the weekend with her family, and left it a couple of days before knocking on his door when she got back. When there was still no reply the following day she phoned his son. He came straight away. She hadn't seen the son visit him for some time."

"Yes, I am not surprised; he is not a good son," Margaret scoffed.

"I've been thinking about his message and I have an alternative theory to the one you suggested."

"Yes? What is this alternative?"

"Well, as I said, a few people have been left for a while undiscovered in their homes, and possibly Graham wanted someone to know that he was ill, so if the worse came to the worse he could be found quickly. It wasn't just a cold, or seasonal flu, which he might not want to worry you about; he would know the seriousness of it and the possible outcome. He was concerned enough to break his usual rule of not admitting to any weakness. He probably sent a text to his son as well."

"And his son ignored it!" she said angrily. "He could so easily have visited his father to see if he was alright, and taken him to hospital in time! I would have come straight away if I'd been in London, but I was in Poland looking after my mother. I tried to contact him many times. I even thought when he did not answer my calls that maybe he has changed his mind about getting married. Was Graham tested for the virus?"

"No he wasn't, although it was named as the underlying cause on the death certificate. There's more," said Krill.

"Yes?"

"I went to see Graham's solicitor, who as it happens is also mine, and while he couldn't give me any details, or even confirm whether a new will had been drafted, he did say that Graham's children wouldn't have had any reason to be concerned about their father's estate if he remarried."

"He didn't tell you anything about what was in Graham's new will?"

"He couldn't because of client confidentiality. But I managed in a roundabout way to establish what had happened, and I'm pretty sure that there was a new one."

He recalled his intellectual jousting with the lawyer to try to find a way around the rules. Krill had eventually tried a different tack by asking what advice he would give him if he was planning to remarry. The lawyer had smiled and said that he would definitely recommend that all his clients who were remarrying and already had children should draw up a new will.

"See, I tell you this. There is a new will and it is the motive!" she said excitedly.

"Well, I don't believe it was, because it's highly probable that Graham, like a lot of people who remarry later in life, wanted to protect his children's inheritance. He possibly thought that it would help them to accept you, if they knew that the money and his property were safe." Krill recalled the lawyer's advice to him. "So probably under the terms of this new will you would have been entitled to remain in Graham's house for as long as you lived, or alternatively remarried, and would probably have also had a share of his pension. His children would still have received the bulk of his considerable estate on his death, and his house at some point in the future."

"OK, maybe you are right, but this house is still worth a lot of money, and it is better for his son to have that money now rather than have to wait thirty years or even longer.

Maybe he is angry at the thought of me living in this house which he thinks is his?"

"Possibly, but the son is already quite wealthy so I don't think it would be worth the risk."

"You have checked up on him?" she asked.

Krill hadn't done so himself but instead he'd asked an old colleague to investigate both Graham and his family.

"I've had some enquiries made, yes. If his son had been in debt and the will had been different, then I agree he would have been under some pressure to try to stop his father from marrying you. But knowing what I now know, I don't see him risking his liberty in order to be able to sell his father's house. All it would have needed would be for the doctor to refer the death to a coroner, and for them to have arranged for a postmortem to be carried out. In his shoes I would not have taken that risk."

"But you are far cleverer than him, and you know about these things, coroners and such like. Also maybe his son finds out that Graham is changing his will but does not know what is in the new one? Yes, that is it! Maybe he thinks that I get it all. And many rich people want even more and more; maybe he needed all his inheritance now, for some big business deal!"

Krill thought that she looked even prettier when a little flushed and animated. He'd been tempted to try to find out more about her online after her visit to his cottage, but had resisted. He thought it best to get to know her in a more traditional way, a more 'romantic' way, if that was possible. He found that he enjoyed listening to her even when she was completely on the wrong track, as he believed she now was. Hearing her say that two and two made five or six or seven would have been a pleasurable experience for him, given the current state of his love life.

"And this doctor, did he take much care to examine Graham thoroughly when he signs the certificate?" she asked,

Krill now knew that the guidelines had been revised, and procedures for recording and registering deaths simplified, some might say made too easy, in the Coronavirus Act, because he'd looked it up. Given the number of excess deaths it was almost inevitable, or doctors wouldn't have been able to cope. The BMA had asked for concessions from the Government to help their members, including not always attending deaths in person, or referring them to a coroner. Was it a 'charter' for someone who wished to be rid of a troublesome relative? He hardly thought so.

"I'm sure that they took as much care as they could in the circumstances."

She looked confused. "Before, you mentioned children? I thought he only had one son?"

"Yes he did, but his second wife had been married previously and so he also had two stepchildren, both girls."

"Oh! I am so surprised about this; he never mentioned them to me."

"They were teenagers when their mother married him, so he may not have been as close to them. After their mother died he probably saw even less of them than he did his own son."

She looked quite taken aback by these revelations. "I thought that he had only been married one time."

"No, twice; his son Douglas was from his first marriage, and then Carol and Shirley were his stepdaughters. I don't think the second marriage lasted very long."

"How did this other wife die?"

Krill blinked, a little shocked by what she seemed to be implying.

"You think Douglas got rid of his stepmother too? Now you are becoming a little paranoid!"

Realising that he may have overstepped the mark, he put his hand on top of hers in an attempt to counter his criticism. She didn't withdraw hers, but allowed it to remain trapped like a cool soft pouch. He thought a change of topic would be welcome, for him and he hoped also for her.

"You've only been married once, Margaret?"

"Yes, and you, you are divorced?"

"Twice. And you have children?" he asked.

"One daughter, but this is enough because she is not an easy child. I saw photographs in your cottage of a lot of children - these are all yours?"

Krill smiled. "Six of them are grandchildren, but I can fill a small room with my children and their children. They're all wonderful, highly educated, kindhearted. They're more of a credit to their mothers than they are to me, because I only helped to bring them up when they were younger."

"But I think they have your brains and good looks?"

"Possibly, although their mothers were beautiful and highly intelligent."

28

"They are both dead?" she asked.

"No, they're alive, but I meant that they're in the past for me, and I suppose they may now not be as beautiful as they were when I knew them. Probably being married to a very difficult policeman caused them to age prematurely."

She was aggrieved on his behalf. "You have your career and you are conscientious - this should be important to them! They should be proud to be married to someone who becomes so famous for his skills as a detective."

"Hardly famous; maybe one or two cases hit the headlines." He was struggling to take in all her praise: good looks and famous were not epithets he was used to. "The Press like to focus on one person, when really it's always teamwork which solves any case. Both my wives hated my job even though they knew what they were getting into when they married me. They hated the long hours, the phone calls in the middle of the night, the weekends I had to go in, the holidays which were disrupted. They wanted someone who earned a lot more money and worked in a nine to five job."

"And you, you did not hate it?" she asked.

"No, I loved every minute of it! I'd still be doing it now if they'd let me. But I did feel selfish and not a good husband; maybe even not a good father at times. When a case gets hold of you it takes over your whole life - it's all you can think about, so I may not have been there, at home and involved in the children's lives, as much as I should have been."

She frowned. "You think maybe I am obsessing about Graham and his son? You think I should forget what happened to him?"

"Forget, no. You're in mourning and there's a process you have to go through. You were obviously very close to him, so you should never forget him." Krill had a further thought. "Maybe it would help if you spoke to his stepdaughters; possibly they can tell you more about Graham and his son, and also about the funeral, assuming they went. They might know what happened to his ashes. I can get you their contact details if you want me to?"

"Thank you. Let me think about it. It would perhaps be interesting to know a little more about this son's character - whether or not they liked him, what it was like living in the same house as him, how he behaved towards their mother. This would be important information for me."

He suspected that if Margaret did talk to Carol or Shirley she would latch onto any hint of their stepbrother's bad behaviour, any whiff of psychopathic tendencies, and dismiss positive comments about Donald, as it was natural to seek out those views which reinforce our own prejudices. If Graham's son had once thrown a stone at a cat then he would, in her eyes, be capable of cold-blooded murder! He'd experienced the same inclination by some of his less experienced colleagues when examining the evidence they'd collected against suspects, where they'd not followed up leads which led in a contradictory direction until he'd prompted them to do so. He believed wholeheartedly in the scientific method, and thought it equally important to try to find facts which disprove a theory. That was why not a single one of his cases had been overturned on Appeal.

CHAPTER 4

Krill grew increasingly impatient as he went down the same four streets for the third time, looking for a place to park his car. Margaret had assured him that near to her house in North London were lots of unrestricted parking spaces, interspaced with zones dedicated for residents, and it was true, but probably people were reluctant to leave them once they'd managed to squeeze in. He imagined drivers abandoning their vehicles for days or weeks at a time just so they could brag to their friends that they'd got one! He was just thinking that he would have to try farther afield when he saw the rear taillights of a car; he slowed and sure enough it pulled out.

His first reaction when she'd invited him to have lunch at her house was 'fantastic'; his second was - how am I going to get there? It wouldn't have been a problem in normal times, but the furthest he'd travelled in the past few months had been the fifteen miles to his daughter's, and he hadn't been on any public transport since lockdown. Would he have to take a train and then a bus? He didn't want to use the Underground if at all possible, not that there was a station very near to her house in any event. Then she'd suggested that he drove and explained about the parking.

Her house was a fairly typical Victorian three storey villa; well maintained with lots of flowers growing in window boxes and planters. He wondered if it always looked so pristine or whether it had been 'tarted up' for the sale? His mantra as he approached the front door was: 'take things slowly, one small step at a time'. He knew that he had a tendency to rush things, to try to get from point A to point B as soon as possible; point A generally being a crime and B the confession, but it also applied to his romances. He'd married too young the first time, when he had just graduated, and then after that marriage ended, had met and fallen in love with number two without any noticeable time for reflection.

After their lunch at the pub, they'd taken a walk along the canal and Margaret had unexpectedly put her arm through his like they were a proper couple enjoying the sunshine glinting on the murky water. His mind had raced, wondering what it meant? Had she done it because she was in need of his help and support? Was she naturally effusive and outgoing? Was she telling him that she liked him? Was she trying to encourage him?

She opened the door and greeted him; he gave her the box of chocolates he'd brought with him. He wanted to kiss her right then and there, on the cheek at least, but of course couldn't. She seemed flushed and possibly a little excited, but maybe they were the effects of the heat and stress of preparing their meal rather than his sudden appearance on her doorstep. Her dark hair was held in a tidy clump behind her head, and it seemed to accentuate the smooth curve of her slavic cheeks; he saw her neat ears for the first time. There was a bicycle propped up against the wall in the hallway and she apologised, explaining that it belonged to one of her lodgers.

"I have to make allowances otherwise people will not stay with me; and he is a very quiet boy. Please, come into the front sitting room and I will get you something to drink. Did you find a parking place OK?"

"Yes, just like you said; very close." Which he thought was a truth hidden within a larger lie, as it had seemed anything but OK at the time.

"Good! And now that you have seen my house you will believe me when I tell you that I have no need of Graham's money. I am not the gold digger that his son believes!"

"Did he really think that?" he asked. "He doesn't sound like a very nice man at all, and just for the record I believed you before when you told me."

"Yes? But policemen like to see the evidence with their own eyes, don't they, so that they can put it on the record, in their little notebooks?" She laughed, "Of course, I am joking. I still cannot believe that I have the great Inspector Krill here in front of me, in my house!"

He sat down on a large sofa opposite an ornate fireplace, which had pale cream tiles on either side, each decorated with a section of one colourful elongated tulip. There was a large display of dried flowers in the hearth. She positioned herself not quite next to him, leaving space for an invisible chaperone. He'd rehearsed a few opening remarks and potential topics, but for once was a little lost for words. She came to his rescue:

"I can show you most of the house except the rooms which have guests. When I first came here, many years ago, it was in need of a great deal of work, but now it is nearly as I want it, so in some ways I am pleased that I do not need to sell it. Graham did not want to leave the village, and it was silly to have two large houses and be travelling from one to the other all of the time."

He could understand Graham not wanting to leave the peace and tranquility of the village; Krill thought that he would also find it hard to sell his cottage and buy somewhere new with a partner or move in with them. He'd already lost two roofs over his head, and what guarantee was there that it wouldn't happen a third time? None. Maybe unlike Graham, he just wasn't good marriage material? His preferred choice would be to find someone like Margaret and do exactly what she was dismissing: spending time in each other's properties - a few nights midweek in London, followed by a weekend in the country. That sounded perfect to him.

The door opened and a woman in her twenties came in. She looked surprised, then confused, and finally somewhat perturbed, as she glanced at Krill. Margaret stood up and approached her.

"This is my daughter, Nikola. Nikola, I tell you that I have an important visitor today; that Inspector Krill is coming for lunch."

There was a lengthy and rather agitated exchange in Polish between mother and daughter. He heard the word

34

'Mama' a few times, and what he assumed was 'no'. Margaret repeated something twice, her tone growing more insistent, and Nikola finally smiled, said hello in English, and left.

"She is going out to meet her friends. I tell you that she is difficult and now you can see this for yourself!"

Krill wondered what Nikola had thought about her mother remarrying and what would have happened to her?

"She lives here, with you?" he asked.

"Yes. She is twenty eight and still she stays with her mother! Of course when I am her age I am married, I have moved to a new country, and I have a child of my own. She has a boyfriend for a while but she cannot keep them. I was buying her a nice flat in Greenwich when I sell this house; then, just as she is starting to accept that she will be on her own, everything is back to before. Maybe I should still sell this house, buy the apartment for her, and return to Poland? This would serve her right, and there I could buy a castle!"

This no doubt flippant remark got Krill contemplating regular trips to Warsaw; he'd never been to Poland. He now wondered whether Margaret's interest in Graham was in part motivated by a desire to finally free herself of a clinging daughter?

"Does she see much of her father?" he asked.

"Yes, occasionally." She paused and tilted her head to one side as if weighing up some pros and cons. "But I have a big secret to tell you, which is that her father is not my English husband! Perhaps you now think how wicked I am! But the marriage was not a success and the final straw was when I met this nice looking gentleman at the Polish Club, and I find

I am pregnant. Of course it cannot be my husband's, this we both know. Perhaps I think for a while that I will be with this man who fathers my child, but he is not interested in marriage."

"Oh, that's quite a story." He tried not to look shocked or even surprised at such a turn of events.

"Yes. And I'm sure you have some romantic stories to tell about all the ladies in your life. Such an attractive and successful man must have many conquests! Maybe there are people you meet at work or in the village? Maybe I am not the first to come knocking at your door like a … a damsel in distress? Maybe you are a magnet drawing defenceless women in need of your help?"

It was the second time that she'd said that he was attractive, and it pleased him to think that she might be flirting with him. Was she fishing - wanting to find out about his own past or present relationships?

He laughed. "I'm not sure that I've ever been a magnet! And there haven't been any conquests lately, even before the virus stopped us meeting people."

"This is such a shame. You should not hide yourself away in your cottage, hidden down your lane. You see, I have drawn you out of your shell and made you come all the way to London! This is good. Now I promised you a drink and have not got you one. I have wine or beer or some Scottish whisky?"

Krill felt in need of a drink but he would be driving. "Maybe just a small beer?"

While she went to fetch their drinks and check on the lunch, he looked at the photos on a large circular table near the bay window. He assumed the elderly couple in the silver frame were her parents, and those of a child were of her daughter, as people seldom had photos of themselves when very young on display. However, the women in their teens and twenties could have been either her or Nikola, as she obviously took after her 'Mama'. He would need a magnifying glass to check their features more closely but thought he could separate most of them based on fashion styles and backdrops. There were no photographs of her with Graham, or with any other man; had she removed them or were they kept in her bedroom out of sight from Nikola?

"Is this you?" he asked when she returned.

She took the photograph from him and smiled. "Yes. I am twenty one and still at university. It is just before I meet my husband, when he came on holiday to Warsaw."

"You were stunning."

"Thank you! Some photographers wanted me to be their model, but I am a serious girl interested only in science."

"And you've kept your beauty," he quickly added.

"Thank you again! It is my genes. My mother, who is eighty five, is still very beautiful. This is her with Papa; he was a handsome man too." She lifted the silver framed photograph and looked from it towards Krill. "Now I see you both, I think that you have my father's eyes. Maybe this is part of the attraction? Yes, there is a close resemblance. The nose and mouth are a little different but if I put my hand up here in front of you, and my thumb across the photo, then you could be brothers! I did not realise it before. Let me take a photo of you and I will show Nikola."

He tried not to pose too self-consciously as she used her phone.

"I think the eyes are the most important feature. Now, maybe the two of us together?" she suggested. Margaret lifted the camera above them and he just managed to resist the temptation to put his arm around her waist.

"Very good. Now we eat. Please come through to the dining room."

"More coffee?" she asked later, when they returned to the front room.

"Yes please. How did your meeting with Shirley go?"

She refilled their cups and put some cream from a small china jug into her own.

"This was interesting, as I thought it would be. It was a good idea of yours to suggest I meet Graham's stepdaughter. She was quite fond of him and was happy to talk about him. She was also very sad when he dies."

"How old was she when her mother remarried?" Krill was still trying to get the chronology of events right in his head.

"She was fifteen and her sister was seventeen; Douglas was eleven. It was difficult for all of the children to adjust to the new situation. Better if they had been older and had left home, or maybe younger. Graham was kind to them and tried to be the same as he was before with Douglas, but even so perhaps his son does not like the new family very much, as suddenly he is no longer a spoilt only child. I can't imagine what my daughter would do if she suddenly had two siblings to cope with! I think it would drive her crazy."

Or perhaps 'more crazy', he couldn't help wondering?

"Did the girls see much of Graham or Douglas in recent years?"

"No. Graham sends them presents on their birthdays and at Christmas, and sometimes messages, but they have busy lives and do not live very near to him. They saw Douglas for the first time in a long while at the funeral. He was there with his wife and children. Of course none of Graham's friends can go, just the close family."

"Did you mention your suspicions to her?" he asked.

"No, because you tell me that it is unwise to do so. I asked how Douglas was, and of course she says that he too was sad. She did not know that Graham was ill, and did not receive a message from him or Douglas about it, so it is a shock for her too when she finds out he is dead."

"I don't think Graham would have alerted everyone, just told you and maybe his son that he was feeling unwell. Did you get the impression that she liked Douglas?"

She thought for a moment. "No, not liked or disliked; these are both too strong, but she didn't say anything good or bad about him. It was like he wasn't important to her when they were living in the same house, or afterwards."

"That's maybe inevitable. Even if they had been brother and sister the age gap would have probably stopped them from becoming close."

"Yes."

"What happened to his ashes?" he asked.

"She does not know."

"That's a shame. Maybe you could speak to her again and ask her to contact Douglas? If there's a ceremony to scatter them somewhere, and you could be there, even in the background, it would help to give you closure."

"Yes, perhaps."

"So how do you feel about it all now? I'm not sure that I've been able to help you very much."

"Oh but you have John! How do I feel? That his death is still suspicious, and I do not trust this son to tell the truth about anything, or do the right thing."

"You can't bring him back."

"No," she replied, with some sadness still in her eyes.

"If I could speak frankly, both as a retired policeman and hopefully your friend?"

"Yes?"

"You've run out of options Margaret. If, as you believe, Douglas did kill his father, it could never be proven, not without a body. Even if we had access to his computer or phone and found incriminating evidence to support your suspicions, it would not be enough to bring a case against him, let alone secure a conviction. We could find that there had been arguments about the new will and his father's future marriage. We could discover internet searches about poisons. We could show that he visited his father just before he fell ill. But even all that would be insufficient, without the concrete proof from an autopsy to overrule the doctor's signature on the death certificate."

He'd deliberately kept from her the fact that it was not Graham's usual GP who had signed the MCCD form, but a retired doctor from another practice, and even he had not actually attended in person but via a video link. He knew that such a revelation would only fuel her belief that something very untoward had occurred. He could see how she would add it all up, as indeed he might have done in other circumstances: no hospitalisation of the patient, no Covid test carried out, no doctor's visit to certify the cause of death, and finally no autopsy. However, he considered that it would be best for all concerned if she could now let the matter rest and try to move on.

"I think you should accept that you've done all you can to find out what happened, and that unfortunately we can't take this any further."

She bowed her head and he saw a tear drop from her chin into her cup.

CHAPTER 5

"I thought we might review some of our old cases, Moss; visit a few of the crime scenes."

The two men were sitting in the garden of Krill's local, which was handier but far more basic than the one he'd visited with Margaret, and also considerably less expensive than the pub by the river - a steak here was half the price and almost as good. It had a dilapidated climbing frame complete with a slide, which might not pass a health and safety inspection, and the seating scattered randomly hither and thither consisted of old weather worn wooden tables and picnic benches. There was an absence of any colourful flowers or shrubs, and the customers appeared to be less affluent and far more in need of a drink or three.

Ex-sergeant Phillip Moss sipped his pint and looked at his old chief with more than a modicum of affection. They'd worked together for so many years that they probably knew one another better than many married couples. They'd vowed to keep in touch when they both retired, but their resolve had gradually dwindled, until they only met up once or twice a year, sometimes with other members of the old team, and there was a lengthy spell after Krill moved to Scotland to try to save his second marriage when they had hardly communicated at all.

No one would ever think that they were even distantly related. Krill was much taller despite Moss gaining an inch or two due to the thick hair he'd inherited from his Spanish grandmother. However, apart from his curls - which were still mainly black, and his broad shoulders, it was an absence of features which most defined Moss: short neck, stubby nose, narrow deep set eyes, and rather thin pale lips. Give him a facial scar and you might have expected to see him on a 'most wanted' poster!

It was Moss who had named his boss 'Killer'. Not because he had any violent tendencies - if anything Krill was quite sensitive and more softhearted than the average copper, but because he could 'kill a case, stone dead!' Every 'gov'nor' had to have a nickname, and 'Killer' was the obvious one which his unusual surname demanded. It was also quite apt as he'd put away more killers during his twenty years in charge than any other senior officer at the Met. The arguments were so overwhelming that Krill had reluctantly been forced to accept the title while being toasted by his colleagues after a particularly difficult murder case. Even though he'd wanted to be on first name terms with everyone, they'd never once called him 'John', not to his face or when he was away from the team; it would have been like calling the Queen, 'Liz'.

Moss had refused several promotions because it would have meant leaving Krill's side, but he didn't regret it. He'd been a Derby County supporter as a teenager, and saw himself as having a role similar to Peter Taylor's, the assistant manager, who had flown in the slipstream of the great Brian Clough. He'd enjoyed being Krill's wingman, his 'tail end charlie', his 'minder' - fighting off the doubters and the critics, and making sure the Inspector and then Chief Inspector always got what he needed to achieve results. After Moss had retired from the Met he had run a moderately successful private detective agency for several years, and he still dabbled here and there, finding out info, and helping out friends with their little problems.

"What's brought this on Killer? I thought you already had enough material for your memoirs?"

Krill looked rather sheepish, even embarrassed.

"I got a phone call last week from a BBC researcher. She said that there was the possibility of a documentary, or, as she put it, a 'docudrama' about the Canal Killings. She said it was in the very early stages of development; just an idea really that someone had come up with, but they wanted to see if I would cooperate before they took it any further."

"And you said that you would? I thought you hated being in the limelight?" Moss recalled the nervousness his boss had displayed every time he had been forced to appear in front of a TV camera, usually outside court after the successful conclusion of a case, or during an investigation to prompt possible eye witnesses into coming forward.

"I said I would help them, I didn't say I would appear in it! Besides, talking to my Polish friend about Graham's possible murder got the old brain cells working again. It felt like I'd been woken from a deep sleep. You don't have to help or take part in the programme if you don't want to."

"Would we get any say in who would play us in this docudrama? I mean, it wouldn't be fair would it, if your part was played by Hugh Grant and I got some numpty!"

Krill laughed. "You could never be played by a numpty. Anyway, I thought we would do some research ourselves, to remind us of the facts; take a trip back to 1978, so it's fresh in our minds when Alice comes back to me, assuming she does."

Moss looked confused. "1978? I thought it was '77?"

"Well the murders were in '77 and earlier, but we solved it in '78."

"Right. And that was pre DNA."

"It was 'pre' almost everything, apart from analysing blood groups and fingerprints, and there weren't even any of those at the crime scenes. We had to do it the hard way, taking statements from hundreds of potential witnesses, including almost everyone who owned a barge near to the murder scenes. I mean you and the team had to do all that donkeywork."

"A few shoes were worn out that winter! The Canal Killer, it's all coming back to me now, especially that murder in Hampshire when foul play was first suspected. Initially it was thought to have been an accident, an unfortunate trip on the towpath, and the man's head hitting the prow of a derelict barge. Then the eagle-eyed pathologist spotted a puncture wound on the victim's neck. What was she called? Didn't it begin with a 'V'?"

"Veronica."

"Yes, that was her name. I'm not surprised you remember. Very tasty, she was. You dated her, didn't you, after the case?"

"We had a few drinks together," Krill admitted.

Moss thought he knew what that probably meant. "It was just after your first divorce wasn't it, so you were needing some female company."

"You make me sound like a serial divorcee!"

"Sorry Killer, just trying to recall the facts. The local police got nowhere so they called us in. I remember you were not too chuffed even though it was your first big case."

Krill nodded. It wasn't just the location of the murder, in one of the remotest parts of Hampshire, it was all the problems they found when they arrived, and the reaction of the local force to them coming. Krill had repeatedly complained that by the time they saw the crime scene it had been virtually ruined by dozens of 'uniforms' poking about, and by reporters, runners, cyclists, and even sightseers. Plus it was several days after the body had been discovered, so any witnesses were much harder for his team to locate.

"I remember your curses got louder, more frequent, and more profane as that first day progressed."

Krill smiled. "You're 'effing' right they did! It would have been hard enough to solve even if we'd been called in immediately. If you wanted an example of how not to deal with a suspicious death then that was it."

"But you always liked a challenge Killer, and that case, mainly because of its complexities and the fact that it turned out to be a serial killer, made your reputation. Everyone - in the team, the local population, back at the Met, and the media

- all thought you were bloody marvellous and could perform miracles. That was when the cult of Killer Krill really started!"

Krill looked even more embarrassed. Was Moss right? Could he perform miracles? He doubted it very much. He preferred to call it luck, and being in the right place at the right time, which he supposed was really the same thing.

Moss looked at the dark lines under Krill's eyes and his overly wrinkled brow. "Your neighbours been bothering you again? Is that what this is really about? That you need to get away? Take your mind off things?"

"No, not bothering me any more than usual."

"Still no signs of them moving?" Moss asked.

"Nothing definite, just the odd hint occasionally in phone conversations. I sometimes think they know I'm there in my garden and can hear them, and they say it to bait me."

"I'm sure me and the boys could encourage them to move on, or mend their ways."

Krill laughed at the thought of several burly ex-coppers turning up with baseball bats. "What did you have in mind?"

Moss looked affronted. "Obviously nothing illegal Boss, perish the thought! But I don't like to think of you not enjoying your retirement, not after what you've achieved. Maybe if they knew who you were they would be more considerate. Perhaps if we had a chat with them to let them know that we don't like what they're doing, and that they should show some respect? A bit like a solicitor's letter only more in their face, upfront, and personal like. Who's worse, him or her?"

Krill didn't have to think very long about it. "Him definitely. He's the one who plays the piano the loudest, like he's trying to demolish the keys, and he's more often talking in the garden on the phone, and not just to his friends and relations but on business calls too. I appreciate your concern but I doubt if anything would do any good. They live in their own narrow world with hardly a thought for anyone else."

Moss wasn't as pessimistic as Krill; he'd talk it through with the lads. "I suppose it's been worse since lockdown because they've both been at home, and no nursery for the wee one."

"I'm not sure," Krill replied. "Yes they're in the house and the garden more often, but they've had far fewer visitors, and there's been a drastic reduction in barbecues and parties - none at all for several weeks."

"Changing the subject Killer, was that information I got for you about the chemist useful? He didn't seem to fit the profile of a murderer from what I could see. Does your friend still think her fiancé was killed by his son?"

"No, you're right, he didn't fit the profile, and thanks it helped a lot. One thing I've learnt, given my two divorces and numerous other encounters, is that once a woman has made her mind up about something it's very hard to get her to change it. She'll probably always believe that the son polished him off somehow. But if it was murder, then in my view it's just as likely that her daughter did it. She can't have liked the idea of her mother selling the house where she'd been born, being uprooted, and having to live on her own. If anything I'd say her motive was the stronger of the two, and I gather that she's also a little crazy. Perhaps her mother had a key to Standish's house and her daughter secretly copied it? It's not any more far-fetched than the son killing his dad."

Moss whistled, impressed as usual by Krill's thought processes.

"So, best to let sleeping or dead fiancés lie, eh? And you had no chance of proving anything anyway without a body...."

"Exactly Moss. Same thing could easily have happened with the murder in Hampshire - presumed an accidental death, body disposed of, and no one the wiser. Lots of pathologists might have gone along with the verdict of the local police and just rubber stamped it, with only a cursory check of the remains, because that's exactly what had happened on at least three previous occasions - in Lancashire and the Midlands. It was only when we started checking canal deaths and saw the possible link that those crimes came to light. There were undoubtedly others which we couldn't prove - four that we know of which fitted the MO but the bodies had been cremated."

"Could have been dozens before we caught him, and who knows how many more if we hadn't? Is Crow still protesting his innocence?"

"As far as I know he is. Maybe he's hoping to be let out one day, but there's no chance of that happening, not after a 'whole life tariff' was imposed on him a few years ago. Anyway, it was talking to Margaret which got me thinking again about murders and victims, and a bonus was that helping her certainly took my mind off my neighbours for a while. So, following the BBC's inquiry I've decided that I need to get out more! I thought that maybe we should visit not just Hampshire, but all our old crime scenes; check the files again if we can."

Krill noticed that his companion didn't seem very enamoured with the idea; maybe he was enjoying his retirement far more than he was? He remembered how Moss spent much of his leisure time, so perhaps a little 'bait' would help?

"What do you think? And maybe we could combine it with some fishing? I know how you've been trying to 'lure' me onto a riverbank - well now's your chance!"

It was true, every time they met for a drink or spoke on the phone Moss had talked about his latest fishing trip, and tried to encourage his ex-boss to join him. But he suspected that what Krill had in mind would be almost entirely investigation and very little time for recreation, and his constant verbal reflections would no doubt disturb the fish. Still, something was always better than nothing.

"So, we start in Hampshire?"

Krill beamed; he'd known that his sidekick wouldn't desert him.

"And perhaps it will be an opportunity to meet up with the lads from our team, and maybe some of the officers who were based at the local Hampshire station to get their viewpoint."

"You sure about that Killer? We didn't leave them on the best of terms."

"No, unfortunately we didn't, but it was only that one Inspector who was a real problem; we got on OK with virtually everyone else. Eventually at least."

Moss didn't look convinced. "That 'nobhead' almost single-handedly stopped the investigation in its tracks. The showdown with him was almost inevitable, but, and you won't like me saying this Killer, you could have handled it differently, a little more sensitively, and left him with at least a modicum of dignity."

Krill shook his head, but it wasn't in disagreement, because he knew that Moss was perfectly right. It was more an acknowledgement that dealing with people had never been his strong suit, and also a longstanding disbelief, a lack of understanding, and probably guilt, about what had happened.

"Mind you, who was to know that it would be the final straw and he would top himself? He was a devious selfish bastard and probably thought that if he couldn't get you in life he could do so in death. And he very nearly did. OK, I'll do it on one condition."

"What's that?" Krill asked, even though he thought he knew the answer.

"That we have a weekend's fishing *before* we start."

CHAPTER 6

Up close her eyes were enormous - they seemed to fill her whole face above her fine nose. They kissed a little less passionately and far less hungrily than they'd done before. It was 3pm and they were still in bed at his cottage. That unusual circumstance, a rare one for Krill unless he was really very ill, was added to his long list of guilty pleasures. Strangely for both of them, it had been when their mouths had touched for the first time rather than their bodies joining which seemed to be the most forbidden fruit of all! Maybe that was why they kissed so often after that first occasion in her London house.

He'd been nervous and a little worried as she'd calmly taken his hand and led him upstairs, past the parked bicycle, past her daughter's bedroom where the door had fortunately been shut, past the paintings by her friend in Krakow; onwards and upwards they'd crept like mischievous mice. She hadn't spoken any words of passion or desire, she hadn't revealed her intentions, or even asked him whether he wanted to take her to bed, probably because she already knew the answer to that question! She'd just looked at him, decided it would be the right thing to do, and whisked him away.

He was always apprehensive with a new lover, mainly because there would be so many unknown expectations and unseen comparisons, and therefore plenty of opportunity to disappoint. His other concern at the time was that an objective observer might think that he was taking advantage of her present state, and that she still needed sympathy and support far more than she needed sex. But he'd soon discovered that any misgivings about her vulnerability were completely misplaced, as her desire for him appeared to match and possibly even outweigh his own. And if the 'man on the top deck of the Highgate omnibus' had passed by at exactly the right moment and looked in, he would have seen her almost tear Krill's clothes off him! Once he was over the initial shock he'd found that he rather liked being seduced.

When he invited her for the weekend he'd also been a little anxious about the stark contrast between her rather large and expensively furnished house in North London, and his tiny spartan cottage in the sticks. Before she arrived he removed all the spiders he could find and most of the cobwebs, added a picture or two to the blank magnolia walls upstairs, filled a vase with fresh flowers, purchased a new decorative topper and some goose down pillows, refilled lots of potpourri pots, and as a final touch, hung a little red heart from one of the bedposts!

Early in his dalliances Krill couldn't stop himself from thinking about the future, or to be more precise, about 'their future' together, and whether there was one. As long as the possibility of something at least semi-permanent existed he could give free reign to both his lust and his love. His experiences, both in and out of marriage, made it easier for him to cope with the ups and downs of love, so much so that he wondered whether the human heart became more immune to rejection after it had been broken a few times? 'Hard hearted' might equate with being cruel and uncaring for many people, but not for him; it was simply a coping mechanism which enabled him to continue his search for love rather than be forced to give it up. Like the Scales of Justice he found he could balance his hopes about a relationship with any scepticism, his joy with possible disillusionment, and the promise of love with the risk of rejection and loss.

He'd noticed that afternoon that Margaret had seemed more distant, as if her thoughts were elsewhere, or that she was troubled by something. He'd tried to dismiss it by saying to himself that most people had plenty to think about even in normal times, never mind in the middle of a pandemic. He'd wondered if it was something to do with her daughter? So it wasn't a surprise to either of them when he stroked her naked shoulder, kissed it tenderly, and asked, "Are you OK?"

She looked at him with concern, and spoke without hesitation, because she'd also been reviewing the situation.

"You are a lovely man John, but you must not fall in love with me. That would not be a good idea."

Not good for whom he wondered? Presumably for him. Maybe her warning had come a little too late. "Why?" he asked, even though he didn't really want his question answered.

"Because it would not last," she replied.

"No?" He thought for him it could last, at least for as long as she allowed it to. "Why not?"

"Because, sadly, you are not what I need, Inspector Krill. You are nice, very nice, a wonderful person, but only for a short time, a brief affair, not for a longer time."

How brief he wondered? He would accept months or even weeks, but now it was out in the open he suspected that he might never see her again. He forced himself to ask, "Why, what do you need?"

"Someone who I can be with always and for a very long time. I do not want to be hurt again like I was when Graham died. More and more I see that you are attached to your cottage like a limpet; happy in your lane, hidden away, only coming out for a little while, for some romance. You have been alone for too long and I think you like it."

"True, it does have its appeal; I can do what I want, when I want. But this is nice isn't it, being here sometimes and at your house? You could keep me as a pet until something better comes along!"

She laughed. "Maybe, but you would always want more - I know this, and the longer we are together the harder it will be to part."

He was upset, but tried to hide it.

"Perhaps if we are together for a little longer, then we will decide not to part?"

"No, that will not happen. It is not just that you like your life in the village, alone in your cottage, it is also that you are older even than Graham, so I think about how long you will be with me."

He was somewhat taken aback. "Well I'm not planning to pop my clogs just yet!"

"I have heard this expression, and kick the bucket also. No I very much hope not. But Graham thought the same, poor man, and now I think that maybe even he was too old for me."

It was no use trying to pretend that he was younger, even though he liked to think that he didn't look his age, because his career meant that such personal details could easily be found online. She'd never asked him how old he was; he'd thought that maybe it was because it didn't matter to her, but now he saw that it was because she already knew. It was unfortunate, even borderline tragic. He felt that fate had dealt him a cruel blow of mistiming. If they'd met before she'd known Graham, then she probably would have accepted his age and not thought too much about it. The pandemic and her fiancé's death had highlighted to her the ephemeral nature of relationships with older men, and she didn't want to be caught out again. She could easily find someone her own age or younger so why take the risk? Much as he wanted to, he couldn't find fault with her reasoning.

"Are you upset?" she asked.

"Of course I am. But I do understand, and I can see that your mind's made up." He kissed her again, and tried to change the mood, "More champagne?"

"Yes please."

After she'd taken just one sip, he took the glass from her and placed it on the bedside table.

"Well then, I suppose I'd better make the most of you while I still can!"

CHAPTER 7

Several days later Krill's sleep was disturbed at 7.30am by loud shouting in the garden next door. The 'Honeys' were back, and as noisy as ever. He seldom set the alarm, and if left to his own devices could wake up at any time between 6 and 10am; sometimes first at 6 followed by a doze until 10. He could close the window to deaden the noise but he'd slept with it open for most of his life.

After his affair with Margaret had ended, Krill had seamlessly returned to a routine of adjusting his life around his neighbours' habits, and he tried not to dwell on the all too brief peaceful fortnight. He didn't try to write when the piano was being played but instead kept out of the dining room, and took a shower, or ironed, or vacuumed, or listened to the radio. He went on walks during the Honeys' raucous outdoor lunches, when 'Arch' was told to come back to the table twenty times and threatened with various punishments, including having no teddy when he went to bed - as if they would do anything which might make him less likely to sleep! He spent a peaceful hour in the garden from two until three when both children were expected to take a nap. He had no idea what their parents did during this short ceasefire, although he imagined them lying side by side in a darkened room, like aliens from the planet 'Hubbub', with their enormous mouths open, trying to cool their hot swollen overworked vocal cords, and thinking up new schemes for torturing quiet introspective retired humans!

Encouraged by his romance with Margaret, he'd resumed his search for a partner online, and discovered that almost every woman now seemed to desire a 'socially distanced' relationship. How would that work, he wondered? He imagined that it might involve several phone and video calls, some tentative 'bargepole' meetings, mutual temperature checks using snub-nosed technology, and in a few rare instances, taking the bedroom plunge without any of the traditional and now highly dangerous formalities such as hand holding, cuddles, or kisses! And of course avoiding anything 'face to face', upright or horizontally, at all costs! Second dates would depend on the results of lateral flow tests, and if you were lucky you might be accepted into a long-term relationship called a 'bubble'. In his experience 'bubbles' were always just itching to burst.

He wondered if the removal of a face mask might one day be considered 'erotic' depending on how it was undone, a little like a shortened version of the 'dance of the seven veils'? The sexy lady slowly revealing the bridge then tip of her nose, ear fixings stretched like the elastic on dainty thongs, then partially unhooked, a single nostril teasingly exposed - perhaps complete with an unexpected piercing, the ridge below incrementally elongating until the curved crest of an upper lip is seen, a gasp at the sight of the 'O' of an open orifice, and finally the orgasmic hint of a forbidden pink tongue....?

As far as the couple next door were concerned, there seemed to be little evidence of any obvious sweetness in their relationship despite their 'honeyed' tones, at least not in their garden where they spoke to one another more like work colleagues than lovers of either the past or present variety. Maybe it was the pressures of their current situation, much of it self-inflicted - young kids, shortage of funds, big bills, jobs now at risk, lack of sleep.... He found he could still just about empathise with them, at least when they were not being selfish, thoughtless, and downright annoying!

He'd reached a conclusion regarding Graham's demise, based as always on the best available evidence. He now believed that Margaret's vendetta against Douglas was a form of displacement; most likely the result of her own guilty feelings. Her desire to blame someone else for his death was in order to eradicate her subconscious culpability. Because, he reasoned, if Graham had been as careful as she'd claimed he was and avoided contacts with other people, then it seemed highly likely that he had caught the virus either from her or from her daughter. Maybe one of them had been asymptomatic and had been unaware of the danger they posed to others? Maybe Margaret had experienced a slight fever and lightheadedness but had put it down to her age? The only way to discover whether his suspicions were at all justified was by having her and her daughter tested for antibodies, but he thought it better that she didn't know one way or the other; better for her to continue to blame Douglas.

Seeing her and being intimate, had been by far the greatest risk that Krill had taken since the start of the pandemic, and it had undoubtedly been much the same for Graham. However, Graham had had far less choice in the matter than Krill, because he'd known Margaret for some time beforehand, and going into isolation would have been a recognition of his age and his susceptibility to the virus, and would probably have put his relationship with her in real jeopardy. In his shoes Krill would have done exactly the same, accepted the risk, and carried on regardless.

At least Graham had died believing that he had a future with Margaret, whereas Krill had to live with the knowledge that he'd never really got close to winning her. They still exchanged messages, and she occasionally said how nice it would be to catch up, but it was just polite conversation. He would always be too old and too set in his ways for her, and while he could attempt to fix one obstacle he could do nothing about the other. Except, perhaps, remind her when he reached the ripe old age of a hundred, of all the years that they could have spent happily together. By that time she might be on her second or third husband. He only hoped she wouldn't invite him to the weddings, or call on his expertise if they also suddenly keeled over! Mind you, he would always welcome any opportunity to reactivate, even briefly, their very 'socially un-distanced' relationship.

CHAPTER 8

"Are you sure this is the right spot Moss? Everything looks very different."

Krill's former colleague opened the file and checked several photographs in turn. Of course the rotting and abandoned narrowboat had been broken up and removed soon after the trial, the trees and bushes had grown, and it was a different season of the year, but he was quite certain. He could triangulate the exact point using a church steeple in the distance, the bridge upstream, and an electricity pylon behind and to the left.

"Yes, give or take a couple of feet, Killer," Moss said.

Krill remained sceptical. "It seems so peaceful now."

"It was probably even more peaceful then, before it happened."

They both moved off the narrow path, out of the way as two bikes went past them at speed.

"Fewer dog walkers, and not as many cyclists in the 70's," Moss added.

"I wonder how he got his victim to stop?"

Moss checked his old notes again. There was nothing in them to answer Krill's question, as Peter Crow hadn't been forthcoming about any of the crimes he was accused of.

"Easy to stop someone just by passing the time of day."

"Bit cold for a chat though, in December." Krill shivered at the thought of it. "Not sure if I'd want to hang about, not for anyone, let alone someone like him."

"He would only need the shortest of conversations," Moss argued. "He'd no doubt already have checked that the barge was unoccupied, and scanned at the last minute for any witnesses as his victim approached along the path, then a quick 'nice day', and a stab in the neck. It would all be over in less than thirty seconds. Catch him in his arms as he became unconscious - Crow was a big strong brute - and ease him into the canal, making sure to hit his head on the barge on the way in. Quite neat and skilful really."

Krill nodded. "Yes, I remember our reconstruction to try to dig up some witnesses, where you played the part of Crow. I think you enjoyed tossing that poor volunteer into the water."

"He wasn't a poor volunteer Killer, he was a stuntman, and we paid him well. It was one of the many things the ill-fated inspector moaned about to the Chief Constable - how we were misusing public funds. And there's little doubt that he leaked it to the Press, as you so vociferously accused him of, in front of the whole team."

"His red face said it all - you could see the guilt written all over it; and he'd been leaking stuff before." Krill's own face went a shade redder as he recalled the confrontation. "We

63

already suspected that he was attempting to undermine our investigation - he wanted us out of the way so he could solve it himself, not that he would have done. We made history as it was probably the first and last time a stuntman has been used in a police reconstruction! But what choice did we have? Pretend to throw someone in? Throw in a dummy? It was a key part of the crime and none of the local lads were willing to be dumped in the canal."

"No, not in January. It certainly raised our profile on TV and in the Press. I always wondered if you hoped he might raise Cain about it, almost baited him with it, so we would become front page in the Nationals and on the main News as well as locally?"

Krill grinned. "You have a very suspicious mind, but I suppose that's an advantage for a Copper. Far more suspicious than the police here were at the time. I'm still amazed that they initially recorded it as an accidental death. I mean how did the guy end up in the canal unless someone put him there?"

Moss thought his old boss was being far too harsh on the locals, and using the benefit of hindsight.

"Remember there was ice on the path so it was quite slippery, and there was speculation that he'd gone onto the barge to check it out and lost his footing. Plus there were no signs of a struggle or obvious marks on the body apart from the head wound, and there was blood on the prow of the boat which suggested he was unconscious when he'd fallen in. Nothing was missing from his person, so they could definitely rule out a mugging. Easy to put it all together as accidental death, probably ninety nine times out of a hundred."

Krill walked a little way along the rutted path, visualising the crime. "So he waits on the footpath near the barge, maybe with his camera pretending to take photos of the winter scene."

"Possibly; Crow did have incriminating photos of canals, including one of this very spot, so clearly he had a camera with him for some of the time."

"Right, although we never found the camera did we? After he's chosen the barge for the killing, he does require an innocent reason to be hanging about here when people pass, and importantly when his victim comes along, because Crow needs him to be off his guard."

"Here's a harmless man, taking a few photos, or maybe he pretends to be working on the barge, or just tying his shoelace," said Moss.

"Not sure about the shoelace theory, because runners and walkers can come back and would notice if you're still tying it an hour later! Of course we don't know how long he waited for the right moment and the right person."

"Bound to be for a while; thirty minutes at least, probably longer. Even if the right person happened along there may be other people about."

"Fishing - that would be a good excuse for being close to the barge for lengthy periods. Is there a closed season? Can you fish here in December Moss?"

"On the canal, yes you can, but Crow didn't have a licence or any gear, so we quickly discounted that possibility."

Krill mentally stamped his foot, frustrated by even a single missing piece of evidence. "Why won't he tell us? Repeating: 'I didn't do it', or 'that is not mine' when presented with irrefutable evidence, over and over and over again, hardly helps us to fill in the gaps and understand precisely what took place here and at the other crime scenes. Maybe I'll go and see him; maybe he'll be more forthcoming now he's got no chance of release?"

"You can try Killer, but why would he spill the beans now? What's in it for him? Can we offer him a better cell or some privileges? Last I heard he was in charge of the library in an Open prison, so he's probably already got it quite cushy."

"I suppose all we can offer is more recognition and increased notoriety. People have long ago forgotten about the Canal Killer of the 70's, and maybe he does want to be remembered? This BBC film might provide it. Can't do any harm to chat."

Krill cast his mind back decades, turned both ways and looked up and down the path, as he imagined Crow would have done.

"OK, so he's innocently hanging about here, spots his victim a couple of hundred yards away, a middle-aged man - again we don't know why he selects that sex and age group. He waits and watches, decides that everything is perfect - he's good to go - and he gets him to stop. Probably already has taken the syringe out of his pocket and has it in his hand behind him, out of sight. They chat for a few moments, victim says 'cheerio old chum', turns to walk away, Crow checks one last time that the coast is clear, takes a step forward and plunges the needle in."

"That's about it," Moss agreed.

"How long was he in the water before someone spotted him?"

"We thought it was around eighteen hours. The murder took place in the late afternoon, not long before dark, so he wasn't discovered until the following morning. Not easy to see a half submerged body in the dusk if you're hurrying to finish your walk or run."

"I think the timing was also important. Too early in the day and the alarm might be quickly raised, but get it just right and you could be well on your way even if foul play is suspected."

"Which it wasn't," said Moss.

"Yes, which it wasn't for more than seventy two hours, because the forensic pathologist's office was shut over the weekend and she had others to look at first. Maybe choosing a Friday for the murder was a further factor?" Krill felt that he could almost admire Crow's cunning. "By Monday they would have had several bodies to deal with, so why waste time on one which looks like an accident? Just check there's water in the lungs to show that the victim drowned. It increases the chances that a murder won't be spotted. And then another two days wasted once she's notified the local police, with them not doing very much before we get called in. Still surprising though that no one spotted Crow hanging about the barge; he's big and a bit menacing at the best of times, as you said before. I suppose it was quite a while before we appealed for witnesses, and to be honest I couldn't remember who I passed on my walk along the canal near my cottage yesterday, never mind a week ago. You wouldn't remember someone unless you had a reason to do so, like they were doing something unusual, out of the ordinary. I suppose blending in was also part of his MO. Show me again Moss where we think Crow left his motorbike."

"It's just at the bridge. There's a farm track and footpath which leads from the main road to the bridge, and across it to a gate in a field. We found numerous tyre tracks but none that we could definitely link to Crow's motorcycle."

"That's true, but several witnesses reported seeing a man on a motorbike of some description near to or even on the lane, more than once."

"Right. It was a good disguise too because the crash helmet hid his face." Moss glanced at his file again. "Estimated heights of the rider ranged from five ten to over six feet. Nothing usable regarding a number plate: one thought it began with 'M', another said 'N', a third thought it was 'H'. Nothing special about the bike: no distinctive colours, just black; nor did it have any memorable accessories. Probably Japanese, but could have been a Yamaha or a Suzuki or a Honda or a Kawasaki, depending on who you asked. Could have been any one of thousands of motorbikes."

"But it matched Crow's black Yamaha," said Krill.

"True, for what it was worth."

"Another piece Moss, another jigsaw piece. Every little bit helps with a conviction, you know that. And don't forget that according to one of the more observant witnesses the rider's crash helmet was quite distinctive - white with a red and blue stripe down the middle, so it was identical to Crow's. We could also show that he had the means to get to all the crime scenes. It was more than enough to get a search warrant, after we'd initially interviewed him, and that was when we came up trumps."

CHAPTER 9

"Why are you doing this?"

"Stop whining and drink your water before I take it away." The older man paused, already having second thoughts about his plans for this one. He didn't answer questions; he was the one who asked them. But he sometimes had to give a little back, otherwise they might refuse to talk at all.

"OK I'll answer you. I'm doing 'this' because it needs to be done. I'm doing 'this' because you deserve it. And maybe I'm doing 'this' because it satisfies a need in me. There, does that help? No, I didn't think it would."

The young man was seated on a rusty metal chair which had been bolted to the concrete floor; his legs and one arm were taped to it. He was naked apart from his underpants. His would-be tormentor stood next to a table several feet away, drinking red wine from a crystal glass. He picked up the bottle and studied it:

"This wine is rather good: 'Violets, plums, blackberries, cherries and peppery spices'. That's rather a lot of flavours for a few grapes, don't you think? 'Soft tannins and an elegant long lasting finish'. What a load of bollocks! You know I really can't stand pretentious people." He swilled the wine around first in the glass, then in his mouth, before swallowing.

"Nature or nurture - which gets your vote? Are people born pretentious, selfish, and arrogant, or is it their parents' fault? Or perhaps it's the result of years spent at a Public school, or is it the people they subsequently associate with as adults? Maybe it's the pompous women they marry who draw it out of them? What's the root cause of a puffed up sense of self-importance, and a deep-seated desire to impress others? You should know, so please tell me. The question I pose is - would you be so uncaring about others if you'd been born 'Up North' to working class parents, gone to a State school, entered the army as a private soldier, and married the pleasant, down to earth girl on the Tesco's checkout? Maybe one day there'll be a cure for it, or support groups: 'Hi, I'm Richard and I'm a pretentious selfish twat!'" He sipped some more wine. "Anyway, it's a very pleasant medium priced South African Malbec - that just about says it all."

His captive mumbled something incoherent.

"What did you say? Speak up. How can we have a conversation if you stutter and mutter?"

"I said I'm not pretentious."

"Wow. Really? And you actually believe that? What about selfish, arrogant and thoughtless - do you deny having those faults as well? It's the same with alcoholics you know, and those with a gambling addiction. The hardest part is accepting that they have a problem. It's because they've been like it for such a long time and somehow coped, pretended to themselves that they can control it; and also it's been a

71

gradual decline, an almost imperceptible slip into the abyss. I mean, you didn't suddenly wake up one morning as a selfish bastard and start spouting pretentious drivel, did you? It probably grew in you slowly like cancer. But perhaps I shouldn't be too hard on you because it would have been very difficult to be otherwise when living in such a pretentious microcosm. We all want to fit in - in school, at work, with our friends - so even if you had been semi-normal as a young child, you would have had to learn the pretentious lingo and mannerisms or risk being shunned and excluded from the club."

"I don't understand," said the young man.

"Of course you do; it's not difficult. You are what you are, and probably can't help it. I hate what you are and I can't help that either. In fact, if I'm honest, I rather relish the disgust and annoyance which you generate in me. We're both trapped in our own little opposing worlds."

"You can't go around kidnapping people just because you dislike them."

"Is that what you think I am, a kidnapper, out to make some money? Well I obviously can kidnap pretentious twats, can't I, or you wouldn't be here."

The young man sobbed: "You're going to kill me aren't you."

"What? I can't hear you if you blubber. The muttering and stuttering were bad enough. I'm going to kill you, is that what you said? Well maybe I am and maybe I'm not; I'm not sure if I've made up my mind about that just yet. I should warn you that I have killed before, many many times, and enjoyed it, so the odds are not looking good for you. I suppose it depends on how satisfying it would be to remove you from the face of the Earth, or whether I think it is necessary to do so."

"If you were going to let me go, you wouldn't let me see you... but I won't go to the police. I won't say a word to anyone if you let me go."

"No, of course you won't. But don't get hung up about me not wearing a mask; it's not a significant factor. Here, I'll show you."

He put his glass down, limped slowly across the room, and stood behind his captive. "No, don't turn around. Now supposing I let you live and you did go to the police, what would you tell them about me? Let's play a little game: pretend I'm a policeman and you've been released by the horrid kidnapper."

"I don't want to play any games."

"Being a spoilsport is hardly going to encourage me to let you live is it? No. Now try to describe me."

"Describe you?"

"OK I'll help with some questions. How old was the man who kidnapped you? Twenties, thirties, forties?"

"N..no, much older."

"Good. Now you're getting into the spirit of it! Fifties, sixties, seventies; older than that?"

"Probably late sixties, maybe seventies."

"OK. What colour of hair did he have?"

"I..I don't know; I couldn't see his hair because of his baseball cap."

"Ah a cap. That's interesting. What colour was it?"

"Mmmm… blue I think."

"Excellent. And was there a logo or any writing on it?

"Yes, there was!"

"Can you describe it?"

"Em…I can't remember. Some words."

"Saying 'some words' doesn't help the 'boys in blue' very much does it? How tall was he?"

"Quite tall, not short."

"Medium height? Average height? As tall as you? Taller, shorter than you?"

"I..I..I can't say. Maybe around six feet."

"Yes, it's hard to judge someone's height when you're seated and have nothing to compare them against, like a door. There is one here of course but it's behind you. No, don't turn around or you'll spoil the game. Fat, thin, stocky, well built?"

"Average probably."

"Average again. Colour of eyes?"

"I couldn't see them because of the dark glasses."

"Clean shaven?"

"Yes."

"Distinguishing features? Scars, a big nose, bushy eyebrows, high cheekbones, a fat face?"

"No, I don't think so, except quite a full face, not thin."

"How was his voice - he spoke to you didn't he? Describe it. Did he have an accent?"

"Possibly a Northern accent? Otherwise it was quite ordinary."

"Yes, slightly Northern, possibly lived in the North in his youth. However, you've missed something very obvious."

"Obvious?"

"Yes. Do I have to spell it out? Something to do with his gait?"

"Gate? I don't understand. What gate? I never saw a gate."

"I despair! Here you are, a supposedly educated person, and you can't understand basic English. My gait. G.A.I.T. Something concerning the way I walk?"

"Walk? Yes, you have a limp and walk with a stick."

His captor returned to the table.

"US Open. That's what the cap says!"

"Yes it does, but do you think I would continue to wear this cap after today if I let you go? Do you think I might walk up and down outside police stations wearing it? Unfortunately, you've described the vast majority of the male population of this country aged over sixty. They would no doubt show you photographs of possible perpetrators, but as I don't have a criminal record you won't see my mugshot amongst them. In fact you would struggle to find me anywhere; I practically don't exist. They would ask you about anyone who might have a grudge against you - has anyone threatened you, or can you think of someone who might have any possible reason to kidnap you? Was there a ransom demand? They might suspect the husband of a lover, but I don't think you've been cheating on your wife have you? You're too scared of her to do that. Or a business connection gone wrong - plenty of possibilities there. Or someone from your past - perhaps you bullied or buggered a younger boy at school, or both, and they've waited and waited to get their revenge? All useless speculation because I have no discernible connection to you, none whatsoever. It's like Strangers on a Train - did you see that movie? They'll think it was a random act because the link between us is so tenuous, so far-fetched, that even the great Sherlock Holmes wouldn't find it. So you see, I could drop you right outside a police station and they would have no hope of ever finding me, with or without your useless description."

"You're insane."

"Possibly. I think of sanity as a continuum rather than a black or white concept; there's a very grey area in the middle which is confusing. And while it may be easy to spot those who are obviously quite mad, there are other abnormal or unusual individuals, special people, who can and do avoid that description. Am I insane because I've brought you here and have held you against your will, or because I've killed before? Obviously not according to our legal system, otherwise there wouldn't be any murderers or abductors in our prisons."

"My family will pay you a lot of money if you let me go. My parents are quite wealthy."

"I'm sure they would if I asked them, but I won't. I'm not doing this for financial gain, and money doesn't interest me. I'll tell you what, I'm a fair-minded individual, and you did take part in my little game, so I have another one for you: you have three guesses, and if you can tell me why you're here, I'll let you go, now, today; I can't say fairer than that. Take your time, there's no rush; neither of us is going anywhere.

Oh, please don't start screaming and shouting again, you'll only force me to gag you, and there's no one nearby who can hear you even if you had a megaphone. Besides, there's no reason for you to panic; if I do decide to kill you I can assure you that it will be quite painless. There isn't a workbench out of sight with saws and drills, or knives and pliers. I may toy with your mind but I'm not going to torture your body; that's not my style - I'm not a monster. Well maybe I am, but not that kind. So there's no reason for you to shriek and wail like that. Come on now - 'man up' as they say."

His prisoner became quieter.

"That's better. You really do have a lot to be thankful for, you know. You're quite fortunate to have the chance of two kinds of release - both quite painless. Not many people in your situation, abducted by a serial killer, could even dream of having those two rather palatable alternatives."

CHAPTER 10

Krill allowed his mind to drift a little as he sped unhindered along the mainly empty motorway roads, oscillating between memories of his sadly brief affair with Margaret, his expedition with Moss and their discussion about the Canal Killings, and a review of some of the other crimes they'd cracked together. Progress with his memoirs had been incredibly slow, not helped by the neighbours or the Beach Boys! Perhaps he should go on a writing retreat when the pandemic ends, assuming it ever does, to speed up the process? There seemed to be quite a lucrative market for such books, and if successful, he could give the proceeds to his grandchildren. The extra publicity from the BBC programme would no doubt help. Also, it would resurrect his profile within the Force. Maybe it might even get him back into police work in some capacity - teaching at the Police College perhaps, or reviewing cold cases that no one else had the time to look into? Although he'd known even as he'd tentatively broached the idea with Moss, that they would both be considered to be far too 'long in the tooth' for such casework. He suspected that it was officers at the end of their careers, or very recently retired, who would be offered such roles, rather that the likes of them.

Murders had always been his special forte. 'Suspect a murder? Then you need to get the Killer!', had often been the cry up and down the land in the 80's and 90's. He remembered one particularly robust headline - 'It takes a Killer to catch a Killer!' Moss had liked it, particularly as he'd given his boss the nickname. But Krill hadn't been very enthusiastic about any publicity, unless it helped them with a case

He hadn't realised how much he'd missed his sidekick in the intervening years he'd spent in Scotland, until they met up again and renewed their friendship. In some respects, they were far closer than siblings could ever be; maybe on a par with 'blood brothers'? Thirty years working together was indeed a very long time.

He felt unusually maudlin about Margaret, because he had also sensed a bond developing between them, whereas clearly she hadn't. He wondered when it was that she had decided he was too old for her? He had a horrible thought that it might have been when she'd first seen his naked body or experienced his lovemaking? He quickly dismissed those nasty niggles, assuring himself that his body was not yet old and wrinkly, and that his passion and bedroom skills remained at least as good or as bad as they'd always been. No, he didn't think that she'd been put off by anything as personal or intimate.

Perhaps she'd had such a concern at the back of her mind almost from their very first meeting, maybe from the time he'd put his hand over hers in the pub garden and the possibility of something happening had opened up? In which case, why had she allowed things to develop? He would be eternally grateful that she had; he respected her decision and he had no regrets.

When Krill parked his car, put on his face mask, and approached the high security fence topped with razor wire, he wondered how the prison could be described as 'open', because it looked anything but. Maybe it was relatively open and accessible within the guarded perimeter? In a way, he was relieved that Crow was still securely locked up, because he believed the serial killer would continue to pose a risk to the public despite his advanced years. Once a killer always a killer in his book.

He'd arranged with the prison governor to speak to Crow early in the morning, outside normal visiting hours, so he felt quite invigorated despite the long drive the previous day from Berkshire to the North West. The nearby B&B had looked after him well, and he'd enjoyed eating the local produce at breakfast - bacon, eggs, and sausages, while gazing out at the Fells beyond the garden wall. Moss had offered to come with him and share the driving, but Krill was looking forward to having some thinking time on his own. Although he was both refreshed and replete he was not optimistic; he had little reason to believe that Crow would now talk about the murders, but there was no harm in trying.

He had a 'courtesy' pre-meeting with the governor and was shown straight into his rather minimalist office.

"I must admit I was a little surprised when I got your call," he said. "Surprised both that anyone in authority still remembered Peter never mind would want to see him, and also that the legendary Chief Inspector Krill would be willing to come all this way! Anyway, welcome, welcome. I did wonder if there might have been some new developments even after all these years? Perhaps additional crimes you want him to admit to; some potential new victims identified? Maybe some old unsolved cases which have his DNA or modus operandi?"

Krill smiled to himself. It seemed that even prison governors enjoyed CSI and other TV crime dramas.

"No, sorry to disappoint you Governor, I just wanted to talk to him about the original murders, in the hope that he might fill in some of the gaps."

"Oh I see; so there's still some aspects which worry you about the murders even after all this time? How intriguing, and how very conscientious! No stone unturned - I understand, and quite right, quite right. I'm not sure how well you'll fare with our Peter though, he's not the most talkative inmate at the best of times. Very much keeps himself to himself, and the others leave him alone. Still waters and all that." He looked sheepish, "Although I suppose one shouldn't use that phrase given the nature of his crimes! You'll find him a changed man, both physically and mentally. He's not one hundred percent, health wise, has had the odd bout in hospital. But I suppose very few age well in prison even when they're doing far shorter stretches. The 'whole life' verdict was a bit of a blow. He came here soon after, perhaps as a form of consolation prize? But he's never any trouble, no drugs or any problems like that. Of course he doesn't often get visitors which is a shame; probably wouldn't have many even if we weren't located in the very back of beyond."

They walked together down a short corridor and out into the open air. The Governor continued his monologue:

"I know they look like old army barracks but they're quite comfortable inside. The prisoners have their own TV and toilet, and some, like Peter, even have their own shower. They can personalise it as much as they want to, but I don't think Peter has done much of that beyond a few books on his shelf. He still likes to read about canals and has quite an extensive video collection - isn't that interesting? Truly loves those programmes about canal journeys with the husband and wife actors - now what are they called? You'd think, because of what happened, he'd not want to be reminded of them and why here's here; they were his downfall weren't they, the canals? But I suppose his mind doesn't work the same way as ours does it? You would know a lot more about those sorts of things - the criminal mind. Well, here we are. As the weather is fine, well quite fine for here, I've arranged for some chairs to be put outside as you can see, and we'll bring you coffee or tea. I know Peter likes what he calls his 'builder's brew'."

It was a long time since Krill had interviewed anyone 'inside', and he'd never before been to an Open prison, so he wasn't sure what to expect as he waited for Crow to appear. He knew that they were allowed to wear their own clothing within certain limits, and that they were even permitted to buy items from the likes of Argos. What did Crow remind him of as he slowly approached, accompanied by a prison officer? A very careworn, tired, decrepit old man? Krill's grandfather not long before he died? Someone recovering from a life threatening illness? An ancient, slightly well-to-do, tramp? As he later said to Moss, 'one foot in the grave would have been an improvement for poor Crow!'

Krill didn't even think about offering his hand - he wouldn't have done so at any time under any circumstances, and Crow sat down next to him, silently and with hardly a glance in his direction. They waited while the tea, coffee, and biscuits were delivered by another inmate.

"It's been a long time Peter."

Crow concentrated on dunking his shortbread into the dark brown tea.

"It will soon be forty three years. Imagine that." Krill almost said 'how time flies' but suspected that it didn't have any wings for Crow, despite his name.

"What do you want Krill?" Crow continued to stare straight ahead as he spoke. "Why did you come here? As you can see, your work and that of the Crown Prosecution Service is nearly finished: I won't be subject to Her Majesty's Pleasure for much longer. Come to have one last gloat, have you?"

"I'm sorry if you've not been well."

"Really Krill? I'm not. Do you know how many times I've thought about committing suicide since I was convicted? Dozens of times. Hundreds of times. But I'm sure you're not here to say 'sorry' or to enjoy the Governor's biscuits, so let's get down to brass tacks: why are you here?"

Krill was a little surprised by Crow's astuteness and the strength of his voice. Somehow his manner of speaking and his body didn't seem to belong together. Crow had never struck him as an intelligent or educated man; maybe he'd studied and read a lot during his time Inside? He'd been expecting to be met by a sad defeated dullard.

"OK Peter. First things first: do you still say that you're innocent?"

Crow groaned forcefully, his whole body twisting with discomfort.

"Oh what's the point? For God's sake Krill, what on earth is the fucking point?" Crow's cup and saucer wobbled in his hands as he spoke. "There was no point all those years ago when I first told you I was innocent, and there's certainly even less of a point in saying it now. I can't see why you would even ask that question, let alone expect me to answer it. What good will an answer do you or I? No good; none whatsoever. And why would you believe anything I said now, when you didn't believe a word of it then? Huh? I think that of the two of us, you're the one who should be locked up, because you're certainly guilty of being incredibly crass and stubborn!"

Well, well. thought Krill, was he guilty of being insensitive and pig-headed? Probably. He wasn't sure why anyone would want to show any sensitivity towards a criminal guilty of multiple murders. And maybe he was being obdurate in his belief that justice had been done, because there had been more than enough evidence to remove all reasonable doubt. The Jury had thought so too, returning their unanimous verdict after only two hours, which was almost a record for a murder trial at the Old Bailey.

"There was a lot of evidence against you Peter."

"Virtually all of it circumstantial. No eye witnesses, no fingerprints, no 'smoking gun'; nothing concrete apart from that small piece of cloth with the drug residue."

"Yes I agree, that was crucial. If you're innocent, how do you account for it being found hidden in a drawer on your barge?" Krill asked.

Crow closed his eyes trying to control the anger and frustration which rose up inside him. The dam which had been slowly built by forty years of despair and resignation threatened to burst.

"Obviously planted, most likely by one of those conducting the search. You needed something to pin it on me, to go with the other rather inconclusive evidence, and so, like a miracle, it was found. I'm not saying that you did it Krill, or that you asked someone to do it, but it's the only explanation. That sergeant of yours, Moss, he gets my vote, acting on his own perverted initiative. Ask yourself this Krill: if I was clever enough to literally get away with murder for years and years, why would I keep that incriminating rag? It doesn't make sense. But as I say, too much water has now gone under too many canal bridges to even worry about it. I no longer care that I was innocent and somehow 'fitted up' for the murders, so why should you think twice about it?"

Crow finished the last of his tea and stood up.

"I've become a Buddhist; you didn't know that, did you? So I believe I will come back in another form. And as I've been so cruelly treated in this incarnation and never really harmed a living soul, it will be a far better life than this one. I therefore look forward to it: dying as this man, shedding this shell. Anyway Krill, I've said all I'm going to say, so I would like you to leave now. Being with you is very bad for my karma."

CHAPTER 11

For each and every mile of the long tedious journey home, Krill's thoughts kept returning to what Crow had said, particularly his vehement claim of innocence. Could he have been wrong about Crow all these years? Was there a possibility that the key evidence had been planted, and if so by whom? While he'd never had even the slightest reason to doubt Moss's honesty and integrity, he couldn't really say the same about every one of the other members of the search team, mainly because he'd hardly known some of them. Or could it have been an outsider, someone unconnected to the inquiry? Someone who had access to Crow's barge and wanted suspicion to fall on him? Either because they desired to see him put away - there were probably a number of people who wished Crow harm at the time because he'd been a bit of a troublemaker, or because they were the real serial killer and what better way to evade justice?

Although it was not unknown for evidence to be fabricated, Crow's claim seemed very far-fetched, and as such he didn't want to give it any credence. But neither could he totally dismiss it as others might - that was not Krill's style.

On the one hand, Krill believed that Crow was just playing with him and enjoying making him doubt his achievements and abilities, but countering that view was the fact that Crow had sounded very convincing.

Krill tried to set aside any prejudices which he might have due to preconceptions and self-interest, because believing in Crow's innocence would have a profound impact on his reputation and even his self-belief, and also went against his long held opinion. How would someone independent respond to what the convicted serial killer had said? They would have serious doubts about his claim to be innocent of course, because of the circumstances. There would be scepticism because a jury had originally convicted Crow, and legal appeals had failed. Any impartial observer would probably presume that they themselves knew far less than the people who had heard the detailed evidence at the trial, and that they were not as well informed as the professionals. Krill's own record since Crow's conviction would no doubt also hold sway, and push him or her towards disbelief. Therefore, the vast majority of people would probably think that Crow was lying.

But it wasn't enough. Krill also considered himself to be a good judge of character, and he believed that he could tell when someone was lying; or even more importantly perhaps, when they were telling the truth. He recalled Crow's words and mannerisms, and concluded that if he knew nothing about Crow, or the circumstances of the case, then he might be inclined to say that he was telling the truth, or saying what he believed to be the truth, which was not necessarily the same thing. There seemed little doubt that Crow believed he was innocent, and that was very worrying.

He mentally reviewed the case to analyse whether Crow would have been convicted without that telltale piece of cloth, which held traces of the chemical used to render the serial killer's victims unconscious. Crow certainly had the opportunity to commit the murders: he lived alone and didn't have an alibi for any of the dates in question; he also possessed a black motorcycle and a distinctive crash helmet similar to one seen by a key witness. Motive could also be established: Crow had been severely beaten as a child, so had a reason for taking revenge on anyone who reminded him of his past suffering, particularly middle-aged men. Not only did he have a difficult upbringing, he was frequently in trouble as a teenager and young adult, and had been arrested for causing an affray outside a pub (the case was dropped due to a lack of evidence as witnesses failed to come forward), and he'd been charged with using threatening behaviour towards his stepfather, who, probably under pressure from Crow's mother, later withdrew his complaint. During cross examination, the prosecutor had therefore been able to show that Crow had a tendency towards violence. 'Means' was also reasonably strong, as he was diabetic and had access to needles and syringes, and he lived on a barge and knew the canal network well.

Without doubt Crow ticked a large number of boxes for Krill and for the jury, however the chemical on the cloth was the clincher. It was both the icing and a very large cherry on the cake, because it removed any possible shadow of doubt.

Despite Crow saying there hadn't been one, it was the 'smoking gun' of the case. He had to admit that without it there was a possibility that Crow might have been found not guilty. Take away some of the other evidence and Crow would without doubt still have been convicted, but make that rag vanish and the case might start to crumble.

Would the stained cloth still be held somewhere as evidence, and if so, could he have it checked for Crow's DNA? Evidence in serious cases was always kept for at least thirty years, and probably longer in Crow's case as he was still incarcerated. Showing that Crow had handled that cloth even once, would refute his claim that he knew nothing about it, and would certainly put Krill's mind at rest. He still had enough contacts in different departments of the police to have such a check carried out, probably without too many questions being asked, and if he didn't know the right people then Moss would. While an absence of Crow's DNA, or finding someone else's, wouldn't prove Crow's innocence, its presence could certainly confirm his guilt; in which case Crow might not wish to cooperate with such a procedure. However, Crow's DNA should already be on file, probably from a sample taken in the 1980's when the power to collect and store it was first authorised by UK legislation.

He could almost hear Crow laughing as he sat in his cell, visualising Krill being tormented by doubt, and being forced to look again at forty year old evidence. He probably knew that Krill wouldn't be able to ignore what he'd said. However, he'd also claimed that he no longer cared whether Krill or anyone else believed him, and Crow was right, because what good would it do him now after all these years? It therefore felt wrong to assume that Crow was just toying with him.

The one truth which Krill acknowledged, whether universally or otherwise, was that his journey north had certainly opened a particularly nasty can of worms!

As soon as he parked next to his cottage he phoned Moss on his mobile.

"How was the visit, Killer?"

"Interesting and somewhat unsettling."

"Unsettling? How?"

"Come round for a beer and I'll tell you."

"OK, will do. I was planning to pop in to see you anyway, because I have some rather unsettling news of my own."

"What news?" Krill asked.

"Your neighbour's husband has apparently disappeared. I thought it was important to tell you before you found out for yourself, and started wondering if me or one of the lads had been up to no good: such as dumping him stark bollock naked in Prague, like a groom on a stag outing."

Krill couldn't help smiling as he considered that image.

"Which of course you haven't."

"Perish the thought!"

CHAPTER 12

"How much longer are you going to keep me a prisoner?"

"Don't knock it - at least you're still alive, which is a bit of a surprise as I don't normally keep my victims for as long as this. The short answer, strange as it might seem, is that I don't know. What happens to you, and when, doesn't actually depend on either of us, but on another person."

The young man was now fully clothed and chained by his ankle to a ring set into the wall. There was a mattress on the floor, a metal chair for him to sit on, and two buckets. The concrete walls and floor were pitted, stained, and cracked.

"Is it something my father's mixed up in?" he asked.

The other man put down the newspaper he was reading and looked up. "Why, what does he do?"

"He's an investment manager. Maybe he's lost you money? If so, I'm sure he'll reimburse you or even double your initial investment."

"I've already told you that this is not about money, but now you've mentioned your father, let's explore the possibility. Does he often lose people's money?"

"It happens, especially when the market is so volatile," the young man replied.

"Have you personally invested your savings with him?"

"Me? No, I don't have any spare cash."

"I wonder if you would trust your father with it if you did? I suppose he takes advantage of people's greed - the 'get rich quick' brigade, so maybe they get what they deserve. How do you make your money?"

The young man hesitated. "I help people with their financial affairs, with the amount of tax they pay."

"So, like father, like son."

"I suppose so," he admitted.

"Aiding the 'haves' to pay less tax is hardly assisting the poor is it? It doesn't help to pay our nurses and teachers if you set up some offshore accounts for the wealthy. I've never had much time for financiers, especially bankers. Just like you they don't produce anything tangible themselves, anything objectively meaningful, only more money. True, they might once in a while help a business by giving them a loan, but they never get their own hands dirty or risk their personal capital. And for every individual or company they help, there's probably a dozen they turn away or actually harm. It's curious that while they deal in balance sheets, their own is not a very positive one: far more red negative crosses in their lives than black positive ticks. Maybe it's an area I've ignored for too long? Here's another proposition for you to mull over, how about if I take your father or the manager of a local bank, or both, and put them here in your place? Would that be acceptable to you? A swop?"

"I don't think you should take anyone."

"But do you think your father would willingly sacrifice his own freedom, and in all probability his life, to save yours?"

"Probably."

"Well that's something positive isn't it, even if he is a bad broker. Does your wife work?"

"I don't want to talk about my family."

"If you're worried that they might come to some harm then I can assure you that they won't. I've never harmed a woman or a child in my entire life."

"But the people you kill are someone's child."

"Now you're being pedantic and splitting hairs, which is not a good tactic. Telling me about your family might encourage me to take pity on you, for their sake."

"Would it?" he asked, half-hoping.

"Well, it hasn't so far; almost the opposite in fact, but you never know. So, does she work?"

The young man sat down, trying to keep the conversation going, while his captor continued to straddle his own seat, his elbow resting on the table beside him, his walking stick hooked over the arm of his chair. In some ways the tableau resembled a scene from the stage production of a psychological drama, by someone such as Arthur Miller or Tennessee Williams. The only missing element was an audience, but during the pandemic they were now always absent in any event.

"Yes she does, part-time, as an editor."

"Oh, so she's a literary person? That's a good thing: helping people with their writing. I like that. And you have children?"

"Yes two, and they're quite young, so things would be very hard for them if they no longer had my income to rely on."

"So no public schools for them then, if you vanished?"

"Not unless my father paid the fees."

"Which he might well do, using the proceeds from other people's money."

The young man tried a different approach: "How long have you been doing this?"

"Killing people? Oh, for a long, long time; nearly fifty years in fact. But not constantly - I sometimes take a break for a few months or even for a year or two, like a sabbatical, so I come at it again refreshed and eager."

Again the young man hesitated. "How many people?"

"I just knew you were going to ask that next! I'm not sure. I suppose I should be sad or at least sorry to have to say it: sad for myself and sorry for my victims. At first, I could remember each and every one: their names, what they did for a living, what family they had - wives, children, parents if they were still alive; everything important about them. But then, probably about twenty years ago, they started to merge together, the edges became blurred, and I got muddled up. Was it Bill or Dave who had two kids named Sarah and Peter? It used to drive me crazy trying to figure it out, because of course I never wrote any of it down, but then I just gave up.

Maybe it's because of the sheer number, and maybe it's my failing memory?"

"More than fifty, which would be one a year?"

"Oh, a lot more than that. Fifty would hardly make a worthwhile career would it?"

"Did you have another job, an ordinary job?"

"Of course. I don't make money out of killing people; I could have if I'd wanted to, probably lots, but I didn't. That wouldn't seem right or fair to my victims."

"What did you do? I assume you're retired now?"

"Careful now, if I tell you too much about myself isn't it less likely that I'll let you go? In any case, that's more than enough about me. Tell me the kindest thing you've ever done."

"Kindest?"

"Yes, like helping someone in need, something charitable. Let me give you an example: I remember when boy scouts had their 'Bob a Job Week', when for a shilling as it was then, five pence, we would help someone by mowing their lawn or cleaning their car. That was kind in a way wasn't it? We didn't keep the money ourselves of course; I can't recall what it was used for - probably to buy new toggles and badges."

"You were a boy scout?" The young man seemed amazed.

"Does that surprise you? Yes I was for a couple of years. A lot of kids were in the fifties and early sixties, because there wasn't much else for them to do. It was supposed to be good clean healthy fun: learning skills, encouraging teamwork, and keeping us out of mischief. So, tell me how you've behaved like a boy scout, about what you've done for other people;

and I don't mean your friends or family, or how you've helped someone for monetary gain. Make a case for yourself as a 'good' person, one who doesn't deserve to die."

The young man panicked, overwhelmed by the enormity of the situation; how he might save or more likely condemn himself with his answer.

"I...I...I can't th..th..think."

"Oh, now you've started stuttering again. Remain quiet until you know exactly what you want to say and can do so clearly, that's my advice. Think and then speak; unfortunately so few people seem to follow that rule. Maybe I'll leave you to contemplate your short life and consider the best possible answer to my question. It's unfair to rush you. Take your time. In any case, I have other work to do - you're not my only project."

"No, don't go. Don't leave me here. I've thought about my third guess."

But it was too late - the door had already been closed and locked, and he was alone once more.

CHAPTER 13

"I found this on my doorstep when I arrived home."

Moss eased on the latex gloves which Krill handed him. Only then did he pick up the brown plastic urn from the kitchen worktop and carefully remove the lid. He saw that it was two thirds filled with a grey ash. He put his nose near to the lip and sniffed, but there was no smell.

"Have you checked whether there's anything hidden inside?" Moss asked.

"Yes, but see for yourself."

Krill passed Moss a long thin screwdriver which he used to stir up the contents until he was satisfied that it only contained ash.

"No note with it?"

"Yes, this."

Moss read the short typed note out loud: "'Are you enjoying the peace and quiet Krill?' Peace and quiet? What does that mean?"

"Well, the implication being that you're possibly holding my missing neighbour in your hands."

Moss looked shocked, then disbelieving,

"How can it be your missing neighbour? There hasn't been sufficient time to kill him, cremate the body, and deliver it to you."

"No?"

"Not in a couple of days. Well I suppose it's theoretically possible but extremely unlikely." Moss shook the urn again to disturb the contents. "This looks professionally done to me, not someone using a funeral pyre in the backyard or there'd be larger pieces of bone and fragments of wood. How would anyone who took your neighbour have access to cremators?"

"Someone who works in a crematorium, or perhaps deals with hospital waste?" Krill suggested.

"Let's not jump too hastily to conclusions Killer. These may not even be human remains. We should get them analysed and the urn checked for fingerprints. And even if they are human, they're not necessarily from someone recently deceased."

Krill nodded. "True. My first thought when I saw the urn on the doorstep, before I read the note, was that it was 'Graham', Margaret's fiancé, because we were talking about his ashes just a couple of weeks ago."

"Why would anyone send you his ashes? Sending them to her might make some sense, not placing them at the door to your cottage. However, whatever they are, human or animal, old or recent, or even from the tray of a wood-burning stove, it's definitely someone sending you a message of some kind. But why and about what?"

"I think it's far more likely to be a practical joke, and one which is in very poor taste. Perhaps from someone who's heard about my neighbour and knows about my past. Why do you think someone would send me ashes as a message? You think they're possibly saying that I could be next?"

"Maybe. There are bound to be lots of people on the wrong side of the Law who don't like what you've done to them or their relatives. We should check who's recently been released. I'm worried, Killer."

"Worried? Why?"

"Worried that you're beginning to treat this like an interesting puzzle or game. If it is, then you're the mouse and we have absolutely no idea who the cat is, or what he or she will do next. Worried for your safety, quite frankly. I think we should take precautions."

Krill laughed. "You sound like my mother before I went on my first date! What sort of precautions? An armed guard sleeping in the spare room? 'Hoping I'm enjoying a quieter life' is hardly threatening, Moss. Now if they'd said - 'you're next', or 'do you regret what you've done', or 'I'm watching you', then I could understand your concern."

"Don't joke about it, Killer. I think it is threatening: the implication being - enjoy it while you can."

"You seriously think that I should be worried that I could end up in an urn, ahead of my time that is?" Krill asked.

"If you were a member of the public who'd had some remains, probably human, left on your doorstep, and received a dubious note, what would you do? You'd go straight to the police, and fast."

Krill's phone alerted him. It was a text from an unknown number: 'Did you believe Crow? Maybe you should.' He showed it to Moss.

"How does anyone know I visited Crow?"

"Did you tell anyone apart from me? People connected with your visit would know - those in the prison service for example." Moss thought for a moment. "Easiest way of course is to track your car. You pour the beers Killer and I'll have a look."

Ten minutes later Moss was back holding a small metal device.

"Under a wheel arch. Looks quite sophisticated. I can have it checked out: where it was made, who supplies them, maybe who's recently bought one, even try to trace the signal if that's possible. But I wouldn't get your hopes up."

"No, don't do that; they'll soon realise we've found it. Put it back until we know more about who placed it there."

Moss hesitated, then decided on a compromise: "OK, but I'll take a photo of the serial number and manufacturer."

The mysterious urn had been placed in a Waitrose plastic bag and put inside Moss's car boot for later analysis, and while outside he'd replaced, a little unwillingly, the tracking device where he'd found it. Moss had been tempted to put it on his own car in an effort to draw any danger away from Krill, but had decided that it was unlikely to achieve the desired result, and would only serve to annoy his ex-boss. He looked all around him on the walk back, checking the street where he'd parked, and the gardens and empty vehicles down the narrow pebbled lane which led to Krill's cottage, but all seemed quiet and totally unthreatening.

He wished Krill lived, like he did, in a top floor flat in a block which had a single public entrance and a decent door entry system, because that was far more secure and much easier to 'defend', whereas Krill's cottage had lots of rickety ground floor windows, old inadequate door locks, and despite his troublesome neighbours, was located in a quiet remote spot at the end of an unlit lane.

The nearest police station was also miles away, so any 999 calls would not be responded to quickly even if he had a word with the local senior officer, or one of his higher up contacts at Thames Valley. They also couldn't do a regular drive past to check for anything suspicious or as a deterrent. Maybe they would have to resort to him and the lads taking it in turns to be in the spare room after all? He could almost hear Krill's complaints about the intrusion and how ridiculous he was being. It wouldn't be the first time that Krill had accused Moss of trying to 'mother' him.

He found Krill still in the kitchen when he returned, stirring something in a pan with a wooden spoon.

"I've taken some vegetable soup out of the freezer; there's more than enough for two, and I'm also defrosting some rolls to have with it."

Moss inwardly groaned as he looked at the earth coloured concoction - he tried to avoid all vegetables whenever he could.

"Great," said Moss, unconvincingly. "So what was so disturbing about your trip North? Visiting Crow can't have been a pleasant experience at the best of times, but especially now that he knows he will die in prison. And why should you believe him? What did he say?"

"He's known for a while that he'll never be released. At least where he is, he's quite comfortable; it's probably not that different from student accommodation during lockdown."

Moss laughed. "Did you see the signs they'd put up in the windows of their Halls of Residence? 'Help - bring beer', and another said, 'HMP'."

"Poor sods, they're really missing out; it took me quite a while to recover from the excesses of my Freshers' Week. Yes, Crow will definitely die in prison, and from the look of him it won't be very long now."

Krill poured out the soup and passed a bowl to Moss. They both went through to the dining room.

"What was so disturbing about my visit? First, he's a changed man, apparently quite educated and well read. He's also resigned to his fate. He even told me he's become a Buddhist and was looking forward to his reincarnation."

"Blimey. A Buddhist! Old Crow? Still I suppose a lot of long-term prisoners take courses and some find religion. Did he give you any more details about his crimes?" Moss asked.

"No he didn't, and in a way I wasn't expecting him too. The somewhat perplexing aspect of our conversation was that even now, when he has absolutely no hope of release, he still says he is innocent," Krill paused, "and that, if anything, I was inclined to believe him, even before I received that text."

Moss was aghast. This was heresy. "You can't be serious, Boss. Crow innocent? Never in a million years!"

"He says someone else placed that piece of cloth on his barge."

Now Moss was angry and aggrieved. "Of course he would bloody well say that! They all shout it from the prison rooftop - I've been framed! The evidence was planted! Police corruption! I'm innocent! We've heard it so many times before."

"That cloth worried me a little at the time, because it didn't feel right. Why would he have kept it? For what purpose? It's not a trophy and it was the one direct link to the crimes."

"I assumed that he needed a cloth to carry the filled syringe around with him. He could hardly have it unwrapped or unprotected in his pocket, or he might accidentally anaesthetise himself. Keeping the cloth would save him having to find a new one each time," Moss reasoned.

"True, but which is more likely: taking a huge risk and keeping the same cloth for weeks or months, or simply cutting a new piece each time? We never found the original material that it came from on the barge, nor did we find any of the drug itself."

"OK, I see what you're getting at, but how did it get in his bloody drawer if he didn't put it there? I oversaw the search and I kept a very close eye on what was going on."

"But you couldn't watch everyone all the time." Krill tried to placate Moss and tone down his sense of outrage. "However, I don't for one moment believe that any of the team planted it. I think someone else put it there as soon as they knew we were looking for a murder suspect. And it has to be someone who knew that Crow would fit the profile."

"Well, that again points the finger at those involved in the investigation because who else would know?" Moss waggled his sparsely filled spoon at Krill in emphasis.

"Not necessarily, as most of the details were in the press: the motorbike, the crash helmet, the injection of a chemical, and obviously the link to canals. Someone who knew Crow's background - that he lived on a barge, was diabetic, and had a bike - could easily see that he might become a suspect. If we accept that it was some unknown person then there's only two alternatives: it's someone who knew Crow and wanted to harm him or get him out of the way, or it was the real killer wanting to lay a false trail. Obviously the text saying Crow is innocent could have been sent by his enemy, who's still gloating about Crow's incarceration, or by the real killer, who for some reason is wishing to point out my mistake."

"Or the text could have been sent by Crow himself, just to wind you up? He definitely knew about your visit and what was said. Isn't that the most likely explanation?" said Moss, looking for a far simpler solution.

"That obviously can't be ruled out either, but it doesn't get my vote, nor does the first of the two alternatives I mentioned. And what's more I think that recent events are all somehow interconnected."

Moss was a little stunned both by what Krill believed to have happened and by his calmness in stating his opinion.

"So, if I understand you correctly Guv, you're opting for the absolutely worst case scenario: namely that Crow is innocent, that there's a serial killer still on the loose, who for some reason is baiting you, and that they're linked in some roundabout way to your neighbour going AWOL, the urn arriving on your doorstep, the tracking device being put on your car, and the text you've received?"

"Unfortunately yes, I think I am saying exactly that."

Moss understood a little about the way Krill's complicated brain worked but even so it was a lot to take in. He had no choice but to run with it for the time being.

"Assuming that you're right, what do we do now?" asked Moss.

"I have absolutely no idea."

"Shit! This is getting serious, Killer, and I think we should definitely consider going straight to the police."

"And tell them what? That I may be the victim of a practical joke? That I'm being followed and spied on, but as yet have no idea who is doing it or why? That Crow could be sending me text messages from prison? Or do I go even further and say that someone else may have committed the Canal Killings, when we have no concrete evidence for it to be the case? Do I say that my neighbour may have been kidnapped, rather than the more likely scenario that he's had a row with his wife and taken off in a huff for a few days, which is probably what the police presently believe? If I tell them even half of my suspicions they're likely to think I'm crazy. No, we have to find out more before we go to the police, and probably have no choice but to wait for the serial killer's next move."

Moss didn't like the sound of that last comment, and thought that it was wrong not to report all that had happened. However, he could see that it was no use arguing with Krill at the moment, and also if he went to the police himself then his friend would never forgive him.

CHAPTER 14

Crow was in the prison library dealing with a few requests and putting the books onto a trolley, when a prison guard came up to him.

"Here's another email for you Peter. This one's even longer than the last."

He handed Crow three sheets of closely typed print.

"Mind telling me what it's about?"

"You've read it?"

"Of course. Personally, I'm surprised the Governor has allowed you to see them because they're a bit weird aren't they? But I suppose he thinks they're harmless enough, especially for you to have Peter. Is it a story someone's writing, or is it about you, when you were younger? This one's about some lassie called Marie and her boyfriend, and how jealous this other boy was; how he even thought about doing away with him, so he could have her himself. Did you own a scooter like this lad Paul? Did you know Marie?"

Crow folded the pages in two and put them in his jacket pocket, ignoring the man's questions. The truth was that he had no idea who was sending the emails and couldn't remember knowing anyone called Marie or Paul. Maybe this email would solve the mystery?

He started to read it as soon as he'd finished delivering the books, and returned to his room:

I became infatuated with a girl called Marie - even her name fascinated me, and she was also very beautiful. She had short golden hair and very blue eyes; they were the colour of the sky on the most perfect day of your best ever holiday. She was my first unrequited love.

Looking back, it's curious that right from the very start, when I had absolutely no experience, I wanted it to look like an accident. What better way to make certain that I didn't get caught than if no one even suspected that a crime had been committed?

I imagined myself consoling Marie about the tragic loss of her boyfriend, saying how awful it was that such a young life should be cut short, and therefore able, almost naturally, to take my victim's place. I knew she fancied me, because of how she looked at me every time I went into the local supermarket where she worked after school and on Saturdays; it was a mixture of curiosity and anticipation. I never understood what she saw in Paul - he was seventeen, the same age as me, and he certainly wasn't better looking, or richer, or cleverer. Maybe he was the sensitive type; maybe he read poetry to her or she felt sorry for him? It made no sense to me, but I respected her loyalty and didn't think any less of her when she said she couldn't go out with me because of him. But I could sense that she seemed sad to have to say it. I think she was yet another person who was trapped, and like the others needed to be freed.

Paul and I both had Lambretta scooters - his had lots of mirrors attached to the front. I can't remember what colour it was, but mine was bright yellow, which made it difficult to follow him without being seen. However, I managed it; perhaps I was virtually invisible even then? I followed him home, I watched as he parked it in the supermarket car park, I tailed the two of them as they rode around the Town, and a few times into the countryside.

I already knew a little about the mechanics of scooters, but bought a manual just to be sure. I thought the easiest way to remove my rival would be by tampering with the brakes - loosening the nuts which held the cables or slackening them off. I'd had problems with my own, so I knew how temperamental they could be; the brakes were barely sufficient on my 125cc scooter and his was the more powerful 175. It was really an accident waiting to happen - kids came off them all the time, and he liked to go fast.

The problem was how to ensure that the accident was fatal, and importantly, that it didn't happen when Marie was with him? The start of a school day would be best because he was generally late leaving home and in a rush, plus he wouldn't be seeing Marie until much later, so there would be plenty of opportunity for my plan to work on the trips to and from school and to the supermarket, without endangering her. Fate lent a hand because he lived at the top of a very steep hill, probably the steepest in the Town, and right at the bottom was a busy main road. He also left his scooter very *conveniently parked in his parents' drive. He seemed to be asking for it.*

What I remember most is the exhilaration: of following him, of the planning, which included adjusting my own brakes to see how easy it would be to fix his, and in particular, knowing that his life was now in my hands. I could decide each day whether he would live or die! I think it was the excitement and the novelty of it all which made me delay - it became almost an addiction, and that hiatus brought another factor into the equation - Susan.

I was quite popular, especially with girls, and got invited to all the parties. I suspect they could sense my inner strength, my power; or maybe it's like they say, they were attracted to me because I was a 'bad boy'? Some women find that irresistible don't they? I seldom had anyone to take, but that didn't matter, because most people seemed to be in the same boat. I would always check to see if Marie and Paul were there, but they never were; perhaps he didn't like parties, or maybe he knew that he risked losing her if she had the chance to meet other boys? He wanted to keep her hidden away, like his own private property. He probably didn't like the idea of her working in the shop. He almost kept her a prisoner.

Susan was by far the prettiest girl at this particular party, and very sexy too, although I didn't realise it then. I knew she was a few months older than me and seemingly going steady with an eighteen year old, so I didn't pay her that much attention, beyond the odd admiring glance. At some point a group of us were relaxing on the sofa, including her boyfriend, and she came over to join us, and sat at his feet.

That was when she surreptitiously started putting her hand inside the leg of my trousers! Nothing else happened that evening - she left as expected with him, but I got her number and we soon started a relationship. She unknowingly saved Paul.

But I never forgot Marie, and how I let her boyfriend off the hook. It took me a while to put matters right, or as right as they could be after all the years which had elapsed, and what had happened in the meantime.

Looking back at my life, I think all the foreseen and unknown consequences of my actions mattered as much if not more to me, as the deed itself. I'm sure some of the children went on to have very successful careers despite what happened to their fathers, and some of the wives no doubt remarried. I don't begrudge them their good fortune; I wanted to alter lives, not spoil them.

Crow put the pages down on his bed. He'd thought of himself more as a 'Rocker' in the 60's and 70's, so had never owned a scooter, only a battered moped, and then several secondhand motorcycles. While he had slicked back his hair and worn leathers, he hadn't joined any gangs or ridden to the seaside for fights on the promenade with 'Mods'. Besides, they happened more in the South, in Brighton and other resorts near London, not near his Northern town.

He'd asked the Governor about the source of the emails when the second one had been sent, and was told that they were from someone called Andy who lived in the Wirral. Crow's stepfather had been called Andrew and was born in

Lancashire, but it couldn't be him because he'd been dead for twenty years. The Governor had asked him whether he no longer wanted to receive the emails, but they'd sparked his curiosity, and besides it helped to relieve the boredom. Each missive had been longer than the one before. The first had been just a couple of paragraphs about a 1950's murder trial. Crow couldn't stop himself from taking it out of the drawer and rereading it:

'I think the anger was always inside me, waiting to be released. The seed was probably present when I was born, but I believe it first germinated when I was just a child, in 1957. Had I been ten years older that year, seventeen instead of seven, then things might have been different. I might have been more interested in girls than in the spectacular true crime revelations on the front pages of the newspapers. It was the trial of an Eastbourne doctor who was accused of murdering his patients, and benefitting from legacies in their wills. The notion that anyone might be able to get away with not just one but multiple murders both intrigued and excited me.

I quickly saw the mistakes he'd made, including the telltale trail which led to his bank account, and also the paper records he'd unsuccessfully falsified. He wasn't my hero as such because he'd been stupid enough to be arrested, but I was impressed by the fact that he was acquitted of the murder charge, perhaps helped by his friends in high places who could vouch for him and possibly manipulate the system. All those thoughts lay dormant at the back of my mind, incubating.'

What stood out for Crow now were two things: the fact that the writer of the emails apparently wanted his crimes to be seen as an accident, and in some ways even more strange, was that he had been born the very same year as himself. He had a vague recollection of someone he'd known as a teenager dating a girl called Susan, and several of his friends at that time had ridden scooters, but he struggled to put it all together. He was tired and it was a very long time ago.

The second email had been quite different, and had dealt almost entirely with death. How, in the author's view, it would be like an endless sleep but without the troublesome dreams that often plagued us in this life. It said that for many people their fear of death was the ultimate fear of missing out. They couldn't cope with the knowledge that life would go on happily without them. Or it was the act of dying and whether it would be painful which frightened them most. These were far more significant than any worries about what might await them in an afterlife, which in any case, according to the sender, did not exist. Clearly whoever it was, was not very religious, and most definitely not a Buddhist.

Crow had had more than his fair share of bad dreams and nightmares in this life so could identify with the author's hopes for an untroubled sleep. Unlike most people, Crow had not experienced FOMO for decades, if at all, because his lengthy incarceration and the absence of a normal life had made him immune to such worries. In his case it was more a fear of the same dreary life continuing ad infinitum. He reread the paragraph at the end of the email:

'And does it really matter that much how and when you die, providing it's relatively quick and painless? Surely deep down most people fear the passing from a state of being to one of not being, more than they worry about the outcome? If someone is killed suddenly, unexpectedly, and painlessly, before they even start to worry about illness or death, and before they've had to experience the inconveniences of growing old, is that not the optimal way to die? They don't even have any worries or guilt about what the consequences of them dying might be, and they certainly don't have any time for regrets. It is their families who suffer, not them. For they are caught up in the ripples caused by their death, which in some cases might endure for the rest of the lives of those they leave behind. My solitary actions changed the future for many people; I became important to them all - the relatives and friends. I was obviously a very significant person in the life and death of the 'one'; in fact second only to the mother who bore him.'

Crow believed that there were far worse things than death. A living hell for one. A wasted life another. And it wasn't the death of his father but him leaving home, and the arrival of a stepfather, which had so drastically affected his own life.

CHAPTER 15

Krill cursed as the phone buzzed loudly at his bedside. He'd struggled to get off to sleep anyway because of his conversation with Moss, and then he'd forgotten to mute it yet again. What now, he thought? Moss with more worries and thoughts? He switched on the light and looked at his watch: it was only twelve thirty. He must have fallen into a deep sleep very quickly. When he checked the caller's identity he saw that it was Margaret.

"Hello? Margaret?" he asked, still half-asleep.

"Yes hello. I am so sorry to ring you this late but I had to speak to someone."

"That's OK. What's happened? Is it about Graham?"

"Graham? No. It is one of my tenants, Colin. He's been found dead."

Krill sat up, suddenly wide awake.

"You're at home?" he asked.

"Yes, here at home. The police, they have just left."

Krill made a quick decision. "OK. I'll come right away. I should be there by three. Make yourself a cup of tea Margaret, and maybe have a brandy."

"You will come? Oh, thank you, thank you."

"I'm leaving right now. Try to stay calm."

As he joined the M4, Krill toyed with the idea of speaking to Moss and asking him for help in finding out details of the police investigation into her lodger's demise, but decided to gather as much information as he could from Margaret first. He knew that the first question Moss would ask would be - 'where did he die?'. It would likely be far more complicated for Margaret if the death had occurred in her house, because it could then potentially become a crime scene. He cursed himself for not asking her that very basic question. Was he losing his touch, or had he just been in too much of a rush to get to her?

He parked half on the pavement over the double yellow lines immediately outside her house; he would move it in a couple of hours, if he remembered. Margaret was still fully dressed and looking haggard and unkempt as she took him into the same front sitting room, where he saw a pot of tea, a used mug, and an empty brandy glass on the coffee table.

When they sat on the sofa he took her hand. For some reason, this slight intimacy caused her to burst into tears, and he held her close as she sobbed. He waited while the crying subsided, and wondered where the brandy bottle was, as another measure would probably be needed.

"This is so silly. All these tears. He is a tenant, only a tenant, not my daughter, or even a friend."

"You've had a shock. Do you think that you can tell me about it?"

"Yes, I want to talk about it. This is why I call you. Yes it is a shock when the police come to my door this evening. I immediately think something has happened to Nikola because she is visiting her new boyfriend. My heart is beating very fast as soon as I see them standing there. Then they say can they come inside, and I know it is bad."

"What did they say?"

"They say to sit down, and I am going crazy inside my head thinking Nikola is dead. When they say it is about Colin I am so relieved, and then I think I am a bad person for feeling happy that something terrible has happened to him. At first they say he has had an accident and they want to see his room, so I show them. One of them he stays in Colin's room, while the lady takes me downstairs and we sit here and she asks me about Colin - how long has he been living in my house, when did I last see him? I ask if he is hurt bad, and she says she is sorry but he is dead. Dead I say, how is he dead? How can this happen? She does not answer. Then the other policeman comes back and asks how he seemed the last time I saw him. I ask what they mean - seemed? They say was he upset, or worried? I say no, he hurries out of the door with his bicycle and his satchel like every day. No difference."

"Where's Nikola now?" Krill asked, thinking that someone needed to be with Margaret.

"At her boyfriend's. She tells me she may stay there with him last night. I have not spoken to her. If I ring her she will just be angry."

"I can stay here until she comes home, or is there another friend who could be here with you?"

Margaret thought for a moment. "Yes, I can go to the Polish shop when it opens, and the owner or her daughter will probably come here to be with me. What is going to happen?"

"I'm not sure; it depends on the circumstances. But at some point there will be an inquest of course, and you will probably be asked to give a statement or attend the hearing, or both. I'm not sure when the inquest will be - there's bound to be a backlog just now. What did the police say when they left?"

"That someone will come here tomorrow, today I mean, and take a statement."

"I could use my connections to find out a little more about what happened, although I may not be able to share any information with you. Did he have a family?" he asked.

"Yes, it is terrible, because he has a wife and children in Scotland. He was going home at the weekend."

While Margaret went to make some more tea he rang Moss; despite the hour it was answered immediately.

"What's up Killer?"

"Don't you ever sleep Moss?"

"I was asleep, or as asleep as I ever get these days. Have you had another text?"

"No, it's Margaret. I'm in London now, at her house. She rang me because one of her tenants has died and the police have been here."

"What, died in her house? Was it Covid?"

Krill smiled, at least Moss was very much on the ball even when half-asleep.

"No, not here thankfully. The last she saw of him was this morning, when he left to go to work on his bike. They didn't say what had happened, or where, only that he was dead. Doubtful it's Covid related; evidently quite a young chap with a family in Scotland. They asked about his state of mind, so it sounds to me like it could be a possible suicide."

"Jeesus! It's a laugh a minute with you at present isn't it Killer! How is she?"

"Understandably upset."

"And no doubt in need of some consoling?"

"This is no joking matter, Moss!"

"Sorry Boss. Want me to make a few enquiries?"

"Could you? I'll text the details: his name and her address. Do you need any more?"

"Names and numbers of the officers attending would help?"

"I don't think she knows those, but I'll ask her."

"Shouldn't take long. I'll ring you later."

"No, could you come to my cottage this evening? I should be able to leave here by lunchtime at the latest."

There was a slight pause before Moss replied, "I will if you don't force me to eat any more soup."

"I'm very offended, Moss; that was my grandmother's recipe. Margaret is coming back; we'll speak later."

"Anyway, what's wrong with my soup?" Krill asked that evening when his friend arrived at the cottage.

Moss screwed up his face. "Everything if you don't like soup or vegetables. But this chicken sandwich is just what the detective ordered."

"Good. Now what have you found out?"

They waited until Moss had finished his next enormous bite. He checked his notes: "Colin was twenty eight, and as you told me, from Scotland, family in Perth. Married, with two kids - five and one. Worked as a low level lawyer for Scottish Government, on secondment to HMG, supposedly to liaise with the PM and his team about Covid regulations and restrictions."

"What happened to him? How did he die?"

"You were right; initial thinking is suicide. His body was found at the bottom of a multistorey car park."

"Good grief! They think he jumped?" asked Krill.

"That's the general view. No unexplained marks on the body; nothing stolen; unlikely to have been an accident - you don't usually fall off the top of a multistorey car park accidentally, not unless you're repairing it."

"Any suicide note?"

"No."

"A family man, employed - he doesn't sound like a typical suicide victim, especially as Margaret said he was looking forward to going home at the weekend."

"True Killer, but there may have been a history of depression which we don't know about, or he could have had financial or marital worries; no details on any of that yet. I suppose anyone might jump off a roof if they had to liaise with Number 10 about Covid - can't have been an easy job. Not as bad as Brexit but close."

"You're right, sometimes there aren't any obvious signs, are there? Maybe something happened during the day - a meeting or a phone call - which upset him and he just couldn't take any more."

"They're still speaking to his colleagues, but so far all they've had from his wife and the others is total shock and disbelief. And I'll tell you another funny thing," said Moss.

"What?"

"No one knows what happened to his bike. You said that he definitely left Margaret's riding it, just as he did every weekday, but there was no sign of it at the multi or at his work."

"Could have been nicked of course if he left it at the multi? But I'm getting more and more alarmed about this. When is the pathologist going to take a look?"

"Not sure - I'll check."

"Do you think we're being paranoid, Moss? Putting two and two together and making twenty two?"

"Probably, but we need to rule out even the most unlikely of possibilities. Maybe it was a suicide and we'll never know why he jumped, but given what's happened it's best to err on the safe side. Without the recent events connected to you, I would say that our thoughts about a possible murder of her lodger were borderline looney, but what you can't ignore is that whoever fitted that tracking device to your car not only knew that you visited Crow, but also in all probability was aware that you were seeing Margaret. So it appears that he may be targeting you, or at least people connected to you."

Krill thought about other possible victims if it was a form of vendetta. "We may need to warn other people. There's my family, and there's also you and the others who were on our team."

"Me and the lads can take care of ourselves. I think your family should be OK, but you could ask them to be extra cautious because one of your old cases may be trying to get revenge?"

"I'll do that."

"I also got you this."

Moss took a revolver out of the carrier bag at his feet and placed it gingerly on the dining room table.

"I don't want that!" said Krill, shocked. "Where did you get it?"

"Don't ask. I'll sleep easier in my bed if I know you have it. Put it somewhere safe - in the drawer of your bedside table or under your pillow. Hopefully you will never need to use it." Moss picked up the gun, "I think you have a limited choice Killer, it's either this or someone in your spare room."

Krill welcomed the concern but not the result of it; apart from anything else he'd never used a firearm.

"Please take it away just now and let's wait for the full autopsy to be carried out, especially the toxicology results, before we jump to too many conclusions. If they find drugs in the body similar to those used in the Canal Killings then we'll know for sure that our worst fears are correct." The tension in the room eased slightly as he watched Moss put the firearm back in the bag.

Krill picked up their plates and took them to the sink. He started to rinse them then paused and turned round. "Of course there is another aspect to all of this which we haven't spoken about. It's almost the craziest notion of the lot."

"Go on, I'm all ears," said Moss.

"Well, it's just that whoever is behind it may believe in some insane perverted way that he's actually helping me - giving me peace and quiet by removing my noisy neighbour, and improving my love life by pushing Margaret back into my arms. It's a bit like a very dark fairy godmother with her three wishes. And if I'm right, is that it or will there be a third?"

"Or has there already been a third and we missed it at the time?"

"What do you mean?" asked Krill.

"What if he gave your career a boost by handing you Crow?"

"Good God I didn't think of that! Yes, it would certainly fit. That would mean he's been watching and waiting all these years. But why do something now? Why proclaim Crow's innocence and kill Colin, now?"

"Maybe it was our trip to the canal in Hampshire, or you seeing Crow, which triggered a reaction? Or something else?"

Krill's phone beeped. He checked it and shook his head.

"And why is he breaking cover now, after successfully hiding for all this time?"

124

He handed his phone to Moss. The message said: 'Give Margaret a kiss from me x.'

Moss grabbed a shopping list Krill had started and left on the worktop. He took the pen conveniently placed next to it, and turned the paper over to the blank side. Looking very anxious he quickly wrote and showed it to Krill: 'Don't say anything! He may be listening.' "Let's go for a stroll, Killer, I need a smoke after all these mental gymnastics."

The two men walked down the lane towards the river, neither speaking until they were near a gate which led into the churchyard. At that very moment the clock bonged out the hour somewhat solemnly. They paused while Moss lit a cigarette and Krill wondered when he'd started smoking again.

"You don't really think my cottage is bugged do you?"

"If there's a chance that it is then we should get it checked out. He seems to know not only where you are and where you've been, but what you're saying and thinking. It was almost as if he heard you say that you and Margaret are back together, and that's why he sent the message."

"Hardly together; not yet at least. How would he have done it, bugged me?"

"Easy to break into your cottage when you're away because your security is total crap. We should get that looked at too. I could get inside in five minutes, leave several hidden devices, and you'd be none the wiser."

"Does that mean he's close?" Krill asked, concerned.

"Not necessarily, not these days. If we find something then we'll know the range. I'll get onto it first thing tomorrow. We also need to check your computer and other electronic devices. Hand me your phone and I'll check it now."

Krill was going to object, thinking the situation was becoming increasingly like something in a John le Carré novel, but he put in his password and handed it over. Moss took just a few seconds to look for malware and returned it.

"That seems fine. You still using your date of birth as a password?"

When Krill didn't deny it, Moss shook his head thinking that he was almost a lost cause.

"It'll be very discreet when the guy comes. Last time I used him, my electronics chum was driving a plumber's van."

"Maybe while he's here, he could also fix a dripping tap? What are you looking at me like that for? I am taking this seriously, Moss, very seriously."

CHAPTER 16

"You don't seem to be interested in knowing my third guess?"

"What third guess?" the older man asked.

"You said if I guessed why you'd brought me here then you would let me go."

"Did I? I was probably just teasing or maybe giving you something to think about, to take your mind off your perilous situation. I already told you, whether you live or die depends on another person. But don't ask who, let's just say it's someone I've had a connection with for a very long time; since before you were even born."

"If I can't ask that question, can you at least tell me why you brought a bike with you today?"

"No."

"Is it yours? Do you ride a bike?" He was still hoping against the odds to establish some kind of rapport with the man who'd kidnapped him.

"No, and no. Now shut up about guesses and bloody bikes!"

"OK. I just thought it was something else to chat about because I enjoy cycling."

He was silenced by his captor putting his index finger up to his own lips and by the threatening scowl on his face. He tried a different approach:

"When will it happen? When will you know about this other person?"

"When the time is fucking right! When I decide it's right." The man seemed to calm himself. "But soon. In a day or two this will all be over, one way or another."

The young man couldn't decide if he was more relieved than frightened, or vice versa. "You seem a little distracted. A bit on edge."

"Do I? I suppose I am. How observant of you; you can have one 'brownie point'."

"Not a scout badge then?"

His captor managed a slight smile while he unzipped a large canvas bag.

"Maybe another time. Now give me peace for a few minutes while I get this equipment ready."

The young man watched as a tripod was set up with a fixing for a smartphone.

"Am I going to be filmed?"

"No, I am, but you will be in the background. You and the bike are sort of props."

"Oh. Won't they need to see and hear me, to know I'm still alive?"

"No, they'll just have to take my word for it, assuming

that you are. However, if you keep pestering me while I'm working, then you probably won't be."

The man threw him a roll of duct tape. "If you would like to sit on the chair and tape your legs and arm to it I will not have to sedate you again."

He did as he was told.

"Now I am going to have to gag you and put a hood over your head just for the recording, because I don't want you talking or mouthing words at the camera. It won't help you and it will certainly annoy me."

"OK. I definitely don't want to annoy you."

After he'd checked the restraints and secured the young man's one free arm, his captor returned to the canvas bag and took out a black hood and some white cloth. He gagged his prisoner and put the hood on him. He then turned on the phone's camera, pressed record and stood to one side of his victim. After he'd checked the images he moved the bicycle a few inches to the right before putting on a dark medical face mask and the peaked cap. Satisfied, he spoke for a few minutes and then examined the final recording.

"Good. Thank you Richard for cooperating. I'll now remove the hood and gag, but maybe you could remain seated for a little longer while we chat? You appear to want to talk so we will, and I feel more comfortable when we're both seated. There, that's better. I'll send the video clip later today, and that should move things along nicely. You asked about the bicycle? I suppose it's wrong to see it just as a prop as it clearly proves my credentials. It demonstrates that I am what I say I am - a murderer, because it belonged to a very unfortunate young man who, through no fault of his own, was living in the wrong house."

"Why, what happened to him?" the young man asked, rather hesitantly.

"He fell off a very high building, or rather I threw him off it. Like all my victims he didn't feel a thing as his life ended. He didn't panic or scream as he plummeted to the ground, and he was still unconscious when he hit the pavement. Messy but painless. The police presently believe it was suicide, although I'm sure that view will soon be corrected, but only because I want it to be. He was married and had two children, similar in age to yours in fact."

"The police think it was a suicide, that he jumped?"

"Yes, they do, because there is presently no reason for them to believe otherwise."

"Shouldn't there have been a note or some obvious reason why he killed himself? If you drop some bloke off a roof completely without warning, and without a note, won't they be suspicious and wonder why?"

His captor smiled, pleased to be able to show off his superior knowledge.

"No they won't. I've used 'suicide' quite a lot in recent years, probably as much as I've manipulated 'accidental' deaths. So I've had cause to study them, and most people who kill themselves don't leave a note, and a good proportion are totally unexpected and unexplained. Therefore, in answer to your question, no they would not normally be suspicious because of the absence of a note; not even if he kissed his wife goodbye, smiled happily, and said 'see you this evening darling'."

"Oh." The young man was both horrified but also curious in a macabre way. "Do you always use tall buildings? I don't think I would want you to do that to me, even if I am unconscious."

"Well we'll see, won't we? Perhaps I might let you choose - that would be a first. Yes, I do like tall buildings, but train tracks are even better. They both help to destroy any evidence of foul play. If I were in America, I would probably have to use firearms as it's by far the most common method of suicide there, but fortunately we're far more creative this side of the Atlantic. As far as accidental deaths are concerned, I've always loved drownings. There's a certain romanticism involved in launching the body into a current, and seeing them drift away like Ophelia. Fires happen all the time. Drug overdoses occasionally, if the victim is a user. You see there's a lot of opportunity out there to kill and have the body dealt with by the unsuspecting system, if you know how to do it. I've always steered clear of burying my victims, because unfortunately bodies do have a tendency to become discovered, be dug up. Too many get caught that way. Similarly, putting body parts in bin bags, under floorboards, or down sewers is very inadvisable. Acid baths are also a no-no because I believe that you're left with a disgusting sludge which is hazardous to your own health and hard to get rid of. And why go to all the trouble of dismembering and burying or boiling or dissolving, when some other kind person will quite happily do the job of disposing of the body for you? Getting rid of the evidence has long been the undoing of most unsuccessful murderers and serial killers. That's what makes me different from all the others."

"You drug your victims don't you? I mean you injected me with something when you brought me here?"

"Yes of course I drugged you, and yes I always drug my victims so I can dispatch them painlessly. Is that wrong? Would you prefer to experience pain? Are you a masochist? I suppose those weirdos might be disappointed if I made them unconscious."

"No, of course not. But don't they find those drugs at a post mortem?"

The man nodded. "You're curious about my methods aren't you? I like that. I can tell you that I've made it my business to know how the police and pathologists operate. It should come as no surprise to you or to anyone else that they don't routinely test for every possible drug at a post mortem, as that would be virtually impossible, hugely expensive, and by and large unnecessary. So they wouldn't find it unless they were specifically asked to look for it. Also new drugs come onto the market all the time - it's just a question of having the right connections and staying one step ahead of the opposition. But let's assume that I do make a mistake and that this error is combined with the presence of a particularly conscientious and fastidious pathologist or coroner." His mind wandered back for a moment to 1978. "Aren't they just as likely to believe that the victim took the drug himself? I mean, wouldn't you want to be drugged up to the eyeballs and ideally unconscious before you got hit by a train? People see what they want to see Richard. They are also very busy people, and like all of us, have a tendency to accept the purported facts presented to them by the police, unless they have a very good reason not to do so. It's human nature."

"Don't you feel any remorse for that poor guy you killed, or guilty about his family, and how they're suffering?"

"No. Not one iota. Not for one instant. It was necessary. It will serve it's purpose, which incidentally could include saving your life. I accept that saying I have no remorse or feel no guilt separates me from the norm, that it marks me out as different from those who you would describe as 'normal', but let's look at the facts. Did you know that on average around two people die in the world every second of every day? Which means that somewhere a family is losing a loved one just now; oh dear there's another one gone, and now another, yet another, and so on, ad infinitum. Death is a part of life, and we should be grateful for it. What I add to this immense death toll is inconsequential. It's a few drops in an ocean of blood. And before you condemn me, consider others who cause far more suffering. Am I worse than the drug dealer, the arms manufacturer, the warlord, the drunk driver? No I am not. I am just more direct, and far more honest. You should also be honest - if it was a choice of you or another person, what would you do? If I had the two of you, you and the erstwhile cyclist, right now up on the roof of that multistorey car park, and one of you had to die, wouldn't you plead with me, beg me in fact, to throw him over the edge rather than you? Wouldn't you even throw him off the roof yourself if it was the only way to save your own life? Of course you would.

Again it's human nature to want to survive at almost all costs. Just as it's in us all to kill if we have to. What I do is human nature too, because it's a driving force inside me, and like it or not, I am human." He sighed, it had been a long day. "Anyway, what is it?"

"What's what?" the young man asked, confused.

"Your third guess, since you seem so keen to share it?"

"OK. I think my kidnapping is somehow connected to Youtube. There was a speech I recently gave at a Chartered Institute of Taxation conference, which was uploaded and viewed quite a few times. I think you saw it and that's why you chose me."

The man shook his head. "You couldn't be more wrong. I'm disappointed but not surprised. Unlike your generation, I'm not glued to my phone, or constantly checking websites such as Youtube and Facebook, or that other one, what's it called - Ticktack or TokTik? I use the Internet only when I have to. But don't be disappointed. If I gave you 3000 or 3 million guesses you still wouldn't get close to the truth."

"About what you said on the film - what will happen if the person you spoke to refuses to do as you ask?"

"It means that you will die, and that I will have to find someone else to use as my lever to get what I want. I might even have to break a long held rule of mine never to harm a woman, if he pushes me far enough."

CHAPTER 17

"This is so very nice John."

Krill took Margaret's hand and nodded in agreement. Indeed it was very nice in lots and lots of ways; far better in fact than just 'nice'. He'd been pleasantly surprised that she had accepted his invitation to have dinner with him at an exclusive hotel near to the British Museum. He'd been delighted after he'd told her that he was staying there, that she'd asked if she could see his room; and elated - there was no other way to describe it - by the way matters had developed from that point onwards. He'd felt like a teenager again as they'd excitedly searched the nearby shops to purchase the items she would need in order to stay the night with him. He'd already paid for a double room because he was ever the optimist.

The waiter came over to their table and asked if they would like him to prepare some freshly squeezed juices or 'smoothies', and gave them a choice of orange, grapefruit, apple, carrot, cranberry, strawberry, blueberry, raspberry, mango, beetroot, avocado, and spinach - singly and in whatever combination they fancied. Margaret beamed, her eyes glowing with pleasure.

"Surprise us. Give us two of your best smoothies." He quickly looked at Margaret. "Is that OK?"

"Oh yes, I love surprises."

When the waiter had gone he smiled wistfully. "I have a confession."

"You do?"

"Yes, my memory is not as sharp as it was, and I couldn't recall half of the fruit and vegetables he'd listed. I'm afraid that he lost me after 'carrot'. I didn't want to ask him to repeat them, so I thought we might let him decide."

"It was such a big choice."

"It reminded me of the tray of objects, a game we used to play, when you had to remember as many of them as you could when the cloth was removed for a few seconds. I was never much good at that either."

"Doesn't a detective have to have an eye for detail?" she asked.

"Yes, but clues usually come singly rather than in confusing groups of ten or a dozen! Besides, I could rely on Moss to do most of that."

"Moss?"

"Yes, he was my sergeant, my second in command. He was more concerned with the details of an investigation, whereas my job was to sort the wheat from the chaff, to focus the investigation on the key areas, to see the big picture, and occasionally to think outside the box."

Krill thought he sounded like some management guru,

and if he wasn't careful he would soon be talking about running things up flagpoles and 'game changers'. Fortunately he was saved by the waiter bringing over their concoctions: greenish for him, reddish for her. He hovered nearby while they tasted them and demonstrated their suitably effusive satisfaction.

"Can I try yours?" he asked.

They swapped.

"Mine is nicer," she declared.

They swapped back.

"We could do this again tomorrow morning; have breakfast together?"

"A lovely thought John, but I have to get back this afternoon, or at the very latest by this evening, for my daughter. It is such a shame because I am loving this time away from my house with its so sad memories, and of course I am loving this time with you too, my wonderful detective." He looked a little sad so she stroked his hand. "Of course when your cottage is repaired I could soon come there again."

Krill felt a twinge of guilt about the lie he'd told regarding the reason he had decided to stay in London for a few days. He'd said that his boiler needed to be fixed and there was no hot water at his cottage. In reality he didn't want her there, or anyone else for that matter, until Moss had checked it for bugs. He hoped that if there were any listening devices, they were confined to the living room and not any in his bedroom! He'd blushed at the thought of anyone overhearing their antics during her visits there.

"So you will see me again? I thought you might not want to because of what you said before, about me being too old for you?"

She smiled sweetly at him.

"Yes, I do want to see you again. Of course. The more I am with you John, the more I want. It is true that you are older than my ideal, but I have changed my mind and do not now think that you are 'too old'. I am very sorry that I said such a thing to you."

"Well that's good. Great in fact! That last afternoon, when we were talking in bed at my cottage, and you said I was not right for you because I was older than Graham, my mind filled with all sorts of arguments to try to persuade you that it wasn't true, but I thought you'd already made up your mind and wouldn't change it."

"What were these arguments of yours? I would like you to tell them to me now."

"OK, I'll try to remember. Right - the most important one was that all the men in my family seem to live to a ripe old age. For example, my father was ninety five when he died."

"Really?" She seemed impressed. "That is such a good age. I am very relieved. You have more?"

"That was definitely the main one. After we'd split up I imagined inviting you to my hundredth birthday celebration, just to show you how long we could have been together. I thought you would be very regretful and so disappointed that we'd missed out on thirty years of happiness, which we could have shared."

She laughed. "But maybe I do not live so long that I can see this great day!"

"Apart from that, it was the usual stuff about looking after myself and being younger than my years."

"So you think we could be together for many years?" she asked.

"I certainly hope so. But it wasn't any of my arguments which caused you to change your mind, so what did?"

"I think it was poor Colin dying, so young and unexpectedly. It was such a shock. It made me think that there is no guarantee for anyone, young or old; not for me and not for his young wife. It is true that I could easily become ill and die before you, and you could be left on your own rather than me. His death made me want to grasp whatever happiness I can have now, and for as long as it is there. And I think Inspector Krill, that you could make me very happy."

His phone trilled on the way back to their room; he apologised and went to a quiet corner of the corridor.

"You OK Killer?"

"Yes Moss - found anything?"

"This guy is good. Any normal tracing device wouldn't have found it, but fortunately my friend has the best equipment there is."

"Where was it?"

"In an old BT box you no longer use, on the windowsill in your lounge."

"Just the one?"

"So far, but we'll do another thorough sweep just to make sure."

"Any indication of its range?"

"Yes, apparently pretty infinite. He could be listening from virtually anywhere in the world. I didn't even know that that was possible."

"Me neither. I suppose in a way that's reassuring - that he's not necessarily been waiting and listening in the village, just around the corner."

"Hopefully not," agreed Moss, "although he or someone else has obviously been inside your cottage recently to put it in there. Incidentally, I've taken the liberty while we're here, to change your door locks and put some extra security on all your windows. I'll also get him to install a camera so you can check who's at your door, or in your garden. He's also going to improve your exterior lighting."

"That's all OK, thanks. I've been intending to get around to doing some of that myself anyway."

"What do you want us to do with the bug?" Moss asked.

"Leave it there somewhere accessible for now, so I can easily get rid of it later. We might be able to use it somehow, if he doesn't know we've found it."

"False messages and trails? Misleading conversations?"

"Possibly, I'm not sure. Any news on the suicide?"

"Not yet, they're still waiting for toxicology. I did

however get the results from the lab which analysed the contents of the mysterious urn."

"And?" Krill asked, a little impatiently.

"Almost certainly they're human, as there's a high concentration of calcium phosphate. Based on the volume and weight of ash they're probably of an adult male; but no idea when the person was cremated. Could be very recent or fifty years ago."

"So not an early Halloween prank then, using the contents of someone's fire?"

"No, definitely not Killer. And what I would say is that whoever left the urn on your doorstep definitely wants to be taken seriously." Moss took the silence to indicate agreement. "However, if they leave any more surprises then we should now catch them on camera. When are you back?"

"Late tomorrow. I thought I might have a quiet chat with a couple of people at the Met while I'm here."

"OK Killer, let me know when you're on your way 'cos I'll have to meet you there with your new set of keys. Oh, and you'll need to remember whenever you're in your cottage that he could be listening. Maybe we should put warning notices up on the walls as a reminder? Some antique posters with 'Walls have ears'?"

"Don't worry, I'll remember; I'm not quite senile yet! Bye Moss."

"Bye, Killer. We'll have everything sorted at your cottage by the time you get back; not quite Fort Knox, but close."

CHAPTER 18

"Are you sure we're safe in here from prying ears?"

"Yes, as long as we keep the radio on in the lounge, the door to your kitchen shut, and the cooker fan on."

"OK, well he's shown his hand, just now while you popped out for a fag."

"Is that good or bad?" asked Moss.

"Bad or very bad probably; I don't think there's much good about it."

"What happened?"

"He sent me a short video clip via WhatsApp. Here, I'll play it for you. Oh shit!"

"What's wrong?"

"It's been deleted, the video - I can't play it anymore. How did he do that after I'd already opened it?"

"It's not difficult. I'm afraid it's gone - what was on it?"

Krill scratched his head trying to remember all the details.

"He was there, our mystery man - face mask, hat, sunglasses, so no chance of identifying him. Looked to be in a cellar of some kind. There was someone seated behind him on a chair and hooded, and possibly even more sinister, there was a bicycle propped up against a wall."

"You're thinking it was your neighbour who was hooded?"

"Yes I'm certain; for one thing he called him Richard."

"And you think that the bike belonged to Margaret's lodger?"

"Most likely. It was there for a purpose - to show he means business. To prove that he's killed before, and will do so again."

"What else did he say?" asked Moss.

"Oh he was very precise: if I wanted Richard to live then I have to release a statement by 6pm this evening, to all the National newspapers, to Sky, and to the BBC, saying that I made a mistake in the Canal Murders case, and that I now believe Peter Crow to be innocent."

"That's it? That's what he wants?" Moss seemed incredulous. He checked his watch, it was already 4pm. "That only gives us a couple of hours!"

"He also said that I shouldn't make any reference to the kidnapping, or imply that I had somehow been coerced into making the statement. I had to sound like I believed it. His final comment was that we would chat again soon."

Things were moving far too quickly for Moss. He was used to the steady snail's pace of an investigation, or since he'd retired - the quiet nothingness of the riverbank while he fished. It was as if the water in front of him had suddenly and inexplicably become filled with sharks. He wanted it to stop; he wanted normality to return. And more than anything he didn't want his old boss being stalked and receiving video clips from a possible serial killer! He searched for a more palatable explanation.

"Couldn't it still be someone playing a prank? You don't know for certain that it was your neighbour, and maybe the bike wasn't Colin's? Or maybe it's someone linked to Crow trying to upset you? Wouldn't that make more sense? Why would anyone apart from Crow want him exonerated? It could still be him who's behind it. Did the guy in the video say the bike belonged to the man who fell from the multi?"

"No he didn't Moss, but I'm almost certain that it is the missing bike. I saw it once at Margaret's, and the one in the video looked pretty identical to me. I don't believe that this is down to Crow. This is about me, not him. Anyway, how would pranksters know my neighbour is called Richard?"

"They wouldn't, not unless he was in on it. Don't get angry, I'm just trying to rule out other possibilities. It's still weird though; I'm confused. Why would he want you to make such a statement?"

"To embarrass me, that's why. To ruin my reputation. Maybe to cast doubt on all my other cases - you know how these things can grow and grow. Where there's smoke…"

"I suppose it's possible. Did he say that he was the one who committed the Canal Killings?" Moss asked.

"Not in so many words, no, but right at the end of the clip he picked up a distinctive patterned cloth from the table next to him."

"You think it was the same as the piece of cloth we found on Crow's barge?"

"I do, yes. Speaking of which, did we ever get the DNA results back from the original cloth used in evidence?"

"Not yet Killer, but I'll speak to my contact at the lab again. Never mind about that, what are you going to do?"

"There's only one thing I can do - exactly what he says."

"What about going to the police, now we definitely believe that he's kidnapped your neighbour and may have committed a murder?"

Krill thought that there wouldn't be sufficient time to involve the police; it would take far too long even for him to manage to see someone sufficiently in authority. He'd then have to make them take the threat of the deleted video seriously, which would have been hard enough even if he could still play it to them. And what could they do in the time anyway?

"There's no time, Moss, and by deleting it he's made sure there is no evidence, only my word about what I saw in the video."

"But your word should count for a lot."

"Well it will count for far less once I release my statement!"

Moss shook his head to try to stop it from spinning.

"Got any whisky? I need a drink."

"In the dining room; get me one too would you - a large one."

145

They stood in the kitchen sipping their malts.

"What was your impression of the man in the video?"

"He only spoke for a few seconds but I would definitely say that he means what he says. He came across as intelligent, articulate, completely ruthless and determined. He was clearly enjoying himself. I think under the mask he was sneering at me."

What Krill didn't say was that the hairs on the back of his neck had risen as he'd watched and listened. He'd sensed an evil the likes of which he'd not met before; certainly not when he'd interrogated Crow, who had come across as rather lost and bewildered.

"Do you think he will really let your neighbour go even if you do as he asks? Maybe, if he's so ruthless, he'll kill him anyway? Maybe he'll go to the press himself and say it's in revenge for what you did to Crow; an eye for an eye."

"Thanks Moss, I hadn't thought of that possibility! It would be a logical next step if he wants to disgrace me still further; let's just hope he doesn't."

"But as far as we know he's never released a victim before, has he, if he is the Canal Killer? This would be a first."

"Yes, but so is sending the video, so are delivering the urn and the texts. In a way they're what give me hope. And also because if he did kill Richard then I wouldn't agree to talk to him again would I? I did get the distinct impression that the two of us communicating is important to him."

"Well no, you wouldn't agree to speak to him, not unless

he took someone else to force you to do so."

"Thanks again, Moss."

"Sorry Killer. Difficult at present to see the bright side. I'd better let the lads know about the Press Release. They'll be shocked and very upset, especially for you. So much for our theory that he was your fairy godmother granting you three wishes!"

"Correct. He's now turned into the one with a poisoned apple."

"No, not Snow White's stepmother, the wicked fairy with a spinning wheel is far more appropriate, given his penchant for sharp needles!"

"Very good Moss. Ha, ha! That would normally have me in stitches. In some ways what he's asking me to do was becoming pretty inevitable anyway, once you begin to doubt Crow's guilt. True, I wouldn't necessarily have done it this way, by announcing it to the Media; and heaven knows what the Home Office is going to say when they find out. I need to speak to them, and the Crown Prosecution Service, and the Governor of the prison where Crow is being held….in fact I'd better make a list!"

CHAPTER 19

"Not long now Richard. Just a little longer to wait and we'll know."

"Who was that man you mentioned in the video yesterday? I think Crow was his name?"

"Peter? He was my one and only Plan B."

"Plan B? What was Plan A?"

"Making sure that my victims were never seen as the work of a serial killer of course. Making sure that they never even came looking for me. However, I was not as expert in those early days as I am now, and unfortunately I always left a telltale sign on the bodies, which could be seen if you searched hard enough for it. I knew that sooner or later it might be spotted, and then they would look at similar cases. Before too long the hunt for a serial killer would be on. So I made sure right from the very start that Peter would be the one they would soon home in on, by fitting my killings entirely around him."

"How did you do that?" Richard asked.

"Quite easily. He lived on a barge, so I chose canals as my hunting ground. He rode a motorbike, so I did as well to carry out my killings. He was diabetic so I used syringes to anaesthetise my victims. I knew he lived alone and hardly ever saw anyone, so there was no chance he would have an alibi for any of the crimes."

"What happened to him?"

"Peter? Well he got what he deserved didn't he? Found guilty and put away for life. He's still in prison, but he won't be there for much longer."

"He'll be released?"

"No, I doubt it. I rather think he'll die before they get round to reviewing his case."

"Why did he deserve it, if he wasn't guilty? What did he do to you?"

"You ask too many questions Richard. Take care because if I inadvertently tell you something that I shouldn't, you know exactly where that will lead don't you, irrespective of what Krill does? What I will say is that in a way I saved Peter Crow from himself. Before he went to prison he was on a very slippery slope - both drink and drugs. He also chain-smoked, he was overweight, and if the alcohol or an accident on the barge didn't get him, then probably a heart attack soon would have. He almost certainly wouldn't have lived many more years, and definitely would not have reached the ripe old age that he has now. And from what I hear, I think that prison may have been the making of him. Which on reflection, is a bit of a disappointment! But enough about him, let's listen to the Six o'Clock News shall we? It may have something of interest on it."

They listened to the usual items relating to coronavirus and the UK economy, followed by an update on Brexit negotiations. There was a report and interviews with various people regarding the US Presidential election, and details of a hurricane about to hit the coast of Mexico. Then...

'We've just received some Breaking News: Retired Chief Inspector John Krill, who was the lead detective in the infamous Canal Murders case of the late 1970's, has released a statement late this afternoon saying that he now believes that Peter Crow, the man who was convicted of the crimes, may in fact be innocent. Krill, a former senior officer with the Metropolitan Police has so far been unavailable for comment. Peter Crow was sentenced to life imprisonment and has remained in prison for more than forty years. Crow has always claimed that he was innocent of the murders of four middle-aged men, which took place on various canal towpaths across England. We hope to have more on this startling news later in the programme. Sport...'

"He's done as you asked."

"Yes, fortunately for you."

"So will you now release me; like you said in the video?"

"Possibly; I haven't completely made up my mind yet."

"But you said you would!" Richard complained, rather like a spoiled child.

"Oh, are you so shocked that a scrial killer may not be a man of his word? Anyway, you and I have some unfinished business: remember I asked you to tell me about an act of kindness, and to make a case for being allowed to live? Well Richard, I can't wait to hear what you've come up with! But first we need to celebrate. I know it's still a little early but we do both have a good reason for doing so: Krill has made an absolute fool of himself, and in addition, he hasn't summarily condemned you to death. So let's drink a toast to him and to Peter, and then you can tell me why you think that you're really such a wonderful human being." He brought two tumblers from the table. "Cheers Richard. Here's to your possible release and Krill's comeuppance!"

Richard looked suspiciously at his glass. Would this crazy person try to poison him? Probably. But he'd been given food and drink before, and of course there hadn't been any alternative but to consume it. But alcohol? A celebration? It seemed so out of character. He waited until his captor had sipped his, then drank his own.

CHAPTER 20

"How are you doing Boss?"

Krill had rung Moss both for an update and some reassurance.

"As well as can be expected, thanks. Margaret's looking after me very well."

"It was definitely a good idea to go and stay with her. As anticipated, the vultures are well and truly camped outside your cottage. They probably think you're inside, as your car is there and the curtains are drawn."

"What's worse is they've been hovering around my daughter's too, trying to get her to comment. God knows what people who know or work with my son will think, as Krill is not a common name. He's probably gone overnight from occasionally being asked - 'are you related to that detective who found the serial killer?' to - 'are you the son of that idiot who cocked up that 70's murder investigation?'."

"Hardly an idiot, Killer; and if you are then I am one too, only more so. How did the Home Office take it when you contacted them?"

Krill recalled the difficult conversations he'd had the previous afternoon and evening, in which he'd been well and truly rebuked by the 'uncivil servant', who in turn had no doubt been hauled over the coals by the Secretary of State.

"They were understandably furious. How could I make such a claim about Crow's innocence when I had no evidence beyond my own gut instincts, and the hearsay rantings of a possible lunatic? The Press have already started looking at other cases which I was the lead on. There'll probably be a spate of appeals."

"But why," asked Moss, "it's not as if you falsified the evidence or even manipulated any of it."

He couldn't imagine Krill ever contemplating such a thing, never mind doing it. He knew Krill was as honest as the day is long, or as he visualised it - as straight and true as a summer's day in Iceland! He would defend Krill against any and all accusers, but especially those misguided fools who questioned his integrity.

"No, but it's clearly what some will believe. How else was the incriminating cloth found on Crow's barge unless I put it there, or persuaded someone else to do so? The Home Office told me in no uncertain terms that I shouldn't release the statement. Hadn't they got enough on their hands without having to reopen forty year old cases? They even mentioned my pension. The Crown Prosecution Service said I should retract it or at the very least make it clear that I was doing so under duress, and explain the circumstances."

"Both of which would have more than likely got the hostage killed. You've had no further contact from chummy?" Moss asked.

"No; just a deathly silence. Maybe you were right about him not keeping his word. I mean, why would he? What does he gain by releasing Richard? Nothing. And as you quite rightly pointed out he could use killing him to rub further salt into my open wound."

"Don't panic yet Guv, wait and see what happens. I think this game of his may only just be starting. And he'll want to keep you on the hook somehow."

Krill almost smiled at Moss's fishing metaphor.

"I do have some news."

"Good or bad? Not sure if I'm ready just now for the bad variety; but tell me anyway Phillip."

Moss knew that Krill only used his first name when he was severely rattled; he could probably count the times it had happened on the fingers of one hand.

"I suppose it's both. They did find DNA on the cloth, which is not surprising, and it isn't Crow's. They're still checking whether they can find a match for anyone else in the database, but so far they've drawn a blank. Maybe it might make the Home Office happier - the fact that we now have at least some supporting evidence that an unknown person committed the crimes and fitted up Crow. Maybe they should be shouting from the rooftops that you're trying to rectify a miscarriage of justice, and free an innocent man?"

Krill couldn't see that happening. "Possibly, when the dust settles. However, that is hardly going to counter the outrage that I allowed a serial killer to remain on the loose and active for forty years."

"Unfortunately, they said as much on the News: 'How many more victims have there been since 1978?' and 'How many lives have been lost because the wrong man was convicted?' But aren't they jumping to conclusions? Maybe Crow is guilty? Or if there was another killer, maybe he decided to stop after the Canal Killings? Maybe he thought it was too dangerous, so he went into premature retirement until something recently jolted him back into action?"

Krill seldom accepted any 'maybe's', even from someone as trustworthy as Moss. "It's possible, although I very much doubt it. I think he's been active. I got the impression from the video that he's been busy. And even if he hasn't then we know of at least one more victim."

"Poor Colin. I assume that you're not sleeping in the dead man's bed Killer?"

Krill was affronted. "Where I'm sleeping is of no concern of yours, Moss!"

"Sorry Boss - couldn't resist it. Has your friend Margaret, found out about it all yet?"

"I had to explain to her the reason for wanting to come to London, didn't I? Besides, I thought it would be better coming from me. I think she sees me now as a hero, trying to save my neighbour's life."

"Well, let's hope for all our sakes that you do." Moss said, then added, "How long do you want us to keep an eye on other people who may be at risk?"

155

"At least until we know what he's going to do with Richard. If he does release him then I think you can call off the troops. I'm hoping to have some form of contact from him within the next twenty four hours; the ball's now back in his court."

CHAPTER 21

"Mr Krill?"

He had just finished brushing his teeth and was on his way downstairs to have a coffee with Margaret when his phone had rung.

"Yes, speaking."

"Ah Mr Krill I'm Sarah Morris from the Met. I don't think I've ever had the pleasure? I wonder if we can meet up sometime today to have a chat about this press release which you issued, and a few other things connected to it?"

"Of course. What do you suggest?"

"It's probably not a good idea for you to come to the Yard as the press are here too. How about somewhere near where you're staying? I assume you're not at your cottage in Berkshire?"

"No, I'm in Highgate." Krill quickly reviewed the options. "What about the Lakeside Cafe in the park next to Alexandra Palace?"

"OK, shall we say two pm? Oh, and why don't you see if Mr Moss can come along too? That way we can save a bit of time."

Krill went straight onto the Internet to find out some information about Sarah Morris, and then sent a text to Moss about the meeting. Moss rang him almost immediately:

"Just getting in my car now Boss, so I'll be there by one."

"Do you know Commander Morris?" Krill asked.

Moss had also done a quick check of her credentials.

"Know of her, but we've never met. She's now in Specialist Crime with a background in serious crime, including abduction and murder. So if I was asked to pick someone at the Met for us to work with it would probably be her."

"Not sure if she'll want us to work with her. She probably just wants to pick our brains clean of info and then dump us."

"Maybe, but how can she dump both of us if you're the one the killer is likely to contact, and it's you that he wants to talk to about your neighbour? Commander Morris will have to keep you in the loop somehow. What would you do if you were in her shoes?"

"Me? I'm not sure. Probably not want some ancient has-been involved in the case, especially someone who's just admitted to an almighty cockup! And definitely not have any input from a potential rival - someone who's used to running investigations his way. Maybe that's why she wants you along."

"What, as the monkey rather than the organ grinder?" Moss suggested, half joking.

"You know I would never think that; we were always equal partners, you and I. No, it's just that she may believe that you will be more willing to work with her in a supporting role, whereas a prima donna like me will want to stick his nose in everywhere it's not wanted."

Krill and Moss were sitting at a table outside the cafe and had just finished their coffees when they saw two people approaching from the other side of the lake. They didn't look like locals or tourists - one was a tall smartly dressed woman in her forties, the other a petite redhead several years younger. The two men watched as they walked past the boats with their swan shaped prows and made a beeline straight for them. Krill stood up and Moss followed his lead.

"Commander Morris?"

The older woman smiled wanly and nodded.

"This is Phillip Moss, my old sergeant and sidekick."

"Thanks for coming. My colleague here is Dr Sharon Knox; she's our top Behavioural Investigative Adviser."

Moss exchanged a glance with Krill, as if to say 'a profiler - so they're taking the serial killer issue seriously, thank goodness'.

"Let me get straight to the point if I can?" said Morris after they'd all sat down on the cold metal chairs. "As I understand it, Mr Krill, you were sent a video yesterday by an unknown person, and in it was someone tied up and hooded, who you believe is your missing neighbour?" Krill nodded. "And apparently the person who sent the video also may have Mr Marshall's missing bicycle? In the clip he said that unless you stated to the media by 6pm that same day, that Peter Crow, the man originally convicted of the Canal Murders, was innocent, he would kill the man seated. This video was subsequently deleted before you could show it to anyone."

"Yes, that's an accurate précis of events."

"Did the man in the video actually say why he believed that Crow was innocent or claim that he himself was the Canal Killer?" Morris asked.

"No he didn't, but personally I have little doubt that he is the man who committed those murders in the 70's."

He told Morris and Knox about his interview with Crow, and also about the cloth which he'd seen in the video.

"Leaving aside for a moment why you didn't go straight to the police Mr Krill as soon as you received the video, what I also fail to understand is why he would admit to those killings after all this time? Or why he would now want Crow exonerated?"

"I have absolutely no idea Commander Morris. Maybe if he gets in touch with me again I can ask him why he wants to 'set the record straight' as he put it in the video."

At this point Dr Knox intervened: "What was the man's demeanour?"

"Demeanour? Calm, confident, threatening, determined, unemotional, ruthless."

"What did he say precisely?" she asked.

Krill took a piece of paper from his pocket.

"Once I discovered that the video had been deleted I made these notes. I can't be one hundred percent certain, but if I remember correctly he said something along the lines of: 'It's been a long time Krill since our paths first crossed in the 70's, too long, and we've both been very busy. I've thought about you often in the past forty years, but it's now time to set the record straight. There's someone here who you can help. His life is very much in your hands. He will die unless you tell the world by 6pm this evening that Peter Crow is innocent. And don't imply that you're being forced to say it - you have to be convincing, for poor Richard's sake. But then you already believe Crow is innocent don't you? Deep down you've known it all along. Bye for now Krill. I'll be in touch.' I can't swear that those were his exact words but I believe so."

Dr Knox was taking her own notes, and when Moss glanced across the table at them he saw that she was using a form of shorthand. She stopped writing and asked:

"He definitely said he's been busy? And by that you assumed he's committed more murders since 1978? Why did you think that? He could have been busy with hundreds of other things; normal everyday things."

"I've gone over it constantly in my mind since I saw the video, analysing it, each and every word, and his mannerisms. It wasn't just what he said but the way he said it. I couldn't see his face because of the medical mask he was wearing, but I just knew he was goading me, and gloating about his crimes, saying: 'look how clever I am and how evil I've been these past decades'. It's hard to put into words, but I had an extremely strong sense of malice as I watched and listened to him in the video. Also, he was saying that it was partly down to me, that I was culpable because I'd fallen for his tricks and not caught him. He was implicating me in his crimes, almost as an unknown accomplice. Oh, there's something else he said which I've not mentioned. He said 'remember that both life and death have their consequences Krill'."

"Consequences? Life and death. That's very interesting." Knox nodded as she wrote it down.

"Yes. There's a few other things which you should be aware of Commander."

Morris quickly jumped in: "We already know about your relationship with Mr Marshall's landlady, Mr Krill. We assume that may be why he was singled out."

Krill began to wonder if any aspect of his life would now remain private, given his recent notoriety.

"OK but there's more: I believe he sent me an urn soon after Richard disappeared. It was left on my doorstep around the same time, and I found it when I arrived back from visiting Crow in prison. I had the contents analysed and know now that it does contain human ashes from a cremation. There was a note with it which said 'Are you enjoying the peace and quiet?' - I assumed that he was referring to the absence of my noisy neighbour. Another text said that I should believe Crow. It appears that he's also been following my movements using a tracking device on my car, and that he's bugged my cottage. That's how he learned about my neighbour and Margaret, and also how he knew I'd been to see Crow." Krill felt like a suspect getting it all off his chest, confessing to multiple crimes. He'd decided not to mention Moss's involvement in any of it.

The two women exchanged looks which were a mixture of shock and disbelief. Then Commander Morris sought clarification:

"You've found some surveillance devices?"

"Yes, and left them in place for now. My car is still at the cottage - Moss brought me to London. I've used my contacts to try to trace where they might have been purchased but without luck. I also had the urn checked for prints."

Sarah Morris shook her head vigorously. "You can't play at being detective Mr Krill, not now! Really you of all people should know that. You should have come to us much sooner, probably the minute you discovered the urn and those devices."

"Of course I realise that now, but when I found them I had no idea what it was all about. It could have been some paper snooping into my life and my old cases, or a prank. The texts were hardly threatening." He quickly turned to Dr Knox in part to try to deflect Morris from her justifiable castigation. "Why do you think he sent me an urn?"

"Off the top of my head it was for two reasons: first of all to grab your attention - like the victim's bike it was to tell you that he meant business; and secondly, and probably more importantly, because he's apparently obsessed with death."

"You don't think it might be a past victim?" Krill spelt out what he'd imagined.

"I wouldn't rule it out, although I've not come across a serial killer who cremated his victims and placed them in urns. I suppose it could be considered a trophy, but if so, why would he want to part with it? A gift to you, as a thank you for letting him escape? To implicate you in his crimes, as you suggested earlier? However, I think the urn has some significance for him; he didn't select it as a message and send it to you for no reason."

Moss had been listening to the exchanges but now asked the question which they'd all been thinking about:

"How can a serial killer go about his business for possibly as long as fifty years and not get caught?"

Dr Knox was ready with an answer: "Yes, it is rare but not unknown, there have been similar cases in the US. How? Possibly by using several techniques. If the perpetrator has no distinctive MO which we can identify and moves from place to place, selecting his victims at random, so the crimes are never linked, which means that from our perspective there is no identifiable serial killer. Secondly, he might follow a specific pattern but the time between killings is so great, months or even years, that there are too few dots for us to join up. Thirdly, by managing to get rid of his victims successfully - without bodies they just add to the legions of missing persons. Finally, if he can conceal the murders as accidental deaths or suicides. I've looked at the Canal Killings and apparently he used at least two of these tactics - he spaced his killings out around the country, across different policing areas, to reduce the risk of them being linked, and he also tried to disguise them as accidental deaths. And now as a suicide, like the multistorey victim. To sum up: no victim equals no murder equals no serial killer. It's quite neat actually. As far as this guy is concerned - I'm assuming based on the video that it is a man and also because the vast majority of serial killers are men - he's most likely continued to try to hide the murders and sneak them past the police and forensic pathologists. It's virtually impossible to check for his victims, because there are thousands of accidental deaths and suicides each year." She turned to Morris. "Having said that Commander, we should examine other recent suicides which involve men falling from a height, especially from a multistorey car park. Mr Marshall may not be the only one he's killed in this manner."

Krill looked at Morris. "So you're sure Colin was murdered?"

"Yes, we got the toxicology report this morning. He was definitely unconscious when he went over the edge."

Moss thought some more about the urn, and asked Knox: "Is it possible that he had some of his victims illegally cremated?"

"Highly unlikely but not impossible. It couldn't happen now because of the very tight security and record keeping at Crems, but thirty or forty years ago who knows what went on?"

Krill shook his head and sighed; he couldn't help feeling guilty that he'd let a serial killer slip through his fingers. He believed that he had to make amends somehow.

"I have a theory Commander."

"OK, let's hear it."

"I'm almost certain that he's closely connected in some way to Crow; that they knew one another at the time of the Canal Killings. Which is why I phoned the prison Governor yesterday to see if he could get Crow to tell me who his friends and associates were at that time, and also to check who's been to see him. I think we also need to check the visitor records for the other prisons Crow attended. And I assume you're looking at CCTV footage for that day and who was parked at the multi?"

Krill could tell from Morris's angry red face and glaring eyes that he'd done exactly what he'd told himself not to do; that he'd overstepped the mark, interfered in her inquiry, and poked his nose in where it wasn't wanted.

As they walked back through the park, Krill could sense Moss's disquiet.

"Go on, say it."

"Say what Killer?"

"That Commander Morris now thinks that I'm an interfering and incompetent old fool! That I'm not only playing at being a detective, but want to be the chief inspector in charge of this case."

Moss laughed. "Well, I have to admit that there was more than a hint just now of 'teaching your grandmother to suck eggs'. I know you had to mention your call to the prison Governor, because she's bound to find out about it, but did you really have to suggest that they check CCTV and car park users? You knew they would, so why say it?"

Krill was angry with himself. "I know. I know. I got a bit carried away. And I suppose deep down I do want to be in charge of the investigation, even though I know I can't be. If only to make amends for missing our killer before. It's so frustrating!"

"And ideally Killer, I would want you in charge too, and not just because you're superb at what you do, but also because of your involvement in the original case."

"Thanks for your vote of confidence Moss, even if it's not deserved.'

"If it's any consolation I was having the very same thoughts just now about what you said, especially regarding Crow's visitors."

"Yes, but you had the good sense to keep your thoughts to yourself, whereas I'm just an old blabbermouth."

"When she has time for reflection, Commander Morris will realise that you were just trying to help with the investigation. Anyway, you were right regarding my role, about her wanting me to liaise with the Met, and she would have gone down that route anyway irrespective of what was said this afternoon. And she did ask Dr Knox to work with you to draw up a profile of the serial killer, didn't she. That makes sense too. So, it's really not that bad Killer; we're still in the game!"

Krill continued to look sheepish.

"Maybe when you next see her you can find a way to apologise for me? Say I was stressed or something, because of all the media attention."

"Of course. You know how good I am at smoothing out the wrinkles. I'll do it when I deliver the urn, the note, and the surveillance equipment. We don't want to be accused of perverting the course of justice do we, by withholding evidence?"

"Speaking of withholding evidence, when do you think we should tell them about the DNA results on the cloth?" Krill asked.

"I'd almost forgotten about that! Maybe let the dust settle just a little; let everyone at the Home Office and the Met calm down a bit? I could suggest that we do a test and arrange for the results to be sent again but with a revised date on the report? It would be quite simple to do."

"Bit deceitful."

"Well, only marginally so, and I have to protect my contact at the lab who did me a huge favour," Moss explained.

"Yes, I understand. But they'll know that the evidence from Crow's case was booked out."

"True, but I can take the blame for that, and thanks by the way for keeping me out of the rest of it. I don't think Morris would have wanted me on her team if she knew the whole truth about what I've been up to."

Krill's phone beeped, so they stopped on the path.

"Another unknown number. It's a photo." Krill hesitated. "Shall I open it?"

"Yes, but can you forward it to Commander Morris and to me immediately?"

They both looked at the photograph: it was of a lit candle, burning on top of a pile of rags. Behind it was a small square window, with what looked like brackish brown water and some trees in the background. The text said: 'Funny how

168

things turn full circle. Crow would have enjoyed the irony. Don't take too long to find him, Krill.'

"Full circle? What do you think that means? And why would Crow find it ironic?" Moss asked.

Krill quickly forwarded the message, and then enlarged a section of the photo.

"Judging by the view from the window, I think he's put Richard on a barge somewhere. Once that candle burns down and ignites the rags underneath, the whole boat could be set alight. He'll burn to death even if the smoke inhalation doesn't get him first."

Krill's phone rang - it was Commander Morris. "What's it mean, Krill?" she asked.

"That we only have a short time to find my neighbour, who's on a barge somewhere. Full circle I think takes us back to the original Canal Killings."

"If I remember correctly, those murders took place on at least four different canals. We don't have time to search them all, even if we knew the exact locations. We're talking hundreds of miles." She seemed exasperated.

Krill thought for a moment. "My guess is that there are two possible locations where the barge could be - that is if he isn't deliberately sending us off in completely the wrong direction. The first is where Crow's barge was moored at the time of his arrest, and the second is where the serial killer carried out the murder in Hampshire, when I was first brought in on the case. I'll text you the two locations."

"Yes, please do that. I'll send police teams, an ambulance, and firefighters to both. Maybe bloody helicopters too if I can

169

get hold of them! Let's hope for all our sakes that you're right and we get there in time."

Later that afternoon the two men sat side by side on the sofa in Margaret's front room waiting for news. She'd insisted that Moss should stay for dinner, and in the meantime had brought them coffee, some cherry vodka in an impressive oval shaped bottle, and slices of honey-spice cake.

Moss took a bite and smiled. "Does Margaret have any single friends? I could quickly get used to being looked after like this." He finished one piece and picked up another. "Mind you, you need to be careful that she doesn't feed you too well, otherwise you'll have to buy some bigger trousers. Those with an elasticated waist should be ideal."

Krill wasn't interested in cake or small talk. "How long has it been now?"

Moss checked his watch. "Coming up to three hours since you got the message."

"Why doesn't she ring? Do you think it's payback for the things I said; for sticking my nose in?"

Moss shook his head. "No, she'll be busy. You know what it's like, assuming they've found the crime scene."

"But a short call just to say they've found him and he's OK? Maybe he's not OK? Maybe he's dead?"

Moss tried to placate him: "Even if the worse comes to the worse, you couldn't have done any more. You did as the kidnapper asked. You tried to point Commander Morris in the right direction."

Krill remained sceptical: "But what if I was wrong? I've been wrong before."

But Moss wasn't having any of it: "You made a judgement call and we acted as quickly as we could based on the best available info. I would back your judgement every day of the week. If the killer has sent us on a wild goose chase, then what happens is down to him. It wouldn't be your fault."

"No? Then why do I feel so guilty?" Krill complained. "Why do I keep thinking that all this is down to me and my pathetic detective work?"

Moss had seen Krill's bouts of self-doubt and negative thinking before, usually when they'd seemingly hit a brick wall in an investigation, or when a highly promising lead had taken them nowhere.

"Because you're human after all, much to everyone's surprise! We didn't make any mistakes back in '77 and '78; we followed the evidence."

Krill shook his head. "We followed the trail that he laid down for us. We bought it, hook line and sinker!"

"We all did: the whole team, not just you; and so did the Crown Prosecution Service, the Judge and Jury, the Appeal Court, the Home Secretary; everyone."

"But I should have seen through his deception Moss! I should have known that Crow wouldn't have kept that cloth hidden in his drawer, waiting to be found, if he'd been the real killer."

Moss had a few 'but's' of his own: "But that's just the kind of stupid mistake that criminals do make, all the time, fortunately for us."

"It was all too easy and predictable." Krill wasn't to be deterred from his self-flagellation. "And maybe I rushed things because I just wanted to wrap the case up and get back to the Met?"

"You're being far too hard on yourself. What would have happened if you'd asked to keep the case open despite all the evidence indicating that we'd found the killer? I'll tell you what - the top brass would have brought someone else in to finish the job, and sent you, and probably me, off to be the local bobbies on some remote Scottish Island, that's what! Everything fitted. Everything. Even I would have questioned your sanity if you'd started looking elsewhere for the killer once we'd found Crow. The case was as watertight as they come. Don't forget that the police college have used it for years as an example of good detective work; as a model of how to conduct an investigation."

"Well they'll have to stop doing that now, won't they!"

"No they won't," said Moss, "because the techniques we used hold true even if we didn't get the right guy. And personally speaking, I'm still not convinced that we didn't. If we were to carry out the investigation now, today, we would do virtually everything the same, including finding and using that damned cloth as evidence. It took weeks of inquiry to trace the other potential victims of the Canal Killer, and you held out for the bodies to be exhumed and reexamined despite all the protests. If you hadn't, then we wouldn't have even

172

been aware that a serial killer was operating, and who knows how many more people might have been killed in the same way. You weren't the only one to suggest the idea that it might be someone living on or near to a canal. We had to narrow the search down somehow, and it made sense to do that. Again it took fine police work to come up with a list of possible suspects, particularly those with a criminal record and owners of a motorcycle. All we lacked was a confession; we had everything else. It was all done by the book, surely you can see that? OK, so we didn't have DNA, and perhaps that would have made a big difference, but even then, not finding Crow's DNA on that cloth and someone else's, might still have secured a conviction. I'm sure the CPS would have said the DNA indicated that he had an unknown accomplice and that Crow himself wore gloves."

"I suppose so," Krill reluctantly admitted.

Moss's phone rang. "Hello? Yes he's here with me now. Shall I put him on? I see…. Ok…. Yes…. Where?… Ok….. Right…. Which hospital?…. I see. What are the doctors saying?…Yes…. Ok I'll tell him."

Krill leaned forward in his seat and looked concerned at his friend. "Well?"

"That was Commander Morris. They've found your neighbour, and he's been taken to hospital. You were right, the barge was moored where Crow had his. They're still checking it. Evidently someone hired it two days ago from a nearby wharf."

"You mentioned a hospital. How is he?"

"Alive at least, and not in any danger. But...."

"But what?"

"Well apart from some smoke inhalation, apparently he's blind. No sight in either eye. They don't know yet if it's temporary or permanent, or what's caused it. Commander Morris wants me to meet her at the hospital in an hour."

Now Krill's phone rang. "Hello.... Yes speaking...Hi....at the NCA? Yes, what time?.....Yes I can make that....See you then."

"Dr Knox?" asked Moss.

"Yes. She wants me to go to the National Crime Agency."

Krill went to tell Margaret that they both had to go out and weren't sure when they would be back.

"Is it concerning your neighbour?" she asked. "You cannot tell me more, John, about what is happening?"

He quickly kissed her. "I'm sorry I can't, not yet Margaret; maybe I will be able to in a couple of days."

"But he is alive?"

"Yes, he's alive. We must go. I'll ring you if we're not going to be back in time for dinner."

She kissed him again. "Thank God that you have saved him! I will prepare everything, a celebratory dinner, and hope that you return soon."

He in turn hoped that she didn't plan on having any candles with their meal.

CHAPTER 22

Dr Knox met him in reception, got him a Visitor's Pass and took him through security to a meeting room which she'd booked at the National Crime Agency. It was small with barely enough space for a table and four chairs, and therefore provided little or no chance of any social distancing. Krill hoped that she had been careful about her recent contacts. If he hadn't been so desperate to be involved in the investigation he might well have refused her invitation to meet anywhere indoors.

"Can I get you a tea or a coffee Mr Krill?"

"No, I'm fine thanks; I've already had too much coffee today. How can I help you, Dr Knox?"

Gillian smiled. "Well, I'm hoping that we can help each other. I could tell from our brief meeting in the park that you're finding it hard to stay on the fringes of our investigation, and I'm not surprised. It must be very difficult for you, given your high profile career, especially regarding this particular case, because of its possible links to the Canal Murders. I know Commander Morris is keeping an open mind about Peter Crow's guilt or innocence, but what is beyond doubt is that the man who abducted your neighbour and probably killed Mr Marshall has an interest in you, and in the earlier crimes. While Commander Morris does not want to have you officially involved in the investigation, apart from asking you to make a statement regarding the video, she's happy to use your knowledge and expertise unofficially. But rest assured I'll do all I can to make sure that it will be a two-way street, and we'll keep you informed as well. After our chat I'll ask someone to take your statement if that's OK?"

Krill thought it was a good move by Morris, but rather than wanting him to help with the case she possibly was using Dr Knox to keep him busy, keep an eye on what he was up to, and as far as possible out of any further mischief. The old J. Edgar Hoover adage about having 'him inside the tent pissing out, rather than outside pissing in' probably applied.

"Yes, of course. I'm happy to help in any way I can, and thanks for keeping me involved."

She looked pleased. "Great. Can I first of all ask whether you have any idea at all who the person that sent the video is?"

"No, no idea. I didn't recognise him."

"You told us before that he sounded threatening, evil I think you said - was that due to his manner, the tone of his voice, or what he said?" she asked.

Krill thought for a moment. "Probably all three. It was just an impression, like sometimes when you meet someone for the first time you can tell whether they're a nice person, or whether or not you might like them and get on with them. Well, with this guy it was the exact opposite, and I knew that if I was a private citizen, which I suppose I now am, I wouldn't ever want to meet him at all if I could help it. Meeting him is very bad news."

"Some serial killers come across as charming, did he?"

"Not really. He wasn't trying to charm me at all, or even persuade me to do something in the video. It was a case of do it or else."

"No, I understand, and he wouldn't necessarily have to use charm on his victims if he only targets men, or if he doesn't need to gain someone's confidence in order to trap them. Going back to your earlier investigation, where there any other promising lines of inquiry in the Canal case apart from Crow?"

"We had other suspects of course," Krill confirmed, "people who ticked one or more boxes, but no one who came close to Crow. I would be surprised if the man in the video was ever interviewed by my team, if that's what you're implying."

"I think we will have to check the file again to see who was interviewed as a possible suspect. It's a shame that he deleted the video otherwise we could have shown it to the other officers involved to see if it jogged any memories. Why do you think he did that Mr Krill? Why delete it when he was heavily disguised, so almost impossible to identify in any event?"

"I've thought about it, and the only answer I can come up with is that it was part of his desire to discredit me, so that I couldn't even show it to anyone to prove that he'd sent it to me. Maybe he also worried that after my neighbour was released I would retract my statement and show the video."

"Yes, quite possibly; it did make it less likely that you would go straight to the police, because you had no proof. Clearly he thinks things through very carefully. I also wondered if it was deleted so that we couldn't analyse his voice and check it against our records or compare it to a suspect's?"

Krill had to admit that he hadn't thought of that. "His voice wasn't very distinctive, but I suppose a computer analysis of the sound patterns would have been useful."

"And thinking back, you didn't recognise his voice at all?" she asked.

"No."

Dr Knox took a document from a file on the table. "We've spoken briefly to your neighbour."

"Richard?"

"Yes Richard. He's still in a state of shock because of the trauma - not just the kidnapping, but he's been told that there's a good chance he may never regain his sight. He says that the kidnapper had a slight Northern accent."

"Yes, that sounds right; there were hints of that," Krill agreed.

"He also says that the man had no distinguishing features other than a limp. Evidently he used a walking stick. Does that ring any bells now or from the past?"

"No, none whatsoever. I never saw him walk or use a stick in the video. I don't think that any suspects in the Canal Killings had a limp or used a walking stick."

"That was many years ago so he will have aged a lot since then. And you've not seen anyone matching that description recently, acting suspiciously, maybe in your village, or near Margaret's house?"

"No. There's frequently elderly people out and about the village using frames and suchlike, but I know all of them. No, no sinister strangers in London or the village with walking sticks."

Knox looked thoughtful. "From Richard's statement it seems that the man who held him captive is about the right age to have committed the earlier murders."

"Can I ask you a question Dr Knox?"

"Certainly."

"Why do you think he's doing this now? Assuming he is the Canal Killer, why, after all this time, has he decided to come out of the woodwork and show himself?"

"In order to determine his possible motives we need to understand more about who he is. OK, let's assume, as I think you obviously do, that Peter Crow is innocent and this unknown man is the real Canal Killer. Also let's assume that he not only committed those murders but others as well, maybe many more, over the intervening years. In which case it would make him one of the most prolific and successful serial killers of all time, not only in this country but possibly in the world. Let's also assume that he is now in his late sixties or early seventies, because that fits the descriptions - unless he was deliberately making himself look older when he spoke to Richard - and it also fits the timeline for the Canal Murders. We can therefore assume that he is coming to the end of his career as a serial killer, and he now has a choice: does he continue to remain unknown and unseen so that his crimes go with him, unheralded, to the grave, or does he have a final 'swan song' and announce his crimes to the world? Many serial killers want to achieve recognition of some kind. Some of them believe that they are artists or skilled craftsmen and want to put their work on display. Many want to show just how evil and clever they are. Some seek fame, others want to terrify the local population. None of that is possible if no one knows that there is a serial killer still out there."

"Do you think that a part of him also wants to be caught?" Krill asked.

"No I don't. It's one of the many myths about serial killers. There's no evidence that any of them have ever wanted to be caught. Some enjoy taking risks, that's part of it, and these risks may increase over time because they need a greater and greater thrill. Or they come to believe that they are too clever to be caught, so they become incautious and make mistakes. But that's not the same as them ever wanting to be caught."

"At the time of the Canal Killings we didn't have access to an expert like yourself, so we couldn't determine whether Crow matched the profile of a serial killer, beyond knowing that he had been violent in the past. I'd like to hear what you think about those crimes, and whether or not you think we were right to believe that Peter Crow could be a serial killer?"

Dr Knox nodded, enjoying the challenge Krill had posed.

"I've read the file and I can completely understand why you would think him capable of those murders, particularly because of his abusive childhood. Without meeting him I can't tell whether he would have been categorised as a psychopath, which is the most common feature of a serial killer. There doesn't seem to be any evidence, for example, that he had a lack of empathy for others, or was manipulative. He was a loner, which again was a misconception about serial killers at the time. What I can say is that if I had been in your shoes, at that time, based on the available evidence and knowledge about those types of crimes, I would have assumed that Crow was guilty. And let's not completely rule out the possibility that he still may be."

"Thanks for that Doctor."

"Oh, one more thing Mr Krill, we would like your permission to put some software on your phone so we can record and hopefully trace a call if he gets in touch with you again?"

"I don't suppose I have any choice?"

"I'm afraid not. Going back to what I said earlier that the killer may now be seeking some recognition of his deeds,"

"Yes?"

"It's quite possible that the only recognition he wants, and I don't as yet know the reason why, is from you Mr Krill."

They both made it back to Highgate in time for dinner, and were joined by Margaret's petulant daughter. They didn't know what was said between mother and daughter when she turned up, but they could tell that Margaret hadn't expected her to be home that evening. The mealtime conversation was a mixture of tense Polish uttered in short sharp bursts, and rather constrained English, all of which wasn't helped by the fact that most of those around the table wanted to talk about the two subjects which were vetoed - Colin's death and the kidnapping of Krill's neighbour.

When the two men took their coffees to the front room they could hear the argument continuing in the kitchen.

"Strange language Polish - sounds very much like Russian to me; although no doubt they wouldn't like me to say that." Moss lowered his voice. "Are the two of them always like that?"

"Yes, seemingly."

"Are you planning to go there?"

"Where, to Poland? Probably when it's safe to do so."

"Well I hope that you manage to avoid having to take her daughter with you!"

Krill hadn't really thought about that unwelcome possibility.

"Never mind all that Moss, tell me what happened at the hospital."

Moss put his empty cup and saucer down on the coffee table and paused while he considered where to start.

"I think your neighbour was trying to put a brave face on it, partly because his wife was borderline hysterical when she saw him and was told that he's blind."

"What do they think has caused his blindness?" asked Krill.

"They're still not 100% sure, but from what he's said and the symptoms they think he was given Methanol. They're also checking for damage to his other organs. Evidently, even a small dose can cause blindness; a large one is usually fatal. His captor gave him a drink to celebrate your press release, so that's probably when he swallowed it."

"Didn't he suspect anything?" Krill asked.

"Most likely, but what could he do? If he'd refused to drink it then he'd no doubt be dead by now."

"Does he know why he was released?"

"Yes. He knows that you were instrumental, both in doing what the killer wanted and in finding out where he was taken. He wants you to go to see him at the hospital so he can personally thank you."

Krill looked shocked. "Thank me? That would be funny if it wasn't so tragic! If he hadn't had the misfortune to be living next door to me then none of this would have happened."

"No I suppose not," agreed Moss. "Still he's not seeing it that way. Like Margaret he thinks you saved his life."

"They won't keep him in long will they?"

"I'm not sure how long all the tests will take or what they'll do when they've finished them," Moss replied.

"Anyway, I'll wait until he goes home; I'll see him then. I don't like hospitals at the best of times but especially not now. I hope you were careful while in there Moss."

"We all were. It was like being in one of those plague movies - 'Outbreak' or 'Contagion'. How was Dr Knox?"

"Very interesting. What she doesn't know about serial killers probably isn't worth knowing. She's even worked with the FBI on several of their cases. From what she told me it doesn't sound like Richard was able to help you or Commander Morris very much. I assume he has no idea where he was kept? His description of the killer was pretty useless apart from confirming sex, approximate age, limp, and possibly a Northern accent."

"No, that's about it," Moss agreed. "In terms of where he was, he can't remember anything before waking up tied to a chair, like in the video. Evidently it was a large room, possibly underground, with no furniture apart from a table, chairs, and a mattress for him to sleep on. He was chained to the wall when not strapped to the chair. He was kept there for several days and then drugged again and taken to the barge. However, he did say that the killer was quite chatty."

"Chatty? What did he say - anything useful?" Somehow Krill didn't think serial killers should be 'chatty'.

"Not really, not from what he's recalled so far. He told Richard that he's killed a lot of people, including the guy who owned the bicycle. Evidently he likes red wine, and possibly golf as he was wearing a cap with the US Open logo on it."

"What did the killer say about Colin?"

"That he pushed him unconscious off a high building."

"Still no sign of the bike?"

"Yes, that mystery at least has been solved. It was found on top of the barge; they're checking it for prints but it's unlikely they'll find any apart from Colin's. Oh, the killer also said that he was once in the scouts."

Krill shook his head in disbelief: "A chatty boy scout serial killer with a limp who likes golf and red wine! Really?

184

Come on! All likely to be false trails; we can't take anything for granted."

"That's precisely what Commander Morris said." Moss sighed. "I'm in two minds about what she wants to do next."

"Why, what does she want to do?"

"Issue a detailed press release tomorrow, stating that you were forced by the kidnapper to say that Crow was innocent, and that you had no alternative because the person responsible was highly dangerous, as has been demonstrated by recent events. She wants to link him to the murder of Colin Marshall. She's also going to say that they have no evidence to suggest that Peter Crow's conviction should even be reviewed let alone overturned, and that we have no idea why the kidnapper made those demands. Finally she's going to say that if you had not cooperated with the kidnapper and helped the police to find Richard, then there's little doubt that he would also have been murdered. They'll obviously issue a description of the person they're looking for."

"Mmmm...not sure how our friend will react to that little lot. Is that what Morris wants - a reaction?" Krill asked. "Is she hoping to force him to make a move of some kind, and if so - what? I assume they've got someone guarding Richard at the hospital in case he decides to finish the job?"

"Of course, there's round the clock surveillance. I think overall I'm pleased with the press release, and its recognition of what you've done, even if there's a risk that it might provoke the killer. After they issue it, they're almost bound to reward you in some way as the 'hero of the day'. At the very least a commendation or maybe a Public Bravery Award?"

"I'm no hero Moss, and I don't want you or any of the lads talking about me as if I am!"

"I like your friend Moss, but this is such a strange name for you to use. Why don't you call him by his first name?"

"I do sometimes, but mostly he was always Moss, or sometimes Sergeant, for so many years when we worked together, and it sort of stuck. He still calls me 'Boss' or 'Guv'."

He'd asked Moss not to call him by his nickname in Margaret's presence, thinking that she might get the wrong idea; not many ladies like to be wooed by anyone called 'Killer'!

After his colleague had left to drive back to Berkshire, the two of them had retired to her first floor 'boudoir'. There was no other word that he could use to describe it: chintz wallpaper and curtains, silk screen, scattered cushions, and lots of soft lighting. There was one wall lined with books, mainly in Polish. If she'd been a man then he might have referred to it as an 'inner sanctum'. He wasn't sure why one sounded very feminine to the ear and the other far more masculine.

As he stood by the oak mantlepiece sipping the last of his Malbec, he thought about her dead fiancé, and how many times he'd been with her in this very room, maybe standing on exactly the same spot, contemplating the surroundings, and like him, anticipating the delights of the night ahead? He wasn't the jealous type but he couldn't help wondering.

Somewhat strangely, the room didn't contain a bed but rather a bed settee, which she could pull out and make up with bedding from a tall cupboard in the corner. It wasn't very large for sleeping on - a bit of a squeeze for two - but he rather liked that. He supposed it gave her more space during the daytime, and the room was probably a refuge from the more demanding guests and possibly from her daughter.

Margaret continued talking about Moss, "He could have stayed here for the night. I said to him that he should do this."

Krill was pretty sure that Moss wouldn't have wanted to sleep in Colin's bed, if that was what was on offer, and when Margaret had suggested that he stayed neither of them had wanted to ask for further details. Moss had made up some excuse about needing to get back to feed the cat. If he had one, then it was the first that Krill had heard about it!

"I think he's very much a creature of habit," Krill explained. "He hated it if we needed to be away on a case - said he could only get a good night's sleep in his own bed. When he goes on holiday, which isn't very often, he takes his own pillow with him."

"No. This is not true!"

"Yes he does."

"Why is he not married? Has he a girlfriend?"

"He's divorced. I'm not sure about his love life in recent years; he's never talked about anyone," Krill replied.

Margaret didn't like to think of any half decent man going to waste.

"It is a shame that he has no woman to care for him; but maybe that is not his taste? He seems very attached to you."

Krill raised his eyebrows at the implication. "Oh I'm sure his desires match my own. I think he's very envious."

She laughed. "Of you? Because you are with me?"

He pulled her to him and kissed her. "Of course. What man wouldn't be. Shall I help you with the bed?"

"Ha. Always so eager! But I like this." She pushed him away. "But first you must tell me more about what has happened. First you must satisfy my…. curiosity. Mind always before body!" She laughed, and pleaded with him, "Maybe you tell me just a little? Please John."

Her face was half pout, half coquettishness. If Krill had known the origin of the word 'boudoir', derived from the French word 'bouder', which means to sulk, then he would have thought it quite apt. He knew that she would find out more tomorrow in the news anyway, once Morris released her statement, so felt he could share some 'titbits'.

"OK, but why don't I tell you while we make up the bed?"

She grinned, and nodded. Just then his phone rang, spoiling the moment.

"It's Moss," he explained. "I need to take it. Hello Moss, yes…..What…. for fu…Why are they doing that?…..They're wasting everyone's time with their useless speculations and worse, frightening the populace by sensationalising it; blowing it out of all proportion…. Sorry Moss, I know it's not your fault…… No, I won't comment if they get in touch. What else?…..he used Richard's credit card? That's no surprise…..Any news from the prison?…A visitor?…Now

188

that is interesting..... Can we find out more about him? ....OK, OK, I know...I still think one of us should go and see Crow again while we still can, to dig into his past. He should be more cooperative now that I've told the whole world that he may be innocent.....OK, do that, see if Morris agrees... She's done what?...Oh I see, well congratulations....Let's speak again early tomorrow...No, not that early Moss, ten will do! Bye for now."

Margaret sat on the pulled out divan with a pillow in her arms, looking expectant.

"Right. Things are moving quite fast now. Several papers are continuing with the story about a serial killer being on the loose. One has photos of dozens of unsolved murder victims on its front page tomorrow, including several women, despite the fact that there's no evidence he's ever targeted women, or that any of the others were killed by him. The Met is issuing a Press release tomorrow, and I'm afraid it will only be a matter of time before they link Colin's murder to your address."

"Colin did not commit suicide?" she asked, surprised.

"No, I'm afraid that there's little doubt now that he was taken and killed by someone who then tried to make it look like a suicide." He didn't tell her the reason why her lodger had been targeted, although he suspected that if the Press found out that they were in a relationship they would soon see the connection. "I will have to leave here tomorrow before they issue the statement, and you and your daughter may also want to be away for a few days."

"But who will look after my guests? Do I tell them to leave?"

189

Again he held back. He suspected that her guests might very soon be departing in any event; after all, who would want to be staying in a B and B where an innocent young lodger had been murdered, especially by a psychopath who remained at large and highly active?

"Maybe you should talk to them about it as soon as you can and see what they want to do? You should warn them that there will be press and photographers soon outside your door, possibly tomorrow."

"But where would we go?"

He hesitated to say it: "Maybe another trip to Poland? Or we can find somewhere in the country, a cottage to rent? I'll look online and suggest some places. I'll cover the cost of course," he added.

"That is kind, but it is not the money that I am concerned about, John. And where will you go?"

Yes where? He could go to his daughter's, but the press had already been there. He could stay with Moss or one of the other members of the old team, or he could stay in a rented cottage with Margaret, and hopefully not with the dreaded Nikola, if she agreed to it.

"Don't worry about me, darling, I have plenty of options."

They both realised that it was the first time he had called her that. He sat down beside her and took her hand.

"Ideally, I'd like to be with you," he said, hopefully.

CHAPTER 23

"Commander Morris wasn't keen but she could see that there was little choice, as Crow will only speak to you."

They'd just passed Worcester on the M5.

"You know how I hate hospitals Moss; couldn't we have done it by Skype or WhatsApp? Does it have to be face to face? Or that other one, what's it called? Zoom? That's how people are meeting these days, not face to face. They could have rigged a screen up next to his bed."

"He said 'bring me Krill'. Besides, he's in no fit state to be talking on WhatsApp; he can barely speak at all. They say he's probably only got days to live."

"What is it? Cancer?"

"No, his heart. He's had heart trouble for several years."

"He'll bloody well say it's all my fault; that I caused it! And he probably won't cooperate. He just wants me to see him in this state and make me feel guilty."

"Maybe, but you're right, we have to try."

"What have you found out about the man who's been visiting him?" Krill asked.

"Not a great deal as yet. Name of David Smith, which of course doesn't help because it's so common. He hasn't been to see Crow since he was moved to the Open prison, and he's left the last address that we had for him. Bit of a mystery man at present. Do you know how many David Smiths there are living in the UK, Killer? Thousands. And maybe he's moved abroad or used false ID."

"Does Morris think that he could be our man?"

"Do you?" asked Moss.

"No; but he's possibly a link to the killer if he can tell us more about Crow's past. I doubt that the killer ever visited Crow in prison, because it would have been too risky. And why would he? Crow had served his purpose; he had no further use for him. Same with my neighbour - he used him and then threw him away without a second thought. No, that's not quite right, he will be imagining what it's like for him and his family, trying to cope with his blindness; but there'll be no sympathy or contrition for what he's done."

"You've not seen him yet?"

"Richard? No. The press are still sniffing around the cottage so I can't go back there yet. And before you say it, I know that's just an excuse; that I'm putting off seeing him. Maybe when he realises why he was chosen by the killer he won't be so keen to see me."

"It was hardly your fault. You weren't to know what would happen. People complain about their neighbours every day, and lots of people live next door to retired policemen, or retired judges, or ex-politicians. I'm sure they'd sooner do that than have a criminal, even a retired one, as their neighbour. He'll recognise that you did everything you could to save his life, even putting your own career and reputation on the line." Moss shook his head.

"What?"

"It's you Killer. The way you are. Always ready to take the blame for things which aren't your fault."

"Better that than refusing to admit that you could be wrong, and never accepting any responsibility," Krill reasoned, thinking for a moment about certain ex-wives and politicians.

"True, but as they say there's usually a happy medium, and I don't think you have found it."

Krill wanted to change the subject. "How's your new job as a 'Civilian Investigator'? I hope they're paying you the going rate?"

"They are, and it's fine." Moss laughed, "I think I've definitely broken the record for oldest employee. I can't say that the money isn't useful, and it means I'm closer to the centre of the investigation than I would otherwise be."

Moss had been so excited at the idea of working back at the Met that he'd hardly had time to worry if the income might affect his police pension. They'd waived the usual retraining requirements because they wanted him on the case as soon as possible, which suited Moss down to the ground. He'd never been one for sitting down and having to concentrate on what some so-called expert was spouting.

"Think they'll take me on too?"

Moss looked at Krill and laughed again.

"What's so funny Moss? I'm only a couple of years older than you."

"It's not that, I'm just trying to imagine you doing the donkey work."

"I might enjoy it." Krill looked hurt.

Moss shook his head even more visibly. "How's Margaret?"

"She's fine, thanks. I found a very nice cottage for us for a few weeks. The really good news is that her daughter has gone to live with her boyfriend. She didn't want to leave London."

"So it'll be just the two of you? Nice and cosy?"

"Yes, it is, Moss, and if you shake your head any more you'll get a crick in your neck! Why shouldn't we be together?"

"No, I'm pleased that you are, it's just that I thought you enjoyed your own company far too much to put up with someone living with you all the time."

"I don't think it's a permanent arrangement - being together twenty four seven. I think we'll soon go back to living in our own places but seeing a lot of each other. A few days in London, most weekends in Berkshire, and vice versa. That sounds perfect to me. LTA."

"What's LTA?" Moss asked.

"Living Together Apart. Lots of people - more mature people especially - do it. It's trendy. We can each do our own thing, but spend as much time together as possible. She can see her daughter without me, and I can see my kids and grandchildren."

"Yes, I can definitely see the merits of not seeing much of her wayward daughter. However, I'm surprised that Margaret has accepted it; or maybe you haven't discussed it yet?" He could tell from the look on Krill's face that he and Margaret hadn't spoken about the future. "I hope she's happy with that arrangement, but to be frank I'll be surprised."

"Why?"

"Well, didn't you tell me that she was about to marry her last chap, and she was going to sell her house and move in with him? Does that sound like a lady who would be content with just LTA, as you call it?"

Now it was Krill's turn to shake his head. "No, thinking about it, you're probably right."

"Don't look so glum Guv, I can be your 'Best Man'. And you can buy a bigger cottage in the Cotswolds, maybe go the whole hog - a thatched one with a garden full of roses. Sounds good to me."

Krill wasn't at all convinced by the picture Moss painted.

"But she likes to watch 'Call the Midwife', and 'Strictly', and 'The Apprentice'. I manage to squeeze in my foreign dramas very occasionally, but only if there's not too much bloodshed. Even Inspector Montalbano is too violent for her sometimes, although I suspect that she has a soft spot for Luca Zingaretti. And she likes to cook Moss!"

"Well that's good isn't it?"

"Yes and no. Unfortunately she has a limited repertoire. The first thing we had to do when we rented the cottage was to find a Polish outlet. I was brought up on Lincolnshire sausages, not the foreign stuff! And she hates fish. Can't stand

195

the smell of it cooking, or its texture, or how it looks on a plate for some reason. She even 'tuts' when I have it if we eat out. Thinks I need lots of meat to keep up my strength. With LTA I can binge on foreign drama when I'm on my own, and eat what I like. You can definitely have too much of a good thing Moss."

"I wouldn't know Boss, I wouldn't know. I seldom get a little of a good thing. I know, let's stop at the next service station? Maybe you can get some fish and chips?"

"How's the fish?"

"Terrible," said Krill. He wasn't sure whether he'd ever had a really decent meal at any motorway service station in the UK or abroad, but perhaps that was because he was just more fussy about the food which he ate?

"How's the burger?"

"Nice."

They'd bought a newspaper, and it lay open on the table between them, facing towards Moss, who tapped it with his outstretched finger. "At least the story is now relegated to page 4 in this one; and it's a relatively small piece. However, it says that someone has started an online petition to have Crow pardoned. It's already got over a hundred thousand people signed up."

"Do they have anything more about Colin?" Krill asked.

"Not today. Probably the Scottish editions will have."

"What's Commander Morris saying?"

"Just the usual: still no evidence that Crow isn't guilty and that they're following various lines of inquiry regarding the abduction and murder."

"No news about the person who rented the barge?"

"Nothing useful. As I told you, he paid with Richard's stolen credit card, and it's not been used since. Description of the man is pretty useless."

"And the barge?"

Moss told him that because of the pandemic rental barges had to be thoroughly disinfected before any hiring, and so there were literally no fingerprints anywhere. They'd found lots of tyre tracks in the mud not far from the canal, and one set might be from a van used to transport Richard, but as it was probably stolen he thought it would most likely be another dead end. The cords used to bind him could be bought almost anywhere, and the rags soaked in petrol were torn up strips from one of the curtains on the barge. Moss believed that the killer probably spent less than ten minutes on the barge.

Any conversation was almost impossible, as Crow could only speak for a few seconds at a time before he had to replace the oxygen mask; and when he did say something Krill struggled to understand him because of the weakness of his voice, the noise from the machinery which surrounded him, and the distraction of people passing by who were talking and moving equipment. However, it was obvious that Crow knew David Smith, and had struggled to say 'friend', maybe even 'best friend', and definitely 'boys' and 'long ago'. He also said 'doctor' several times, but seemed confused, shaking his head when Krill asked if he wanted him to fetch the doctor.

He appeared to go to sleep or become unconscious for several minutes at a time before suddenly waking up and looking anxiously around, as if he was terrified of what he might see. At one point he gathered all his remaining strength, pulled off his mask again, pointed to the side of the bed and said 'drawer', then more firmly - 'drawer Krill'. Moss watched as Krill took out an old well thumbed book from the bedside cabinet. He didn't get a chance to see the title but it appeared to have a picture of Buddha on the cover.

"Inside," gasped Crow.

Krill did as he was told, and opened it at the place where an old black and white photo was inserted. It was a picture of four boys aged around nine or ten, all quite grubby and wearing short trousers. They had their arms around one another's shoulders like they were the best of mates. Crow took it from him and pointed at one of the boys, saying "David."

The effort seemed to exhaust him and he closed his eyes again. Krill replaced the oxygen mask to ease his laboured breathing. A nurse came up to them and said that they should let him rest for a while. Krill replaced the book in the drawer but kept the photograph.

"Let's go for a walk, Killer. I need to use my phone and have a fag."

"Why don't you go Moss, and update Morris. I'll meet you at the car in half an hour. I doubt whether we'll get anything more out of him just now, but I'll wait a little while to see if he wakes up."

After Moss had gone, Krill asked the nurse where the nearest toilet was. He was still at the urinal when someone entered and stood close behind him. He felt something poked into his back.

"No, don't turn around Krill, and no hasty movements - I have a gun and if I have to I will use it."

Krill glanced towards the door.

"Don't worry - we won't be disturbed: I've put an 'out of order' notice on the door. I think you know exactly who I am, and why I'm here, don't you? Why don't you finish what you're doing and take a seat over there? Slowly now. That's it. Good."

Krill sat down in a cubicle and got his first glimpse of his adversary. He was wearing an old stained raincoat, a brown felt hat which was pulled down almost over his eyes, and a black face mask; he held an expensive looking walking stick in one hand, and a revolver fitted with a silencer in the other.

"I was relying on you having to use the toilet Krill. Men of our age need to more often than not, don't we?"

"What do you want?"

"Don't be like that. I only want to chat, and I won't harm you unless you force me to. I've been trying to find a way for us to meet for a long time now, and here we are. Why don't you take off your face mask so I can get a better look at you. I'll keep mine on if you don't mind." The man waved his gun up and down as a form of encouragement, so Krill did as requested.

His impression of raw undiluted evil was even stronger now that he was close to the killer than it had been when he'd watched the video. Every one of his senses seemed to issue a warning, to scream out - get away, run! As the sweat started to trickle down his back he felt like he had suddenly been transported into the scariest scene of a horror movie. All that was missing was the sinister soundtrack. Previously he'd only confronted killers and those accused of murder on his terms, usually in interview rooms, and with Moss there with him. He'd never really felt threatened before, not once in his long police career, and certainly never by someone who not only had a gun but looked as if he knew how to use it.

"You're looking old and worn out Krill. Maybe too old to still be chasing serial killers? Anyway, I thought that you might have some questions for me? I can't guarantee that I will answer them of course, but I might. However, first I have one for you - do you still think that poor Crow, who's lying out there on his deathbed, was the Canal Killer?"

"No."

"Excellent. He may have been a drunk and a fool, but he's not a murderer."

"Did you send me the urn?" Krill asked.

"Of course I did. I thought it was a nice touch. Maybe a little melodramatic, but I couldn't resist it, and it certainly got your attention didn't it? I think it was a rather unique calling card."

"Is it someone that you've killed?"

"In the urn? No, unfortunately I didn't get the chance to kill him. He was someone I knew a long time ago. In some ways he could be the cause of it all. I would have killed him if I'd had the opportunity, but sadly he died a natural death before I found the time to get to him. Perhaps you want to know what to do with his remains? Tip him in the bin is my suggestion; or down the toilet - yes that would be even better, it's where he belongs."

"Why are you doing all this - the urn, kidnapping and poisoning my neighbour, murdering that poor civil servant, demanding the statement about Crow's innocence. Why? And why now? What made you suddenly do those things?"

"Now those are some very good questions. Why do you think?"

"Possibly that you're reaching the end of your career and want some recognition?"

"Absolutely. Bravo! And why not. Isn't it well deserved? It's time everyone realised, and you in particular, just what I've achieved. Of course, that's why I chose the two of them, because they were linked to you. They didn't fit the usual profile of my victims; you know my penchant for middle-aged men. But hey ho, needs must, or is it 'beggars can't be choosers'?"

Krill winced inwardly at the killer's flippant dismissal of what he'd done to two innocent young men.

"How many have you killed?"

The killer laughed; it made Krill's skin crawl.

"Richard asked me that. I thought you would be more original Krill, more inventive; less boring. But OK, I'll indulge you: let's just say that it's more than anyone else. Many, many more. Too many to count. Unfortunately far too many to remember individually, much as I may try sometimes. How is Richard by the way? A part of me regrets that you found him in time, but he would have been the first one to suffer a painful death, and it's not really my style; well so far at least.

"I don't know how he is. I haven't seen him."

"No? That's a shame; I would have liked you to tell me how he's getting on, how they're all coping. Hopefully, the piano playing has stopped and things are a little quieter? But I suppose you can't go back to your cottage just yet. What is the media like, eh? Don't you just hate them? Maybe I should deal with a journalist or an editor before I finally put away my hypodermic? Of course none of those people they've mentioned in the papers are down to me. Not one. But you already knew that, didn't you?"

"Because your victims are never found, or if they are then no one suspects a murder?"

"Exactly. The perfect crime, each and every time. Give that man a coconut! Admit it Krill, I had you completely fooled forty years ago. You followed my trail exactly as I laid it out."

"You left the cloth and the incriminating photographs on Crow's barge?"

"Of course I did. It was even easier to break into than your cottage. He only ever left it to pick up his dole money and fetch some booze and other provisions, poor sod. Regular as clockwork, he was."

"What if I hadn't found him?"

"Oh I had every confidence in you Krill. Every confidence. But my backup plan was an anonymous tipoff. Now it's my turn: do you like your life Krill? Are you pleased with the way things have turned out for you? Do you have any regrets? How would you change your life if you could?"

These questions were not ones that he was expecting and it took him a while to answer. Why would this insane killer be interested in whether or not he was happy? It made no sense.

The gunman prompted him: "Well?"

"I would describe myself as fairly happy, yes, but like most people I have some regrets."

"Your two divorces perhaps? The fact that you lost touch with your children for a while?"

The killer's knowledge of his private life shocked him even more. "Yes, I would include those on my list, but right now I rather enjoy being independent."

"Excellent Krill. Just like me. What about that police inspector in Hampshire - are you sorry about him too? Maybe you should be. It was a suicide by the way, in case you're wondering. I had nothing to do with his death; well only indirectly."

"Yes I am sorry he killed himself."

"You don't sound very convincing. Surely it was convenient for you? Gave you a free run so to speak?"

"My turn." said Krill. "How long were you listening to my conversations at the cottage?"

"Long enough to put all my plans in place. I have to admit that I had a chuckle when you told Moss that the urn might contain your neighbour's ashes. Sad to say that even I am not that efficient! By the way, I'm pleased that you passed my little test of your moral fibre. It can't have been easy ruining your hard earned reputation for the sake of anyone as worthless as Richard, and someone who had also caused you a great deal of inconvenience. Did you waver at all Krill, even slightly? Weren't you just a little pleased when you discovered that he'd disappeared? How did it feel when you had to admit you were wrong about Crow?"

"Feel? It felt like the right thing to do for all sorts of reasons."

"Such a goodie goodie, aren't we! Even though it put you in a bad light with your previously adoring public?"

"I've never sought fame or publicity, except when it was necessary to progress an investigation." Krill tried one more question, hoping to catch the killer off guard, "Who's David Smith?"

"Who indeed, Krill? Someone from Crow's past no doubt? A mutual acquaintance perhaps? But I don't want to make it too easy for you, do I? I have one last question for you - does the great Chief Inspector Krill believe in Fate? No? That's a shame. What if I told you that two apparently separate lives can be inextricably linked in some way, almost like twins? You see, I believe that you are without doubt the Yang to my Yin - opposites yet connected; and that there's an invisible thread connecting us, which has been there almost since the day we were born, perhaps even before then. I can see from your face that you find the very idea of us being conjoined in some way abhorrent; but not to worry, maybe in time you'll see that I am right."

The killer checked his watch.

"I know you've been trying to keep me talking in the hope that Moss will come looking for you, but I'm afraid that I'm going to have to terminate our little question and answer session. This has been by far the riskiest little episode in my long and incredibly fruitful career - speaking to you in person, but in a way, and somewhat surprisingly, I think I've loved it the most." He bowed. "Thank you Chief Inspector Krill. It's almost made me regret that I've remained hidden all these years, and not done this before. However, it's now time for me to go, I'm afraid. All too brief, but as I say, Moss may be wondering where you are. Now we can do this the hard way or the easy way, because I do need time to make my exit unimpeded."

He propped his walking stick against the toilet door frame and took out a syringe.

"Don't worry, it's a very small amount, probably put you out for twenty minutes. Or I could just shoot you? No one would hear. What's it to be?"

CHAPTER 24

"He's coming round."

Krill opened first one eye and then the other, and struggled to focus. When he could do so he saw Moss leaning over him looking more frightened than he'd ever seen him before, and several people nearby in white and pale blue and green uniforms.

One of the medics spoke: "He probably just fainted, but we should check him out. I'll arrange for him to be taken to A&E and we can ask them to run some tests. This hasn't happened to him before?"

"Not to my knowledge, doctor."

Krill tried to speak but found that he couldn't. A few minutes later he felt himself being lifted onto a hospital trolly, and his head was placed in some sort of neck brace. He watched the ceiling lights flash by in quick succession as he was taken down several corridors, into a lift, then along another corridor. He managed to move his head a fraction and saw Moss out of the corner of his eye, walking at his side.

"Don't move or try to speak, not until we know what happened to you."

"Drug…"

They arrived in A&E and Krill was lifted onto a bed.

"I'm afraid I'll have to ask you to wait in reception while we examine your friend," the nurse explained to Moss.

Krill managed to grab Moss's arm before he could leave.

"No. Didn't faint…drugged."

"Did he say that he was drugged?"

"Yes, I think so, nurse."

"But how?"

Moss looked fearful. "Quick nurse, check his neck for a puncture wound."

The head blocks were carefully removed and the nurse examined first one side of Krill's neck and then the other. She went to fetch the doctor.

"What do we think has happened here, nurse?"

"The patient believes that he was drugged, doctor, and there does appear to be a fresh needle mark on his neck."

He shone a bright light into Krill's eyes and checked his pupils. "Ok nurse, let's run the usual toxicology."

At this point Krill tried to sit up, then laid back down again.

"Can you tell me what happened to you?" asked the doctor.

"Yes…someone… injected a drug…. into me."

Moss moved closer. "Was he here?"

Krill nodded.

"Sorry doctor, but I think we have to call your security and the police - now! There may be a very dangerous man here in the hospital. I have to use my phone." Moss stepped out of the cubicle while the nurse ran to get help.

"How are you feeling now Killer?" Moss asked.

Krill sipped his water; he couldn't face drinking tea or coffee yet.

"Still a little sick, but it's wearing off."

The two of them were sitting in an Inspector's office at the nearest police station to the hospital, which was being used to coordinate a response to the incident. Krill had insisted on leaving A&E as soon as he could stand. He'd already given Moss chapter and verse about his conversation with the serial killer, not just about what had been said but how he'd felt in his presence. Moss had taken notes which would later help with making a statement.

"The Deputy Chief Constable is coming down; he should be here soon. They're checking the hospital CCTV for anyone matching the description. There was no sign of him in the building when we searched it," Moss explained.

"I think he had a large carrier bag with him, so possibly he changed his clothes before he left."

"Maybe Killer, but we can check all solitary males leaving the building around that time."

Krill shook his head, and then pulled a face due to the after-effects of the drug.

"I doubt he'll use any of the regular exits. He might even have been dressed as a doctor or a porter. Check the fire exits and any staff entrances too."

"Ok. We'll do all we can to find him on camera. If we're lucky we might even see him taking a taxi or getting into his car."

"Yes, we have to check everything thoroughly - you know I always like to work by the 'book', but I'll be surprised if you find anything useful on CCTV. He's thought this through very very carefully; probably planned it down to the minutest detail. What I can't figure out Moss, what's really troubling me, is how he knew we would be there? Did he follow us? Did he put a tracker on your car, like he did mine? Or did someone tip him off?" Krill looked alarmed. "Just in case he followed you to the holiday cottage to pick me up, can you get one of the boys to check that Margaret's OK, and keep an eye on her until we get back?"

"I'll get on to it right away." Moss left the room to make the call and get a coffee refill. He came back minutes later. "Someone will be at the cottage in thirty minutes."

"Make sure he doesn't alarm her, or tell her too much about what happened to me so she gets upset. Who'd you send?"

"Jim. He's as solid as they come."

"Good. So who knew that we were going to see Crow at the hospital today apart from you and me Moss?"

"Only the Prison Governor and Commander Morris. Obviously we've no idea who they in turn told, if anyone."

"What did Commander Morris say when you informed her about what had happened?"

"She was quite shocked and very concerned about you. She asked whether we were getting full cooperation from the local police. I think she was disappointed that we didn't need any more helicopters!"

"What if the killer suspected that we were likely to visit Crow again, and perhaps had someone at the hospital watching for me? Or maybe he went there himself to take a last look at Crow and our paths just happened to cross? He did say something about Fate; maybe it was pure chance?"

"All of those are possible," said Moss "We'll check for two people on the hospital CCTV in case you're right. Do you think you could identify him, Boss? From mugshots? Maybe do a photofit?"

"No, and that would all definitely be a complete waste of time because I couldn't see his face. However, I might recognise his voice if I heard it again. It was much clearer today than on that video. I suppose Richard could as well, come to think of it. Would that stand up in court? An old ex-copper and a blind man saying - yes it's definitely his voice, he's your man? I doubt it. He's playing his cards incredibly well."

"So far. They all slip up some time."

"Not the ones we never catch. Having said that Moss, as Dr Knox remarked to me only the other day, it does seem that he is taking more and more risks."

"Can I see that photograph which you took from Crow's book?"

"The photo! I'd almost forgotten about it."

He took it out of the inside pocket of his jacket, looked at it briefly, and handed it to Moss.

"You think one of these is David Smith, the person who used to visit him in prison?" Moss asked.

"That's what Crow said; he's second from the right. I believe Crow is also in the picture."

"Could our killer be one of the four?"

"Possibly. We can try to talk to Crow again, later today or tomorrow, to see if he can put a name to the others. I assume they've put a guard on him?"

"Yes, now they have. They didn't bother with one before because of his condition; he wasn't going anywhere." Moss looked at the photograph again. "It's not a very good print, but if you ask me then two of the boys look as if they might be related: the one who's evidently called David and the one on the far left. They might even be twins."

"Let me see. Twins? Funny you should say that because the killer talked about twins. I wonder if he inadvertently let something slip? Can you get me a magnifying glass?"

"OK Sherlock, back in a tick."

When Moss returned they both used the magnifying glass to check the photo again.

"Yes they do look almost identical, and I think the one standing between them might be Peter Crow. See if we can get the photo digitally enhanced will you? So, if we're right, in this old photo we have Peter Crow, David Smith standing on one side of him, another Smith on the other side - David's twin brother, and a fourth unknown boy. If we find this mysterious David Smith, hopefully he can tell us who they all are in the photo, even if Crow isn't able to do so." Krill had a further unpleasant thought: "We need to speed up our search for him, not least because the killer may also be looking for him. When I mentioned David Smith's name I got the distinct impression he knew who he was."

As soon as they were joined by the local Inspector, Krill asked him whether they'd found anything yet on the CCTV from the hospital.

"Well so far, ruling out groups of people - i.e. three or more leaving the hospital, we've got several possible sightings. Let me show you." He swung the screen round so it faced his visitors and typed on his keyboard. "This is someone being pushed in a wheelchair leaving the hospital main entrance roughly ten minutes after you were attacked. I think you said that you thought he might have an accomplice? The person seated is wearing a hat like the one you described, and you can see that he does appear to have a walking stick on his lap."

Krill studied the screen closely. "Leaving the hospital in a wheelchair would certainly be a good cover for him, but I think it's a long shot. Can you blow it up and print it?"

"Will do, although as you'll see, they're all still wearing face masks in the clips when they leave. Here's another one in a wheelchair, this time on his own, but no walking stick that we can see. I suppose he could have dumped it, maybe with some others - there's lots of them in the hospital."

"The walking stick looked very distinctive; not your standard NHS one. Again I'd like to look at a close up of him."

The Inspector continued: "We have several single males exiting at roughly the right time, but none with a walking stick, and no one wearing the right clothing. I'll show you: there's him.....now him.....this one......here's another....him....and him."

Krill squinted as he focussed on the screen. "I'm happy to look at them all. What about CCTV inside the hospital, near the toilet where he attacked me, in the lifts, and on the way out? If we could follow his route we might have a better idea of the exact time he left."

"I have a list of all the camera locations." The Inspector took out a sheet of paper from a folder. "Unfortunately they're only located in certain areas. There's several in A&E as you would expect, a few near Maternity, curiously some next to the Education Centre and lecture theatres, the dining areas have a couple - again not sure why, staff car parks are covered, so is the store's loading bay, and all the main entrances. Which means that unless he veered off into one of those areas by mistake he could walk from the toilet right to the main entrance without passing a single CCTV camera. Don't blame me or the hospital Mr Krill, blame it on RIPA and the Data Protection Act."

"What about fire exits? Do they have CCTV?" Moss asked.

"No, because they're alarmed. However, we've discovered that one alarm was not working. It leads straight onto a car park and from there you can walk into town."

Krill looked at Moss and they both reached the same conclusion.

"That's probably how he came and went Inspector," Moss spoke for the two of them.

"Yes, that's my guess also." The Inspector shook his head, "It's like he's invisible."

"No, he's just very very good at what he does. Any further news about Crow Inspector?"

"Yes Mr Krill, and I'm afraid that's not good either. He suffered another heart attack and slipped into a coma. They don't expect him to last the night."

Krill slammed his fist onto the desk. "Damnation."

"Don't be too upset about the CCTV Boss, it wouldn't have been of much use anyway because of the face mask."

"I know that Moss. It's just that he's constantly at least one step ahead of us. It would have been a small victory to have caught him on camera just once, mask or no mask." Krill checked his watch. "What time is the video conference with Commander Morris?"

"In fifteen minutes. She says that she would like you and the Assistant Chief Constable present as well, if at all possible Inspector?"

"Fine by me, but I think the ACC may have already left; I'll check."

"Hello Inspector, thanks for making yourself available."

"I'm afraid that the ACC was already on his way back to HQ when we got your meeting request Commander."

"No problem, I'm sure you'll update him later. Good evening Mr Krill, I hope you've now recovered from your ordeal?"

"Yes, thank you Commander."

"Looks like you got off very lightly; he must like you. Anyway, I see Dr Knox is now online too, so as we're all present and correct let's get started shall we? Perhaps we should do this chronologically, starting with the interview with Peter Crow. Mr Krill?"

"I would hardly call it an interview Commander, as he was slipping in and out of consciousness all the time. He only managed a few words."

"But he did identify David Smith on this photograph that you've sent us? And Crow seemed to suggest that he's known him since childhood?"

"Yes, and we also believe that another boy in the group is David's twin brother."

"Based on what?" Commander Morris asked.

"Based on the fact that they look identical," said Krill.

"OK, well that will have to be confirmed of course. Once we find Mr Smith we'll soon know whether he has a twin. Crow didn't say anything about a twin I take it?"

"No he didn't," Krill confirmed.

"Or about who the fourth boy is?"

"No. As I said, he was barely able to speak, and he was totally exhausted by the very brief conversation which I had with him. I was hoping to speak to him again soon."

"But I gather that, short of a miracle, it's not now going to happen?"

"No, unfortunately it appears not."

"If I could come in Commander?"

"Yes Dr Knox?"

"Serial killer twins are not unknown; in fact I can think of at least one set of twins who acted independently of one another without each other's knowledge."

"So, if I understand you correctly, they were both serial killers but neither knew that the other one was?"

"Exactly Commander, strange as that sounds."

"OK, that's interesting, but let's stick to just one serial killer for the time being can we? Finding one will be hard enough, Gillian. Like you, Mr Krill, I don't think the serial killer would risk visiting Peter Crow several times, which would seem to rule David Smith out, but not his twin, if he has one. Are you OK with that logic Dr Knox?"

"Yes, but of course Commander we have no way of knowing at this juncture whether any of the four boys in the photograph is the person we're looking for, even if we accept Mr Krill's belief that Peter Crow knew the serial killer, which I happen to agree with. The photograph may be useful in terms of eliminating suspects, but the killer could be one of any number of people who Peter Crow met before he was arrested. For example, it could be another person who owned a barge close to where Peter Crow moored his, or he could

216

have met him in the betting shop or at numerous other places that he frequented, including nearby off-licences and pubs. It could be someone who passed by regularly on the footpath and got to know Crow. The possibilities are almost endless."

"The killer mentioned to me something about Crow signing on. Can we check the records for the local labour exchange as it was at the time?" suggested Krill, a little hesitantly because of what had happened at their first meeting.

"We can certainly try Mr Krill. One bit of good news is that I'm going to increase the team that we have working on this. Does anyone know if Crow has any living relatives, or whether he was in contact with any relatives at the time he was arrested? They might have known enough about his habits and possibly visited him on the barge. What's on file Moss?"

By now Moss almost knew the file off by heart: "His mother was still alive and so was his stepfather at that time, but I don't believe that Crow had been in contact with them for several years prior to his arrest, not since he ran away from home. He also had a stepbrother. I remember that we did manage to interview him in '78, but I believe he said that he'd not seen Peter since he'd left the family home as a teenager. I'll double check."

"This is developing more and more dead ends. OK, thanks Moss. Turning to you if I may Inspector, have you ascertained yet how the assailant entered and exited the hospital?"

"Nothing definitive. We were discussing that just prior to your call Commander. Unfortunately there doesn't appear to be anything on CCTV. However, we believe he may have left via a damaged fire exit door and walked either to the adjacent car park or into Town. We're going to check any CCTV from nearby shops and offices to see if we can pick him out en route to the Town centre, and check the registrations of all vehicles using that particular car park."

"Excellent. Looking to the future, what do we think the killer's next move might be? Dr Knox?"

"That's very difficult to say, Commander. Having had his conversation with Mr Krill there's a very slim chance that he might decide to stop killing and disappear for good. It will only happen if he thinks that his work is done and that his achievements have been sufficiently recognised. If not then he'll probably look for more victims. If the people in that photograph are important to him then he might target them, assuming he already targeted Crow, but we have no evidence that he's in the photo or that he knows any of them. A further issue, if it is the same man who committed the Canal Killings, is that he may have widened his choice of victims since the 1970's. As I understand it, those original crimes all involved middle-aged men, but as we know the two latest victims were both much younger. Did he temporarily change his selection because he wanted to target people who knew Mr Krill, or has he been killing a far wider age group for some time? We have no way of knowing and therefore any adult male could be at risk."

"He said that he'd changed his MO of middle-aged men just for me. He also mentioned that he might think about killing someone connected to the media," said Krill.

"Did he indeed, well he'd better join the bloody queue!"

218

The Commander shook her head. "Sorry, I shouldn't joke about such things. Even the media deserve better. As two of the victims are linked to you Mr Krill I assume that you and Moss are taking some preventative measures, including watching out for yourselves?"

"We are, yes Commander," confirmed Moss.

"Good. We certainly wouldn't want either of you to suffer the same fate as poor Mr Marshall or your neighbour."

Krill and Moss walked back to their car which was parked outside the police station.

"Margaret's OK Killer. I got another text from Jim while we were on the conference call. Evidently she's just fed him a huge plate of something called 'Bigos'. He wasn't sure if it was named that because of the size of the portions or because of the ingredients. He says he wants to move in. Is she big on 'Bigos' Boss?"

Krill refused to react and just shook his head. He didn't want to admit to Moss that he'd already had the stew several times because he'd made the mistake the first time of telling her how much he had liked it. And he definitely wasn't in the mood for any misdirected and ill-conceived humour - at least that's what he thought it was, nor for any attempt to lighten the rather sombre mood. Moss unlocked the car doors.

"You happy for me to drive back Killer? I don't think you should drive yet anyway, until we're sure that the drug has completely worn off."

"Yes, you drive Moss; I need to think. Let's find a pub halfway back where we can get something decent and English to eat."

They drove for fifty miles in silence. Moss was reluctant, because of Krill's demeanour, even to turn on the radio, so he was relieved when Krill finally spoke:

"Tell me more about Crow's stepbrother; I'd almost forgotten about him."

"From memory we interviewed him just the once. I've a vague recollection that, like Colin Marshall, he was also some sort of Civil Servant. Said he hadn't seen Crow for more than ten years. Didn't seem very surprised that his half-brother was in trouble. Sorry he couldn't help us. That's about it."

"But he's another link to Crow's past and might know about his friends, at least when he was still living in the family home. He might also know about the photo."

"Yes Boss, I'll try to track him down. Can't remember his surname offhand, except that it wasn't Crow because Peter never took his stepfather's name."

"How much younger than Crow was he?" Krill asked.

"Several years, maybe ten?"

"So he can't be in the photo."

"No, not unless he was remarkably tall for his age! What do you think of Commander Morris, now that you've had more of a chance to see her in action?" Moss hoped that Krill had the same positive view as himself about the Commander.

"Good, impressive, very thorough. However, having said that I think she's going to need all the help she can get, especially from you and I. This case would challenge even the great Sherlock Holmes. It's got so many aspects to it which we still don't understand. Take the urn for instance, which the killer left on my doorstep. I asked him about it, and he said that whoever it was had probably been the cause of it all, the multiple murders, and implied that he would have wanted to kill him as well but that he'd died a natural death."

"Yes, you told me earlier."

"I did wonder if the person in the urn was the fourth boy in the photo?"

"That's quite a big leap Killer, even for you. The urn might have nothing to do with the photo, and if the two are linked then we shouldn't forget that we haven't yet found either of the two Smith's alive, so logically it could be one of them. My money's on the urn and the photo not being linked. In fact, I think there might not be any link at all between the photo and the killer. It could just be three boys that Crow played with who have absolutely nothing to do with any of this."

"But my gut tells me otherwise, Moss, and I've learned to trust it over the years. I think that photo could be the key to it all."

"Well I hope you're right yet again Killer, because otherwise we don't have a bloody clue! Do you think he'll contact you again?"

"No, possibly not, unless I can somehow force him to do so."

"How would you do that?" Moss sounded worried.

"Maybe by making him angry? You heard what Dr Knox said about him needing recognition. He won't like it if I make it clear that I don't think he's any different from all the other pathetic serial killers. And by making him want to prove that I'm wrong? Or by making myself a target?"

"Be very careful Boss; remember who we're dealing with here - someone who's already killed scores, maybe hundreds of people. Also you'd be putting anyone close to you at risk, not just yourself; it wouldn't be just you that he might target if you riled him. And think about how easy it was for him to corner you in that toilet. Would you really want to put yourself through that again, or God forbid, anyone you care about?"

"No, you're right."

"I know you Killer. You can't bear the thought of him just going away; vanishing into thin air. You want justice for his victims, and so do I, so you're desperate to catch him. And it's partly to make amends for the mistake we all made forty years ago. But lets find him using good old fashioned detective work, not by employing some highly risky trick psychology. More than likely if you did try to get him annoyed, hoping he might make a mistake, he'd see through it anyway. We'll definitely follow your ingenious gut; somehow we'll track down those three boys in the photo. Hopefully, then you might bloody well shut up about it!"

Krill laughed, much to Moss's relief, as he wasn't sure if he'd overstepped the mark.

"You're keeping me on the right path as usual Moss. Where would I be if I didn't have you?"

"Probably eating 'Bigos'!"

Krill was halfway through a rather tasty sea bass in a pub not far from the M5 when his companion's phone rang. He listened to one side of the short conversation, gathering at various points that Moss was pleased and then just the opposite.

"Right. That was one of the team at the Met. They've found David Smith, or rather Doctor David Smith, who is a retired GP."

"Doctor! That's what Crow was trying to tell me; that his friend is a doctor, and stupidly I thought he wanted me to fetch the doctor. When are they interviewing him?"

"Tomorrow morning at his local station."

"God Moss, I wish I could be in on the interview."

"Well, the best you can hope for is that I can somehow wangle you being able to watch it remotely at the station."

"Where is the interview?"

"Bracknell - so not too far from home thankfully. It should be fairly straightforward: questions about his relationship with Crow, about Crow's friends and those in the photo of course, maybe ask if Crow ever said anything during his numerous visits which might suggest that someone had a

223

grudge against him." Moss paused briefly. "The other news is that Crow's dead."

"I'm sorry to hear that, but in a way it's better for him that his long ordeal is finally over. I'll try to go to his funeral of course. I don't suppose there'll be many mourners."

"You might get another chance to speak to his stepbrother if he bothers to turn up. Speaking of him, I didn't say anything in the meeting today, but the weird thing is that I've already gone through the file from end to end twice now, and there's no record of him being interviewed in 1978. But I'm as certain as I can be that we did see him, as I told you earlier. In which case, where is the report?"

"Obviously missing, which is highly unusual but not a completely rare event. Listen Moss, I know it's a bit deceitful, but Doctor Smith might be more forthcoming tomorrow if he doesn't find out that Crow is dead until after the interview. I assume it won't become public knowledge for at least twenty four hours?"

"I'm sure we can hold it back for a little while. You're right, he may not talk to us at all about Crow if he knew; it might be a case of not wanting to 'speak ill of the dead'. If he thinks we're trying to exonerate his friend, which in a way we are, he should be far more forthcoming. I'll see if Commander Morris is happy with that approach."

"Yes do that; I'd hate to get you into more trouble with your new boss."

"Wouldn't be the first time you've landed me in hot water Killer."

"No, probably not. Did they say who will be conducting the interview?" Krill asked.

"As it's routine it will probably be me, on my own."

"Fine. I trained you well so you'll get all you can out of him. If we ever catch the killer, I would give my right bollock to be leading that interview!"

"I'm not sure if Margaret would approve, Boss. She wouldn't think that you losing one of your jewels was a fair trade." Moss was surprised at Krill's optimism about catching the serial killer, and wondered if it was just putting on a brave face? "Do you honestly believe that we will get him? He's eluded capture for decades, and he easily gave us the slip at the hospital. As you say he's always at least one step ahead of us."

"My head says no we won't but....."

"Your bollock says otherwise?"

"My guts say that we might have a very slim chance."

"And I suppose we did find Doctor Smith before he did; assuming he was also looking for him."

"If he was also looking for him, then I wouldn't be at all surprised if he let us find him first, although don't ask me why."

"Another beer Killer?"

"Thought you were never going to ask. You've been nursing that half inch in your glass for twenty minutes."

"Well I am driving."

While Moss was at the bar, Krill phoned Margaret:

"Hi darling, is everything OK?........Yes, I'm pleased that Jim is looking after you......Had two helpings, did he? Lucky

225

chap............No I won't, thanks all the same; Moss and I are eating just now.......Oh..a nice juicy steak........We shouldn't be too long, but don't wait up....yes of course I've missed you.....night darling."

Moss put the drinks on the table and sat back down.

"So who had the steak?"

"I did, and don't you say otherwise if you're asked! A nice big fat sirloin. Evidently Jim had double 'Bigos', so hopefully there won't be any left for tomorrow."

Moss smiled. "Maybe you could include it in a prenup?"

"Include what?" asked Krill, expecting some smart-arsed answer.

"A clause that you're the only one allowed to do any cooking. Or you could specify a maximum number of days each year for foreign food. Or you could tell her that your doctor has specified a meat free diet for you, maybe just fish and white meat, or even vegan? She'll want to keep you young and healthy, won't she?"

Krill had to laugh. "I'm not sure. I'm beginning to wonder if Polish sausage didn't contribute in some way to poor Graham's demise!"

CHAPTER 25

"Possibly I've been too hasty Moss."

"In what way Boss?"

They'd just joined the M4 and were making good progress towards the junction for Bracknell. As usual Moss was doing the driving.

"In assuming that the killer wouldn't visit Crow. Because it's possible he might have done so in order to mislead us if the case was ever reopened. And of course it would have given him the opportunity to gloat."

"Oh, right." Moss wasn't used to Krill amending his deductions so speedily, and especially not now that Dr Knox had appeared to confirm what he'd said about the killer probably not seeing Crow.

"Which means that we shouldn't rule out Doctor Smith as a suspect."

"OK."

"I mean, a doctor would have access to drugs and syringes wouldn't he?"

"Yes, that's true. You're right, we shouldn't rule out

anyone who is in any way connected to Crow."

"Including his stepbrother," Krill added.

"Yes, him too. Thinking about what you've just said, it will help if we can consider the good doctor a suspect, because then you should definitely watch the interview, in case you recognise his voice."

"Yes, although it won't be the same as being in the room with him. Do we know yet if he has a twin?"

"No, not yet, they're still checking his background. They might be able to tell us when we get there, and I'll ask him of course."

"Assuming that he doesn't have a limp and uses a walking stick, ask him if he knows anyone who does."

"Will do," said Moss.

"And see if he has an alibi for the day of our hospital visit."

"Boss...."

"What? What have I done now?" Krill looked most aggrieved at Moss's tone.

"Now you're treating me like I'm your grandmother."

"OK, sorry, I'll put the eggs away and keep 'mum'. Just trying to help."

"Well please don't. Not in that way anyway."

"Thanks for coming in this morning Doctor Smith. Can I get you a tea or a coffee?"

David looked at his watch. "No, thank you; I was rather hoping that this wouldn't take too long. They said that you wanted to talk to me about Peter?"

As Doctor Smith sat down in the seat opposite, he fiddled with his tie trying to loosen it, and Moss assumed that it was because he might not have worn one for a while. The file said that he would be seventy two in December but he looked younger, partly because he still had a full head of greyish hair. He was smartly but casually dressed in a brown check jacket and darker brown trousers. He looked very much like a retired family doctor.

"Have they asked you to come out of retirement because of the pandemic?" Moss asked.

"I've volunteered, yes, but not in a hospital because of my age. I'm helping out in the surgery a couple of afternoons a week."

"That's good of you. I'm sure it's appreciated."

Moss's phone beeped. He quickly checked it - there was a text from Krill which said: 'It's not him'.

"So how can I help you Mr Moss; I'm sorry but I don't know your rank?"

"That's OK Doctor. I used to be a sergeant in the Metropolitan Police, but now I'm a Civilian Investigator assisting them. As you are probably aware, I was one of those who led the investigation into the Canal Killings in 1978 and '79 which resulted in Peter's subsequent conviction. I've been asked to see if you could fill in some of the gaps about Peter's life before he was arrested."

"I see. Is it to do with what I've read in the paper - that the police may now think he was innocent?"

"Yes it is. While we have no evidence as yet that would prove his innocence, we are looking into the possibility that someone else committed those murders. One line of inquiry is that it could be someone who knew enough about Peter to be able to make it look as if he was the killer. It might be an acquaintance of his from the time he was living on the barge, or even someone from his childhood."

"So does that mean that I'm a suspect, because I probably know Peter better than any other living person?"

Moss laughed. "While we're not dismissing anyone completely at this very early stage, no, we do not presently consider you to be a suspect."

"Well that's a relief! In any event, and for the record, if my memory serves me right I was working in Africa for several years before Peter was arrested and those murders were carried out. We rather lost touch for a while, and it was quite a shock when I returned to the UK and found out what had happened. So how can I help?"

"OK, that's useful to know; so you wouldn't be aware of any friends that he might have had while he was living on the barge?"

"No, as I say we'd not spoken for a while. I wrote to him every few months, and occasionally got a brief reply back. I think it was a very difficult time for Peter - he wasn't working and had a drink problem. I sent him some money when I could, but I wasn't earning very much myself in those days."

"You visited him in prison when you came back to the UK?"

"Yes, quite regularly before he was moved North."

"And he never mentioned anything about the people he knew in those days, just prior to his arrest?"

"Surely you should be asking Peter these questions Mr Moss?"

"Unfortunately we can't. Peter had a heart attack and was taken into hospital last week. We did go to see him but unfortunately he wasn't well enough to answer our questions."

"I'd heard he was ill, but I didn't realise it was that serious. Poor Peter. No, we never really talked about the time when he was living on his barge. I think much of it was a bit of a blur due to his drinking."

"What did you talk about?"

"Oh, mainly the old days, when we were both young - the fifties and sixties; also religion, his life in prison, books, TV - the usual stuff."

"You grew up in the same town together?"

"Yes."

"Did you live close to one another?"

"Actually in the very same street, and we went to the same schools for a while. I suppose I felt sorry for Peter, because he was quite lost even as a child."

"Lost - how?"

"He didn't get on with his stepfather, that was at the core of it I think. Also the family was not very well off. I mean none of us were, but Peter's family had a 'hand to mouth' existence. He looked hungry much of the time, and his clothes were even worse than ours. So I think some of the other families in the street rather looked down on him and his mother, especially when his father left. There was speculation that his dad was in prison, but I'm not sure if that was true. Peter was different to the other kids because he was always up to mischief, far more than the rest of us. He reminded me a little of 'Dennis the Menace', the cartoon character in that comic, the Dandy or the Beano, but you won't remember those."

Moss took the photo out of the file and slid it across the table.

"When we saw Peter recently he showed us this photo. I wonder if you recognise those in it?"

Doctor Smith took out his glasses and put them on. He smiled. "Yes I do. I'd forgotten what we all looked like in those days. My, my, what a sad looking disreputable bunch! We all hated those short trousers and couldn't wait to get long ones."

"Peter is in the photo?"

"Yes, that's him in the middle. That's me next to him."

"And the other two?"

Doctor Smith frowned.

"The one on the other side of Peter is my twin brother, Christopher. As for the fourth boy, now what was his name? He came and went a little - he wasn't always part of our 'gang', if we can call it that. But then neither was my brother, not all the time. It was really Peter and myself who were as thick as thieves, sometimes quite literally I'm afraid - he did rather lead me astray. Our parents used to say to us: 'don't you hang out with that Crow kid'. But for me it was a little like a red rag to a bull, you know what kids can be like. I don't suppose that I can get a copy of that photograph, as a keepsake? I may have it somewhere, but I've had to discard such a lot of things because of my travels."

"Yes Doctor, I'll make sure that we send you one. Can we talk briefly about your brother?"

David fidgeted on his seat and looked at his watch again.

"If we must, but I'm afraid I won't be able to help you very much as we haven't seen one another, or even spoken, for more than fifty years."

"You fell out with one another?"

"I'm not sure if we were ever 'in' with one another. People think that twins are close, but unfortunately that's not always the case. We looked alike but were opposites in every other respect. He thought that our mother favoured me for some reason, which is untrue. I suppose if I'm honest I thought father favoured him. We were never close, not in the least, and when we left home we both decided that we really didn't want to have anything further to do with one another. I think he was working abroad too for a while, from what my mother said. Robin. That's what the other boy in the photo was called. Robin….something animal related….Butcher! That's it, Robin Butcher. Poor boy, his father hanged himself in the woods behind our street. It was quite horrible for all of us, but a terrible blow for him. God, I remember being in class when the Deputy Headmaster of the Grammar school came to the door and asked Robin to go with him. We didn't see him for several days after that. He was never the same poor chap. Tragic."

"Robin Butcher. Thanks Doctor. I don't suppose that you and Robin kept in touch?"

"For a while. As I say he went to the same Grammar school as Christopher and myself. I think he then went on to Oxford, or was it Cambridge? Whereas I went to Edinburgh. He was more arts than science, I remember now - languages that sort of thing. Clever chap. Could be a difficult boy even before his father's suicide. He and Peter had a few fallouts."

"What about Peter's stepbrother? At this stage we don't even know his name. Can you give us any information about him or his stepfather?"

"This is getting embarrassing because I'm afraid that I can't. The one thing Peter absolutely refused to ever talk about, as a child or subsequently, was his stepfather, and I never knew his stepbrother at all really. You see he wasn't even born when Peter and I first knew one another."

"OK, not to worry, doctor. Can I just check for the record where you were on Tuesday afternoon and early evening?" asked Moss.

"Tuesday? I was at the surgery in Bracknell from 2pm until 6."

"Thanks. One final question and it may seem a little strange one to ask, but did Peter ever mention anyone who had a limp, or do you know of anyone from his past who had a disability of that kind?"

"No, he didn't, not that I can recall. Of course my brother had polio as a child. Actually it wasn't long after that photo was taken."

"That was excellent Moss. A textbook interview. And you didn't even have to mislead him about Crow's demise. You skirted around that issue expertly. Sins of omission - always the best ones."

They'd gone to a coffee shop close to the police station, and were still wrapped up as Krill had insisted on them sitting at a table near the open windows. Moss had grabbed a slice of cake but Krill was having to watch his weight, even more so since he'd taken up temporary residence with Margaret.

"What was your impression of the Doctor?" Moss asked.

"Seems an amiable chap on the face of it. Doing his bit during the crisis. Obviously liked Peter Crow despite the latter's faults. I think he wanted to give the impression of at least trying to help us, but I'm not sure that he did very much. Says he's fallen out with his brother 'big time', for some reason that he's unwilling to disclose, and it's very interesting that his twin probably has a limp at the very least - few got off lightly when it came to the dreaded polio. The fourth boy, Robin, now he interests me a great deal, although a serial killer called 'Butcher' would be too good to be true! Could his father committing suicide have been some sort of a trigger?

Did he resent others having a father perhaps? Again it would be a possible explanation as to why middle-aged men were originally targeted. It will be interesting to hear Dr Knox's views."

Moss smiled, content that as usual Krill had taken a tiny morsel of background information and used it to come up with a possible motive. He wondered whether he would have arrived at the same conclusion so quickly, but doubted it.

"Hearing him speak about Crow being an alcoholic and not in a good place, made me think again how we could have believed him capable of committing multiple murders and not be caught? It was another reason to question the evidence, Moss."

"But he wasn't on a binge all the time. He was sober when we picked him up that morning, so maybe he kept his drink problem under control? If I remember rightly the defence raised it at his trial, and it was countered by a medical expert or a forensic scientist, who said that in their opinion he was capable of committing the crimes despite his alcohol problem. Anyway, I'll still check that the doctor was abroad like he said he was during the Canal Killings."

"Yes, you should definitely do that, Moss. At least we now have names for all four boys. Christopher or Chris Smith is not going to be easy to find of course. One thing I would have asked him, Moss, is whether he knew which university his brother went to, assuming he did go to one. It's often a good source of information, especially if he's kept in touch through their alumni association. Same goes for Robin

Butcher, we could check the records at Oxford and Cambridge Universities."

"Alumni?" asked Moss.

Krill explained that it was like an old boys' and girls' association, with the ex-students having annual dinners at the university, and being encouraged to become benefactors. Moss said that he would ring the doctor later and ask him if he knew which university his twin attended.

Krill watched enviously as Moss mopped up the last of the crumbs with his final segment of cake.

"When are you next due to see Commander Morris?"

"Tomorrow morning. Do you think I should tell her that we want to focus on the other boys in the photograph? Assuming that's what you think we should do?"

"That photo is definitely important, Moss, and it may turn out to be the crucial piece of evidence. But I wouldn't emphasise it too much at this stage to Commander Morris or anyone else. Might be best to let her reach the same conclusion herself if we can."

"I still think we're clutching at straws regarding Crow's photo, but when that's all you have to grab hold of, what else can you do? I checked our files again for any known associates and there's nothing. Crow was a recluse, particularly after the doctor went abroad. Who would want to associate with a drunk on a barge, apart from another drunk?"

"As you said earlier, he must have been sober sometimes, Moss; he had to collect his dole money for one thing."

"Right. But thinking about it, who else do we know who is linked to Crow's past, prior to his arrest, apart from the boys in that photo? No one. Zilch. Our only other hope is that we can somehow come up with some new names linked to the places he visited when he lived on his barge in the 70's, like the Job Centre and the nearest pubs and off licence. Dr Smith may have been our last hope of finding some other associate of Crow's, unless his twin brother or this Robin Butcher also kept in touch with him? I suppose if his brother, Christopher, also visited him on the barge then Crow might have kept it from David, because of their animosity towards one another?"

"Yes, that's logical, his twin could have visited him, especially when David was abroad."

Moss frowned. "But the huge time gap really scuppers us. Normally we'd go door to door, checking all the nearby pubs and shops with Crow's photo and ask if they'd seen him, either on his own or with someone. And we'd visit all the other barge users who were on that canal at that particular time. I don't suppose the Canal people, the Trust that runs it, would keep records going that far back?"

"They might, it's worth a try."

"I've also been thinking about what Dr Knox said about twin serial killers," Moss added.

"And?"

"Well, even if David Smith was away for the relevant period when the murders were carried out, he could still have been in league with his brother somehow. Telling us that they had a big bust up would be an excellent way of stopping us thinking that they were working together, like a serial killer 'tag team'. He could easily supply the drugs and the syringes, and carry out some of the killings, while his brother did others, and maybe some they did together. He said his brother also spent time abroad, so if we had picked him up at the time for the murders he would have had an alibi too for some of them - the ones which his twin did. It would be almost a perfect setup."

"Mmmm that's an intriguing theory, Moss. You're really on a roll today! I would certainly like to hear both Christopher Smith and Robin Butcher speaking."

"You don't think his twin will sound very similar?"

"Possibly; I don't know. Look it up on the Internet."

Moss checked: "Seems that some twins do sound identical, but others don't."

"OK, so I need to hear both their voices, and maybe have Richard come to the station as well, as he chatted for far longer with the killer than I did. Let's meet up tomorrow, after you've seen Commander Morris."

CHAPTER 26

The second he took his key out of the lock Moss knew that something was wrong. He'd not had any inkling when he'd parked outside, or used the door entry system to the block of flats, or even as he'd climbed the stairs, because everything was exactly as it should be and just as it had always been. He paused, stopping himself from pushing the door open wider so he could see inside, wondering whether someone was still there, possibly waiting for him to do just that. He considered his options: retreat and call for help, barge in quickly and hope to take them by surprise, or act like a thief himself - silently entering his flat to find a weapon of some description, but what? All this thinking took just a few moments. He stepped one pace backwards onto the communal landing, muted his phone and used it to send a text to Jim. Even if he came straight away it would still take him a good forty minutes to get there.

He stretched his upper body at a sixty degree angle, leaning in as far as he could, and turned his head so that his right ear was near to the door jamb, prepared to run or pounce at a moment's notice, but heard nothing. The phrase 'as silent as the grave' slipped into his mind; he didn't like its intrusion one bit! If someone was there, then he assumed that they would have heard his key turning in the lock unless they were either deaf or incredibly distracted by what they were doing. He thought the odds of either scenario were slim; so much for the chance of a surprise attack.

Just inside his entrance hall, and well within reach of the door, was a tall cupboard where he kept coats, an umbrella, fishing gear, and other odds and ends, but unfortunately not any heavy walking sticks or baseball bats. He thought that he was a good match for most men when it came to a fist fight, even two might not be a huge problem, especially in a confined space with obstacles. If they had a firearm, then a club or a stick might prove useless or even encourage them to use it. A burglar with a knife would be different, and in some respects it was the weapon he was most wary of, having come across several wielders in his career, and so he took off his coat and wrapped around his left arm to give himself some defence against one. He checked his watch: just two minutes had now passed since he'd arrived home, although it seemed much longer.

He put his hand flat against the door in front of him and was just about to push it open when a rasping voice behind him almost caused an embarrassing accident.

"Everything alright Phil?"

He slowly turned round, calming himself as he did so, and spoke as quietly and as normally as he could to his elderly neighbour:

"Yes Patrick. You go back inside. I'll come and see you in a minute." He added as an afterthought: "You should lock your door."

One glance inside his flat confirmed his suspicions: some of the contents of the cupboard were scattered on the carpet, half in half out; boxes upended, a discarded coat, a lone wader lying on top of it. He walked warily down the hall to his lounge and found the carnage there complete: the sofa and armchairs had been turned upside down and their backs and bottoms slashed, every book had been removed from shelves and thrown onto the floor, several pictures had been taken down from walls, and those that hadn't, were now askew. Every drawer and cupboard in the kitchen had been left open, and even the plastic trays from the freezer removed and left stacked on the worktop. Semi-frozen vegetables, a soggy looking pizza, and a packet of burgers lay on the tiled floor. His impression that this had been a search for something, rather than a robbery or just kids having some sick fun, was confirmed when he saw that the lid of the toilet cistern had been removed, and some loose sections of flooring prised open. Also nothing seemed to be missing - ripped open, uprooted, and broken yes - but not stolen as far as he could tell. By far the strangest aspect was that every single one of his fishing rods had been deliberately snapped in two and left in a heap.

He righted an armchair and sat down, more than a little dumbfounded - why search his flat at all, and what could they have been looking for? It didn't make any sense. He phoned Krill.

"It seems it's my own security which I should have been more concerned about Killer."

"Why, what's happened?"

"My flat has been ransacked. Nothing stolen as far as I can see, but they were apparently looking for something."

"God Moss, that's terrible! Do you want me to come round and help you clean up?"

"Thanks for the offer but Jim's nearer, and he's already on his way. It's more a question of restocking my freezer and buying new stuff."

"You're insured?"

"Yes, but it won't be easy to replace everything. Every one of my fishing rods has been broken! One was my Dad's!"

"I'm so sorry, how awful. Any idea who might have done it? Could it have anything to do with your work when you were a private investigator?"

"I doubt it; not now. I'm more inclined, if it's not random vandals, to think it's something to do with our recent investigations."

"Really?"

"Possibly, I'm not sure, but it might make more sense, given everything that's happened."

"But what would they be searching for in your flat, and who would do such a thing?" asked Krill.

"Dunno."

"You don't think it's our killer do you?" Krill sounded concerned.

"No, I doubt it, because this is a bit basic for him. I think he's more into subtlety and subterfuge."

"Well, let's hope you're right; neither of us would welcome a visit from him. Why don't you come and stay here tonight? Margaret won't mind and there's plenty of room. You could leave the mess until the morning? And there will definitely not be any soup, I promise!" Krill spoke more quietly, "I even managed to sneak some Lincolnshire sausages and bacon into the fridge, so you can have them for your breakfast."

"It's very tempting, Killer, but Jim and I had better sort things out here as best we can tonight. I need to get a crime number and make a list for the insurers."

"Well just turn up if you change your mind; you know where I am."

"OK. Strange about the rods though isn't it? Almost like someone was telling me to stop fishing? They didn't smash the TV or break anything else. It was like they knew what would hurt me most and they wanted to make it even more personal."

"Yes, that is strange," Krill agreed.

CHAPTER 27

"Morning, Killer. Are you OK to chat?"

"Yes, Margaret's gone to the Polish shop for more bloody sausages! Never mind that, how are you doing?"

"Lucky you. No, I'm fine, thanks. The insurers have asked me to send photos of the damage and I've already ordered some new stuff. The reason I'm phoning is that we're about to start the update, and Commander Morris has suggested that you join us via Zoom."

"And how do I do that?"

"I'll email an invite; just click on the link. It will start in fifteen minutes. I'm sending it now. Have you got it?"

Krill checked his iPad.

"Yes."

"OK. I think she's going to put you on the big screen so it will be as if you're in the room with us."

"Not for me it won't. Will I see you?" Krill asked.

"You should do. You can choose either to view the person speaking or everyone present. I would suggest just the speaker, because it's going to be quite busy. I was hoping you'd be pleased."

"I am. OK, I'm pressing the link now. It says the meeting hasn't started yet.

"You'll come online when Morris starts the meeting. Just wait, Boss."

Krill went through to the lounge in the cottage he and Margaret were temporarily renting, and selected a comfy, if overstuffed, armchair. Then had a further thought and hurried through to the kitchen and grabbed a coffee. He'd always liked to have one on hand whenever he'd briefed his own team.

The screen on his iPad changed and he selected video, seeing first a preview of himself, which as usual disappointed him because he thought he looked rather tired and ancient, then he saw Commander Morris.

"Ah, Mr Krill, welcome. We've just run through the list of who's present so we won't do that again, but you should see who we all are as and when we speak. To speed up the meeting I've asked for written updates from all concerned, including Mr Moss, so I'm going to summarise the current state of play for everyone who's been working on the case. We can have questions and comments after each update. Is everyone happy with that? Good. First we have a report from Inspector Lewis about the incident at the hospital. Nothing much to report there I'm afraid. No sign of anyone resembling the suspect on CCTV, and they're still checking vehicles which were parked at the hospital that day. Anything to add Inspector? No. OK. Regarding the hospital, everyone should know that Peter Crow died two days ago. The press are now also aware of it, so we can expect renewed media attention about him: whether he could be innocent of the Canal Killings, and if so what are we doing about finding an alternative serial killer? Also probably further pointless speculation about dozens of unsolved murders."

"Can I come in Commander?"

Krill saw a new face, a name he didn't recognise, and that it was the Met's Director of Communications.

"Yes Charlie?"

"It's just that we should be aware that there's already been a lot of activity on the Internet, including YouTube, and it's likely to escalate."

Krill was about to ask 'what sort of activity?' when the Commander did it for him.

"There's numerous videos linked to the Canal Killings. People acting out murders on canal towpaths. Someone's got hold of the original reenactment used in '78 with a stuntman, and that's playing too - getting thousands of hits. There's fake blood, dummies being tossed into canals, people with huge syringes, some dressed up as Crows running here and there frightening others, that sort of thing. I've contacted YouTube and they've said that so far nothing has breached their rules, but they are keeping a careful eye on it. The Canal Trust say there's not much they can do as they're public footpaths, and they have hundreds of miles of them, so how could they stop it even if they wanted to? Also if you search for 'Krill' on YouTube then you get just about every interview that the ex-Chief Inspector gave at the time, and since then; they're also getting massive hits. There's a rapper who's made a recording which features Mr Krill's nickname, which I understand was

'Killer'. There's videos made by self-styled experts talking about serial killers and how to catch them."

Commander Morris came back in:

"OK, thanks Charlie. I suppose all that was inevitable in this day and age. Mr Krill, you need to be aware that you've become something of a celebrity once more. Quickly moving on, we have some new information about Colin Marshall. He's obviously vital to the inquiry as he's the only person that we know of, who has been murdered recently by this person. I think any doubts we may have had ended when we found the victims bicycle at the barge site. That trail at least is reasonably fresh and needs to be our absolute priority. We have CCTV of Colin after he left the B&B that morning, so we know the time and the route he took. For several days now, we've had notices up in the streets where we believe he cycled to work, we've put posters on buses which use the presumed route, and we've been stopping pedestrians and cyclists, asking whether anyone saw anything. We now have a witness who saw an incident involving a cyclist and a van on the morning in question. He was on the upstairs deck of a bus which followed the ongoing incident before overtaking a parked van. He also recorded it on his phone. I'll play the video clip now if I may."

Krill watched as if through the window of a bus looking down at the road in front, and saw a drama unfolding between a cyclist and a white van. There was a running commentary from the witness, which included 'he almost hit him again!', 'now the cyclist is chasing the van', 'they've both stopped'. The bus pulled out to overtake and the witness continued to film as the driver and the cyclist confronted one another on the pavement at the side of the van. He then must have moved to the rear to keep watching as the bus drove off down the street. His final comment was: 'where did the fucking cyclist go?'

"We have some enhanced photos from the video, which I can show you now. From what we can see the cyclist does match Mr Marshall's description. What's your view regarding the bike, Mr Krill?"

"It looks very similar, Commander."

"OK, thanks for that. The van in question was stolen earlier that day, so we're assuming that this is Colin Marshall being abducted. Unfortunately, the driver is wearing a face mask and a hat, but we can tell that he's white, and around six feet tall. I'll now move on to some stills from the CCTV at the multi. This one shows a white van entering approximately forty minutes after the incident with the cyclist."

"What happened to the van?"

"It was found parked on the roof of the car park Mr Krill, which unfortunately does not have CCTV. It has now been taken away for forensics. We're still checking other vehicles and pedestrians who used the car park that day, however this is interesting…."

Krill watched two video clips of a man leaving the car park. He wore a felt hat and a black face mask, and used a walking stick.

"Could this be the man who attacked you at the hospital, Mr Krill?"

"It's quite possible; he's dressed in a similar fashion."

"Identifying the owners of all vehicles using the car park that day is now vital, so we can find and interview this person to ascertain whether he is the van driver, and if not, rule him out of our enquiries. And also to check whether anyone saw the van or someone acting suspiciously. Any questions before I move on? No, good. Next, the barge where Mr Krill's neighbour, Richard, was left. We've drawn a blank regarding any forensic evidence there I'm afraid, and so far have been unable to trace the man who hired it, using the neighbour's credit card. That card has not been used since. A further line of inquiry concerns people who knew Peter Crow, based on the theory that the killer must have had some contact with him in order to make it look like he had committed the Canal Killings. Yesterday, Mr Moss interviewed one Dr David Smith who'd known Crow since childhood, and visited him several times in prison. It appears that he was away working in Africa during the Canal Murders so has at present been ruled out as a suspect. Dr Smith was unable to help us regarding Crow's contacts while he was living on his barge, but has given us some information about Crow's childhood which we're following up. He also confirmed that he has a twin brother, Christopher, and we are trying to track him down. Mr Moss is going through the Canal Murders files to provide a list of those we may wish to interview again. Have I missed anything out? No? Any questions? Yes Moss?"

"Just to say Commander that I think two further priorities should be to find Peter Crow's stepbrother - who is unnamed at present; and another childhood acquaintance of Crow, one Robin Butcher who was identified by David Smith. I believe his stepbrother was seen at the time of the Canal Murders by a member of the team, but I haven't been able to locate the interview report. So if anyone finds it, or comes across the name Robin Butcher, can they please let me know?"

"OK Moss. Noted." Commander Morris continued, "One last piece of news - when the Prison Governor was going through Crow's things he found some very interesting emails. I've already sent them to Gillian, our profiler, for her assessment, and she'll circulate them later."

CHAPTER 28

The next day when Moss was looking through some files at the Met, still trying to find the missing interview with Crow's stepbrother, he got a message to go and see Commander Morris as soon as possible. At first he thought that he might have blotted his copybook at the Zoom meeting, by adding more priorities to the approved list, but when he knocked and entered he discovered that the Commander had a visitor with her, someone he hadn't seen before. Moss wilted a little under the stern and hostile gazes, especially from the stranger. He had an inkling that something important was about to occur.

"Come in, Moss; please sit down. This gentleman is from Special Branch; that's all you need to know. I'm afraid we have a problem."

Special Branch thought Moss? How could they be involved? Was the victim connected to them in some way, and if so how? Little alarm bells started to ring and they soon got louder.

"What sort of a problem?" he asked.

Morris ignored his question. "What it means, Moss, is that Special Branch and their colleagues will take over certain aspects of the inquiry. You can carry on as before regarding Colin's murder, Richard's abduction, and the search for a possible serial killer, but everything will now have to be run through them via me, in case there's a risk to National Security."

Commander Morris took a document from a brown folder and handed it to Moss.

"I'm sure you'll remember signing this form about the Official Secrets Acts when you retired Moss. As you can see, you have to get permission in writing from the Commissioner before disclosing anything covered by the Acts. This includes any information which may be gravely injurious to the State or liable to lead to a serious loss of confidence in the public service. I'd like you to sign it again now, just to be certain that you are aware of your obligations as a retired police officer, and what the penalties would be should you breach the Acts."

"Yes, I remember signing it. Is this really necessary Commander?"

The look on her face said it all. Moss hesitated briefly, then signed it.

"Thanks, Moss, you can go."

Moss walked along a corridor past mainly deserted open plan offices on either side, then down a back staircase and descended two floors until he found somewhere quiet and out of earshot, where he could ring Krill without the risk of being disturbed.

"You'll never guess what's just happened, Killer."

"Are you at the Met? Let me see - you've been promoted to Inspector? I think you deserve it Moss. About bloody time!"

Moss ignored the attempt at humour.

"Special Branch is now involved in the case." He could visualise Krill's eyebrows rising up to his missing hairline, and sense the silent whistle as his ex-boss's interest and curiosity sharply increased. "And I've had to sign another bloody form about the Official Secrets Acts!"

"Well, well. I wonder why they should be interested in the murder of a fairly innocuous minor civil servant, and the kidnapping of my neighbour?"

"Your guess is as good as mine."

Moss heard Krill give a loud 'tut'.

"Anyway Moss, don't worry about their official secrets, if you're ever locked up I'll bring you some of Margaret's cake every week, and maybe even a dozen or so cold continental sausages!"

"It's no joking matter Boss. I was really spooked being in the room with that Special Branch guy! They also mentioned National Security."

"Did they indeed? 'Spooked' could be the operative word, Moss. Clearly someone connected to the case is linked to the security services, or possibly to the Government. But who is it, and how are they connected?"

"But if that's the case, if the killer or someone close to him is connected to MI5 or MI6, or whoever, then we'll never find out what happened will we? It'll all be hushed up and swept under a Whitehall carpet."

Krill thought for a moment. "We shall see. On the positive side it could explain a few things quite nicely. For instance, how our killer has remained undiscovered for so long, and why he knew so much about surveillance techniques. If he was someone in the armed forces, in the S.A.S. for example, and possibly trained at the taxpayer's expense to carry out covert operations and avoid capture, then he would have the necessary skills. Maybe he was undercover somewhere, like in Northern Ireland during the 'Troubles', or he infiltrated terrorist groups? Maybe he's in the protection business looking after a member of the Royal Family or a Minister? There's no end of possibilities. Any number of people like that would have Special Branch keeping an eye out for them. It would fit the facts. And let's not forget that Oxford and Cambridge used to be the recruiting grounds for our spies in the fifties and sixties. Several of the people we're interested in probably went there: Robin Butcher, possibly the Doctor's twin, and maybe even Crow's stepbrother. They haven't said anything about not investigating those people have they?"

"Not so far no, not specifically, but if we do a lot of digging online, or in the records, then we might get another visit from Special Branch. If any of them has links to the security services then we'll soon be stopped in our tracks."

"OK, so we have to tread very carefully Moss; softly, softly as they used to say. Let's see what we can find out the good old fashioned way, starting at the primary school which Crow, the two Smith's, and probably Robin Butcher attended; manually checking the old local authority records. Then go to their secondary schools and universities and search those records too. What we need is more background information, and ideally the current contact details for the missing three suspects - two from the photo and Crow's stepbrother, so we can pull them in for questioning, and I can listen to their voices. Did Dr Smith confirm which university his brother attended?"

"Yes, it was Oxford."

"So an Oxbridge connection again. I think it should be safe to look at any physical records and files without outside interference, but will that be sufficient? Probably not. Let's both visit Crow's hometown. I want to walk the streets where he walked; I want to find the place where that photograph of the boys was taken; I want to visit the schools he went to, if they're still there. Maybe check the cemeteries and find his mother and stepfather. Oh, speaking of cemeteries, what's happening about Crow's funeral?"

"No idea' I'll check." Moss was hoping that Commander Morris wouldn't find out about Krill's 'off the record' activities.

"Sorry Moss."

"What for Killer?"

"Well I always was very good at piling the work onto your all too willing shoulders. Maybe we should divide it up more evenly?"

"No, Boss, let's stick to the usual division of labour: you do the thinking and come up with the theories, while I find the evidence to prove you wrong!"

"How are things at home, with your flat?" Krill asked.

"I'm getting there. Jim's got a key and he's going to take delivery of a new three piece suite and a mattress later this week. There's something else which is strange that's happened, or at least I think might have happened."

"What?"

"I can't be sure, but I think my car may also have been searched."

CHAPTER 29

"So this is the infamous Richmond Road."

Krill and Moss stood side by side and gazed from one end of the street to the other. It looked very ordinary, just like thousands of other low rise council estates built in the fifties and sixties, when the need was great and funds were limited.

"Yes Killer, and fortunately for us the Housing Department has records going way back. So we now know that Crow lived at 35B over there, which is an upstairs two bed flat, and Butcher lived right across the road at 16A - the one with the blue door, which is also a flat but ground floor. The Smith's were more fortunate and had a semi down there on the corner, right at the far end of the cul-de-sac, the slightly posher end."

"I wonder who Mr Smith knew in order to get them a semi?" asked Krill. "These all do look like boring, featureless, bog standard, council properties."

"Maybe the Smith's had just been on the waiting list for longer? Yes, they were all council owned at one time but I'm not sure if there's any left now which haven't been sold off in the intervening years."

"It's a bit grim here Moss."

Moss didn't think it was that bad - he'd seen a lot worse. There were even a few trees still growing up through the pavement on either side of the road, and most of the gardens looked reasonably neat. It was true that there were none of the signs of affluence that maybe Krill was used to. The parked cars were all several years old and most had seen better days, and there was far more dog shit deposited here and there than in leafy Berkshire.

"When Crow lived here the flats would have been fairly new, and they were a vast improvement on the overcrowded rows of terraced houses which they replaced. Far more light and air; much healthier."

"If you say so." Krill looked across the road, and then towards the house where the twins had lived. "I wonder why Crow was friendlier with David Smith rather than Robin Butcher, who was a lot closer? They're practically neighbours."

"It's hard to say with kids, they're a law unto themselves. Maybe Peter and Robin were close for a while but had a falling out like Dr Smith said? By the way, I got a text just now, Boss, to say that Crow's body has been collected from the hospital by a firm of undertakers. They're finding out who made the arrangements and what will now happen to it."

"That's good, thanks. Maybe the prison is doing it, or a prisoners' charity stepped in? Do they still have pauper's graves?" Krill asked.

"There's always a chance that it was his stepbrother or some distant relative that we don't know about. In the absence

259

of anyone else, it could be David Smith who's paying for the funeral."

"Let's hope that rather than him it's someone new, who we can question. What did you think of the emails Crow received not long before he died?"

"Weird," said Moss. "Have you spoken to the profiler about them?"

"No, not yet. I'm trying to arrange another meeting with her, and presumably they'll be on her agenda. How far away is the primary school they all attended?"

"Twenty minutes walk Boss. Do you want to use the car?"

"No, let's follow in their footsteps. What about the place where the photo was taken?"

Moss checked it again; he always liked to be sure of his facts.

"As there are goalposts in the distance, I'm assuming it was at the recreation ground. We can go there on the way back to the car - it's only a short diversion."

"Right."

They set off down the residential street and joined a busier road at a T junction, where they turned left.

"Doesn't this make you feel that you're in touch with those boys and getting closer to the truth?"

Moss wasn't sure, he hadn't really thought about it. He was concentrating on not taking a wrong turn and experiencing Krill's wrath, while at the same time doing his best to keep up, as Krill's legs were several inches longer and he'd always been a fast walker. He hoped that Krill might slow up if they continued to chat.

"We know a bit more now about Crow's mother Boss, but have nothing so far which helps us regarding his stepbrother. Evidently she never remarried after Crow's father hopped it in the 50's, which is unusual because people didn't generally live together in those days. Her husband, Crow's father, is listed on the birth certificate as a US serviceman, so maybe he returned to the States and she couldn't get a divorce? Divorces at that time were hard for anyone to get anyway, never mind for someone whose husband lived abroad. The council tenancy of 35B was always in her sole name - Edith Crow, and it remained that way for the next thirty five years, until it was one of the last in the street to be sold. Maybe deep down she didn't think her relationship with Crow's stepfather would last. So currently we don't know who she lived with, how long that relationship lasted, or the name of the child she had with him."

It had the desired effect, and Krill stopped.

"And it's all down to me Moss. I should have asked Crow about his stepbrother. Damnation! How stupid of me. Still no sign of that missing interview in '79?"

"No, but don't give up hope just yet Boss, we've still to check the records of births. She must be on the birth certificate for both him and his stepbrother, married or not. The father may not be listed, but the mother always is. We'll have the boy's name in a couple of days at the latest; then we can start to track him down and see what he knows about Peter's past, if anything."

"Assuming he's not a spy."

"Yes Killer, assuming he's not that or in any other way connected to Special Branch."

"Maybe it's not the stepbrother who they have a vested interest in, but a fiver says it is."

Moss grinned. "OK Killer, I'm always delighted to take your money."

CHAPTER 30

Krill switched off the radio and checked how he looked in his car's tiny overhead mirror. He hated funerals, but so did everyone he supposed, except possibly those who arranged them. They were incredibly busy again: collecting bodies, preparing them, dealing with grieving relatives, washing their sleek black limousines, and attending services. It had been a long time since he'd attended a funeral, so long that he couldn't find his own black tie and had to borrow one from Moss. He supposed it was an indication that, so far at least, he'd been far luckier than many people during the pandemic, and should be incredibly grateful.

There were only six or seven cars parked at the crematorium; he wondered whether any of them were there for Crow. One that was parked fifty yards away seemed out of place as it resembled the funeral cars much more than the hotchpotch of colours and vintages normally used by mourners. It was new, big, black, and highly polished. It also looked official, like it belonged to a Government Minister or some other dignitary. He watched it closely but couldn't see inside as the windows were darkly tinted. He began to speculate as to whether its occupant could be the reason for all the fuss there'd been when they'd started to look into Crow's friends and relations?

He saw a man in his twenties wearing a dark suit get out of the driver's side and walk around the back of the car to a rear passenger door. He held it open while another man, who looked to be in his late fifties or early sixties, got out. Krill opened his own door and saw the young man immediately look his way. Krill walked towards them and his path was quickly blocked.

"It's alright George, I think I know who this gentleman is. It's Mr Krill isn't it, or do you prefer Chief Inspector?"

"Just Krill is fine."

"Perhaps we can sit together during the service? I don't suppose that poor Peter will get many mourners. Somewhat bizarrely, those like him who have so few to mark their passing, might actually be grateful for the restrictions regarding how many people can attend. I presume you found out about Peter's funeral from the prison? We've hopefully managed to keep it out of the media."

Krill noticed that the man had not introduced himself.

"You knew Peter Crow?" he asked.

"You could say that. Let's chat after the service can we Mr Krill? I feel it might be a little disrespectful to talk about me just now, or how I happen to know Peter. Let's focus on him for a short while, can we? Thank you for coming by the way. I'm not sure if Peter would have appreciated it, but I certainly do."

Close up the man oozed class, charm, and respectability, and Krill began to wonder if he was indeed a celebrity who he should recognise. He walked alongside him, with 'George' following closely on their heels. They entered the building and waited in the foyer while other mourners left and the room was cleaned. Under normal circumstances he would have wished to sit next to the only other mourner, but was shown into a separate pew by an usher. The three men turned their heads as a coffin was brought in; they were now outnumbered by the undertaker and his staff. Krill wondered if the service would be any different because Crow had claimed to be a Buddhist, but it seemed to be similar to another nonreligious ceremony he'd once attended, with a celebrant rather than a priest. It was all over in fifteen minutes, and he followed the other two men back to the car park.

"Maybe we can chat in my car Mr Krill? Can you give us a few moments please George?"

George closed the door and stood to attention adjacent to the vehicle. Krill wondered if the bodyguard was actually armed and dangerous, or just looked and acted that way as a deterrent?

"You've probably guessed that I'm Peter's stepbrother. You asked how I knew him, and I suppose the truthful answer is that I didn't. Peter ran away from home when he was fifteen and I was six, but even before he left he was seldom there - he was out with his friends most of the time, so I hardly ever saw him. When I went to university I tried to find Peter and eventually tracked him down, but he wanted nothing to do with me. I'm not sure whether it was the shame of how he was living, or resentment dating back to the time when his world changed because his father deserted him and mine came on the scene? Or maybe even jealousy because my life was light years away from his own? Not long after I left university he was convicted of those dreadful murders and went to prison. Again I tried to visit him, but he refused to see me. Arranging for his funeral today and being here, was the least that I could do."

"Did you know that he became a Buddhist?"

"No I didn't. I guessed that he probably wasn't religious. A Buddhist, that's interesting. I'm pleased if he found something to believe in, and it gave him peace. My mother used to talk about Peter when my father wasn't around. He was a difficult child and he became a very troubled teenager."

"He claimed that your father was violent towards him," said Krill.

"Did he? I never saw any evidence of that. It's true that my father was not an easy person to get along with, and I had several run-ins with him myself at times. He could be aggressive and he certainly shouted a lot, but he never hit either myself or my mother. You told the Press that you believed Peter was innocent - is that still the case?"

"Yes, it is. My belief is that someone who knew Peter made it look as if he was the murderer. I've been trying to track down anyone who knew him in the years before he was arrested. I was hoping to be able to speak to his stepbrother, which is another reason for coming today; in case you were here."

"You're working on the case?" the man asked, a little surprised.

"In an unofficial capacity," Krill explained. "Can I show you this photograph? I've spoken to David Smith - he's the one to Peter's right, and we're trying to track down his twin brother, unfortunately the two of them have not been in contact for many years. We believe that the other boy is Robin Butcher. So far we know nothing about him. Do you know him?"

The man was silent for a moment, then seemed to reach a decision.

"Yes. Robin was, or I should say still is, my cousin. My mother's sister married a Butcher. I'm afraid I've rather lost touch with him too. Again he was much older - around Peter's age."

"So you have really no idea who Peter associated with after he left home?"

"None whatsoever, I'm sorry. I will ask my family if they know any more about Peter than I do, but I would be surprised if they do. I certainly want to help you if I can, both to clear Peter's name and obviously to catch whoever committed those dreadful murders."

"It's vital that we do so, because we have every reason to believe that the real killer has committed more murders since the 70's, and recently killed a man in London."

"Yes, I read about the murder at the multistory car park. So you believe that whoever did that also implicated Peter in the Canal Killings? Interesting. I understand that you may have actually met the person you're looking for?"

Krill was a little taken aback by the question but tried not to show it. "Yes I did, when I was seeing Peter in hospital last week."

"Do you think that you could identify him?" the man asked.

"That won't be easy because he wore a face mask. I think I would probably recognise his voice though, if I heard it again."

"I see. And how would you describe him, based on that short meeting?"

"It's not just my description because there's another victim who survived."

"That's your neighbour who was blinded?"

Again Krill was surprised by the man's knowledge of the case.

"Yes. Based on what we both saw I would say that he's Caucasian, around six feet tall, aged in his sixties or seventies, and uses a walking stick."

"A walking stick?"

Krill had the district impression that this last piece of information had come as a complete surprise to the man.

"I'll give you my number Mr Krill; ring me in a few days time and I'll tell you if I have any more information for you. And perhaps you can let me know how the investigation is progressing?"

Krill scribbled it down on his pad and got out.

As the black limousine drove off, the passenger made a call on his phone:

"Jo, it's Michael. We have a problem....Yes another one. I've just left the crematorium and whilst there I was collared by Krill......Yes, I know you told me to keep well away from Peter's funeral, but he was my mother's firstborn, and I thought it was my duty. I also didn't want him to be treated just as badly in death as he was in life.....The problem? It's that Krill, and I presume the Met, possibly consider Robin a suspect in their murder and kidnapping investigation ...Yes I know what you did, but evidently they're finding a way around Special Branch.... You could try that but I don't think it will be of any use, as Krill has got the bit firmly between his teeth.....hold on...just wait a moment..... Jo.....I resent what you're implying. I don't think that I was in any way encouraging him!....Will you please listen to me! It's because we may need his help or cooperation at some point in the future, that I felt obliged to speak to him. I didn't want him to find out that I'd misled or lied to him.....What did I do? I told him the truth...if you would just shut up I'll tell you!....Jo! ....Thank you! I'm not an idiot, it was obviously not the whole truth. All I told him is that Robin is my cousin, that's all. I said I hadn't really known Peter at all, and had not been in contact with Robin for some time, which is also almost accurate......Sooner or later they would have found out that Peter, Robin, and myself are related......Well I happen to think that they would....I believe that he's now happy as far as I'm concerned, and ruled me out of the inquiry, which is a huge plus, not just for me but for the Service.....Well that may be true, we'll never know...OK, I hear you......What else? I'll tell you what else - find Robin and do it now.....I don't care what it takes, just fucking find him!.....Well Jo, at this exact moment, doing the impossible as you put it, is precisely what I need you to do. I want to know why he was at that car park for starters. I also don't believe that it's a coincidence he's disappeared just as a ginormous turd is about to hit the fan. He's connected to all this in some way, and possibly not just to the recent events. I want him found and placed in a room where myself and several others can find out just what he's been up to. Ring me this evening after nine with an update."

She'd had many roles within the organisation: those in more common parlance included fixer and go-between, but she'd also organised 'dead drops' where messages could be left, been a 'babysitter' helping to protect others, and a case officer for many years running agents, before finally moving to counterintelligence. She'd known Robin ever since her first year in the Service when the 'old man', as he was then known by recruits, despite him only being in his forties, had helped to train her, and had subsequently taken Jo under his wing. Not surprisingly, a strong connection had developed between them, consisting of a mixture of admiration and loyalty. Put simply Jo would do almost anything for Robin, partly because she believed that the reverse would also be true. If it was a choice between helping Robin or defying the Service then she wouldn't have to think twice about doing whatever was necessary, but hopefully it wouldn't come to that.

As far as she was aware, Robin's disenchantment with their employer had begun several years before he'd been forcibly retired. She wasn't sure what event had precipitated it, or whether indeed there had been one big ruction or several minor ones, or none at all. In reality, Robin had spouted too frequently about the direction the Service was taking, and voiced far too many general annoyances and perceived injustices, for her ever to be able to point a finger at a probable cause. Maybe the malaise had been there for as long as Robin had been employed, and had slowly grown and grown? All she knew for certain was that probably about ten years ago the conversations with him and the rancour displayed, had become far more serious and heated. Her efforts to calm her friend had proved worthless, and if anything Robin's malice and resentment had increased significantly since he'd left the Service.

She'd performed a few unofficial 'favours' for Robin over the years, but nothing too onerous or even very illegal: such as finding people, arranging for buildings and their occupants to be watched, providing equipment, the occasional 'off the record' phone call. Jo suspected that Robin could easily have done all of it himself anyway, but either had other things on his mind, or possibly used these requests as a means of them keeping in touch. At least that is when he'd wanted to be in touch; she hadn't seen or heard from him since the start of the pandemic, and had assumed that, like millions of others, he was not venturing very often beyond his own front door. She should have known better.

Could she find him? No, not unless he wanted her to do so, but she had to try, if for no other reason than to warn him. She opened her laptop, logged onto the dating site, and sent a message to 'Karla' saying how much she'd missed their chats and asking her to get in touch. If that failed she would leave notes in several of the locations they'd used over the years. If that didn't work then there were the various pubs and cafés they'd frequented, that is, if they were open.

Searching Moss's flat had been entirely her own idea, and destroying his fishing rods was a somewhat symbolic little touch, a nuance which she hoped that Krill, if not Moss, would appreciate. Would it stop their fishing expedition? She didn't think so.

She'd not spoken to either Robin or Michael about it, beforehand or since. She wasn't sure what she would find there, or indeed if there was anything to find, she'd just felt that it needed to be done, both as a warning and as a means of distraction. It would have been an added bonus if anything had been discovered which might incriminate Robin in any investigation, but nothing had. She presumed that Moss kept everything at the Met or in that tatty briefcase which he carried around. She could have arranged to have the flat searched without Moss being any the wiser, but that wouldn't have had the same impact. Better for both him and Krill to worry about it, and for Moss to be preoccupied with sorting out the mess she'd left.

And if they persisted? Well then they would soon come to realise just who they had taken on, wouldn't they?

CHAPTER 31

Krill was glad to be back home for several reasons, and he hoped that Margaret was also pleased to be with her daughter once more in London. He'd enjoyed their enforced exile, but had missed his little abode, and the independence which it gave him. Earlier that evening, he'd relaxed on his sofa with a plate of beans on toast and binged on three episodes of a particularly gruesome 'Scandi Noir', which he knew for certain that Margaret would have hated. He expected that he would feel sad later when he climbed into his cold and lonely bachelor bed, with no one to cuddle. Like most relationships, it involved both 'swings and roundabouts', and he still hoped that he could somehow manage to have the one without too much of the other.

He felt that the investigation was making slow but steady progress, and he was now firmly on the trail of the monster who had cornered him at the hospital. The lines of inquiry were narrowing, and he was even more convinced that there was a close connection between the serial killer and Peter Crow. But what he didn't yet know was the exact nature of that linkage. If it wasn't his stepbrother, as seemed to be the case, then who was it? His cousin Robin? The elusive Christopher Smith? Someone thus far unknown? His confidence about finding the serial killer was like the tide - always ebbing and flowing, but what was not in doubt was his determination to do so.

He phoned Moss just before going to bed:

"I met Crow's stepbrother today at the funeral."

"Really? And?"

"Let's just say that I'm quietly confident about my fiver," Krill gloated.

"So you think that he's the reason why our friends in Special Branch became highly agitated a few days ago? And does the stepbrother have a name, Killer?"

"No, not as yet, we weren't formally introduced. But he knew who I was. He had a bodyguard or a minder with him, and he was the nearest thing to a James Bond or an 'M' that I'm ever likely to meet. He's definitely not the person who confronted me at the hospital, so I think we should stop searching the County birth records for him. You're not going to find anything much more about him anyway, not without someone threatening you with a speedy trip to the Tower of London. Interestingly he told me that Robin Butcher is a cousin of both himself and Peter Crow."

"A cousin? You're right, that is very interesting."

"Anyway Moss, that's all the good news. The bad news is that he has no information about anyone else his stepbrother might have been friendly with, any other associates, other than those in the photograph, so those three are all we have. He's going to check with his relatives, but as Crow ran away from home aged fifteen and more or less refused to see anyone from his past, apart that is, from David Smith for some reason, I don't think that we should hold our breath. I'm thinking that maybe we should speak to the good Doctor again? Perhaps he's remembered something since you interviewed him? How many times did he visit Crow in prison?"

"I need to double check, but off the top of my head I'd say ten or a dozen times."

"In which case I can't believe that Crow didn't divulge something about his life on the barge. I mean the prison governor told me that Crow was still a canal fanatic, right up to the end. I think we should push him some more."

"Can't do any harm. Do you want me to ask him to come into the station again?" Moss asked.

"No, let's keep it nice and informal this time. Can you find out where he lives so we can maybe pop round on the off chance? That way I can also talk to him. Any luck with the university?"

"Yes, as it happens. There were not that many Christopher Smiths who attended the university around that time, despite his common surname, so I've narrowed it down to two. One got a joint first in History and Philosophy; the other only managed to scrape a second in Divinity. I've decided to check the philosopher first. They have a recent address, because he's one of those aluminums, so if he's not moved we should also be able to see him tomorrow or the day after."

"It's Alumni." Krill couldn't resist the urge to correct

Moss even though he suspected that he was being baited. "So where does he live?"

"Ascot. There's something else you should know."

"What?"

"Guess whose name is on the list of car users for the multi on the day that Colin Marshall was murdered?"

"Robin Butcher?"

"No, a certain Christopher Smith!"

"That is very interesting!"

"Yes, isn't it. Any sign of the Press at your cottage or Margaret's?"

"No, not any more. They're probably consumed by Brexit and the Presidential election which is hotting up."

"By the way, I had the cottage swept again for bugs just before you came back. We didn't find any more."

"Thanks Moss. This whole affair is becoming increasingly cloak and dagger. First Special Branch, and then the incident today at the crematorium. What shouldn't be a surprise is that the man I met at the funeral not only knew who I was, but he also repeated chapter and verse various details about the investigation. I think he was trying to give the impression that he'd read about it in the newspapers but I believe he had other sources of information. Also why didn't he introduce himself?"

"Maybe if he did, he would have had to kill you!"

"Don't joke about it Moss, I don't think that's a million miles from the truth!"

"Have you had any more texts or videos from our mystery man?"

"No, nothing. I think he may be satisfied for the time being with the confrontation he had with me at the hospital, and is lying low."

"Maybe. Night Killer. I'll pick you up at nine for our trip to see David Smith."

As soon as he ended the call his phone rang again.

"Hello?"

"Mr Krill, it's Sharon Knox from the National Crime Agency. I hope it's not too late to chat about the emails which Peter Crow recently received in prison? I assume you've read them?"

"Yes, and found them quite disturbing; I've been wondering what you thought about them. Actually, I was hoping to arrange another meeting with you? There's something I need to run past you which we can't discuss over the phone, concerning how the killer may have evaded justice for so long."

"OK, that's interesting. I'll check my diary and send you some possible dates, but can we have a quick word just now about the emails?"

"Of course."

"In terms of their origin, who do you think sent them? We've not been able to trace the IP address."

"Our killer of course. I think it has to be him, and I believe he knew that we would find them once Crow died, if not before."

"Yes, I think you're probably right on both counts. In which case it appears that he's not only seeking recognition for his crimes, but also an understanding of how and why he became a serial killer. It's interesting that he appears to have had a morbid curiosity about murders from a very young age. Also his comment about wanting to change lives is fascinating; particularly the lives of his victims' children."

"That's why he blinded Richard. He wanted to have an impact on both him and his family, and couldn't let him or them off scot-free. He seemed disappointed when I told him at the hospital that I hadn't yet been to see my neighbour, as if he wanted to feed off the pain they'd suffered."

"'Feeding off the pain' is a good way of putting it, Mr Krill. The question is why is he fixated on death and changing lives? There's obviously a very strong power and control element, which could suggest a lack of both in areas of his own life, and more than likely a disappointment regarding the way things have turned out for himself. Perhaps he never had any recognition or appreciation from a controlling and bullying father? That would certainly explain his target group. Probably he has a deep-seated sense of frustration, but not a sexual one, and an anger at others who have been more successful than himself. Of course that could partly explain why he's so interested in you, because of your highflying career. If you'd not been so high profile, then he might have chosen someone else, despite your links to the original canal killings."

"Is that why he wanted to damage my reputation?"

"Most likely. However, in terms of finding him, which of course is always our top priority - we can focus on the why's and the personality disorders once we have him in custody - I think the emails may indicate that whoever committed these crimes suffered a serious trauma himself as a child or adolescent, which affected, indeed changed, his own life. I would be very surprised if the person we're looking for had a normal happy childhood, so any background information about the early lives of suspects will be crucial."

This last comment reminded Krill about Robin Butcher's childhood, particularly his father hanging himself. That must surely be one of the most devastating traumas a child could ever experience. How had the Doctor described it in the interview? Something about Robin having problems before it happened, and never being the same after his father's death? They would hopefully have an opportunity to dig deeper into Robin's background when they saw David Smith in the morning. Perhaps they would get really lucky, and possibly he or his twin would provide a lead as to how they could find the elusive fourth boy in the photo, because so far they could write all they knew about Robin Butcher on the back of a postage stamp! He also made a mental note to ask Moss to check the local newspapers at the time, to find out more about the suicide.

The way things were developing it appeared vital that Commander Morris should give top priority to finding Robin, but would she do so? More to the point, would she be allowed to do so? Did she even believe, as he did, that the photo was central to solving the case? She probably still saw it as an interesting clue but not a crucial one. Perhaps she thought that if he and his sidekick were allowed to follow the photo's trail it would keep the two of them out of her hair? Krill smiled ruefully - it was probably the tactic he would use if he was in the Commander's shoes. He wasn't sure how to raise the profile of both the photo and Robin Butcher as a suspect, except by hopefully gaining the support of Dr Knox.

"Thanks Sharon, as always it's vitally important to have your insight, and I certainly agree with everything you've said. Let's see what they come up with when you communicate your views about a childhood trauma to the rest of the team. Anyway, please let me have the dates you're free so we can meet up. This week if at all possible."

CHAPTER 32

He looked at the scene before him, entirely dissatisfied because it wasn't exactly what he'd hoped for. But then perfectionists are seldom happy with any outcome; achieving the best that they can in the circumstances does not resonate with them. Phrases such as 'that's good enough' or 'it's OK' or 'you did your best' were not for him but for losers like his father, and he'd vowed long ago never to follow him in either word or deed. Not one single step down that particular path thank you very much!

When he was younger, he'd searched in vain for a role model, someone he could look up to, and found no one who was worthy; no one who came even close to earning his respect. Other murderers were poor inconsequential imitations, and most of them were also losers. Even Krill, despite being an interesting antagonist, was not someone he could fully respect, partly of course because he'd been fooled quite easily; he'd digested every crumb of false evidence placed before him. No, he'd learnt early on that he would have to rise entirely by his own efforts above the scum that covered the farrago of humanity.

For this finale, he'd imagined four men sitting in their posed positions around the kitchen table, but had been forced to settle in the end with just the two. He'd planned it all so carefully, so diligently, but for some inexplicable reason Fate had on this occasion failed to reward him.

He leaned marginally to the left to see things from a different perspective, and then moved the empty syringes and the three small bottles a centimetre closer to a dead hand. He then knocked one of the bottles over, thinking that it shouldn't look too neat. Should their eyes be closed or open? Open seemed preferable. Ideally he'd wanted them to be looking at one another, gazing into each other's glazed eyes, but their heads had dropped forward at the moment of death and now they both stared at the table almost as if they'd nodded off mid conversation. He wondered whether their necks might become firmer and more manoeuvrable in a few hours time, after rigor mortis had partially set in? He quickly dismissed the idea because he couldn't afford to wait that long, and he suspected that any attempt to reposition their heads would be observable and risked spoiling his fantasy, the lie, which he wanted everyone except Krill to believe.

He'd visualised ensnaring Micky, like he'd tricked the twins, overpowering him and bringing him here; and also about stealing Crow's body from the hospital mortuary. But sadly neither was to be. On reflection, he'd had to choose between meeting Krill or stealing Crow, because of the hornets nest he'd stirred up by going to the hospital, but he didn't regret his decision to see his old adversary.

It would have been the crowning glory - to have all four bodies on display, because he knew that it would have caused absolute consternation in all quarters. The police would try to discover the identity of the fourth victim and what he was doing there with the twins and the corpse of a convicted criminal, and quickly be told to 'back off'. And his former employers would be more embarrassed than they'd ever been before, but what could they do? Nothing. They would want the investigation speedily closed. Would they be concerned that a killer might still be on the loose? Not as much as they would worry about the scandal that a manhunt and a subsequent trial would cause. They would want to bury Michael with full honours, and thank the police for bringing matters to a sad conclusion.

Had his cousin, or any of the other desk jockeys who'd given him orders, ever had an inkling about his extracurricular activities, which went back decades? Had they even thought for one single moment that he would use his training in his own wonderfully special way? No. But they needed to know now. They had to understand what they had unwittingly unleashed upon the world!

Creating ripples on life's pond, changing futures, having crucial consequences - these were key elements of his creed. But would his actions change the Service, and the powers that be, at all? It might stop them for a while from feeling so self-righteous, believing they were the heroes saving the Nation; and it might make it harder for them to sleep soundly at night, especially while he was still at large. But all too soon they would move on, forget about him, and ignore their own guilt, unless he could make it impossible for them to do so.

The much revered Michael - he'd come to hate him the most. He'd put his cousin in touch with the right people just prior to him sitting his finals at Cambridge, and radically changed his life as well hadn't he? He didn't know what Micky's plans had been concerning possible careers after graduation, but they certainly hadn't included the one he'd been channelled into. He'd started Micky on his lifelong career, and he'd watched, somewhat bemused, as he'd quickly progressed within the Service, rising through rank after rank. Had he ever shown any appreciation, any gratitude? Of course not. Although he'd come to hate him, he did not envy him. He wouldn't have wanted to be an office based bureaucrat, even a powerful one like Micky; he much preferred the danger and excitement of his role, particularly when he could supplement it. Jo was different, but even she didn't fully understand; even she was really part of the 'club'.

And what could Krill do when they told him it was all over, that the case was finally closed, and the serial killer found? When deep down he would know it wasn't true. He would mope and fret and wish things could be different, and no doubt condemn himself for not being better at his job. Most likely, he'd feel incredibly guilty because of his blinded neighbour, and about the Scottish family deprived of a husband and father. All because of his inadequacies. Yes, he would most likely go to his grave a wounded and very bitter man - representing yet another important ripple.

He felt like he was travelling over a dark brooding sea, as a powerful gale which was blowing pitilessly, or a giant bird flying fast and low, with wings almost touching the surface. Each one disturbing the calm; each one causing the water to rise up in reaction; crest after crest after crest; countless times, endlessly.

But enough philosophising, he thought. He folded Christopher's raincoat carefully over the back of one of the two spare chairs, put the felt hat on top of the seat, and propped the silver topped walking stick next to it. He'd already destroyed the replica's which he'd used as part of his disguise.

He laughed out loud as another appalling image came to mind - its sound echoing unnaturally and wickedly in the stillness of the room. What if Christopher were to be buried as David, and David as Christopher? What if they were each laid to rest beneath the headstone of the twin brother they'd hated for most of their lives? Surely if anything could make someone turn in their grave then that would be it! Was it too late to swop their clothes and personal possessions? He even moved towards one of the twins before he stopped himself. Such an act might be sublimely amusing but would not serve his true purpose. It was an indulgence and he didn't have any time or energy left for those.

He took an envelope out of his pocket, and pressed the fingers of one of the twins onto it, and on each of the sheets of paper before replacing them inside.

Had Christopher recognised him when they'd met in the supermarket car park? Not at first, not until he was close enough to force him into his BMW at gunpoint. And he'd certainly had no idea why he'd been told to drive to Bracknell, or whose drive they'd turned into. He'd had no idea at all what was in store until they'd knocked on the door and he came face to face with David. The look on both their faces had been exactly as he'd anticipated; each one a shocked mirror image of the other!

He checked the room one last time, apparently reluctant to leave, took several photos using his phone, and then, like a maleficent spirit, departed, leaving no telltale trace that he'd ever been there.

She was surprised to see a large black car parked in front of the garage doors, and wasn't sure whether to pull in behind and block it in, or reverse and leave her own vehicle in the lane. She decided to leave it in the drive for the time being and see who the visitor was and how long they would be staying. In all the years she'd been coming, Dr Smith had never had a visitor on a Friday morning, and she didn't think he had very many on other days either, especially now he'd retired.

As she approached the front door she fretted that whoever it was might make it awkward for her to do her job properly. She liked to be thorough and had a set routine which she was loath to alter. Dr Smith was one of her best clients and he always gave her the run of his house, even more so now since the first lockdown, staying in his study for the three hours that she was there. Before the pandemic, when she had her own fifteen minute break at eleven she would take him a cup of coffee and a biscuit, and they would chat in his study, usually about the weather, his roses, or their families. He'd had a lot of aphids this year. Now, it was a far briefer conversation and with neither of them in the same room. Nonetheless, she'd been anticipating the delight he would show when she told him about her nephew going to Cambridge to start his studies. The alien car had instantly deflated her upbeat mood.

Lillian sensed that something wasn't right as soon as she opened the heavy oak door, because rather than the voices she expected to hear there was a deathly quiet, an unnatural stillness. For this reason she didn't call out her usual greeting of 'it's only me Doctor'; nor did she hang up her coat on a peg in the hallway. A little voice inside her head told her to turn around and leave, but she couldn't. The dining room door was open and she glanced in there first - everything looked normal; so did the sitting room on her left. She wondered if Dr Smith and his guest were perhaps in his study at the back of the house, talking quietly with the door closed? Could that be it? She'd almost accepted this notion and was thinking about taking them both a pot of coffee when she walked into the kitchen.

Moss only narrowly avoided hitting the crazed woman when he turned into the lane. He swerved onto the grass verge and jumped out of the car to see what was wrong. As he approached her, she fell to the ground as if poleaxed, and started crying hysterically; incapable of any coherent speech.

"Get her in the car Moss, while I go and see what's happened."

Krill ran along the lane and through the open wooden gates. He quickly took in the scene in front of him - two vehicles including a BMW which he initially assumed belonged to Dr Smith, an impressive well maintained pre-war villa beyond, a trim lawn surrounded by rose bushes, some of which still had blooms despite the onset of winter.

The front door was fully open. He looked down the hallway, which had several paintings spaced at regular intervals. There were a number of coats of various sizes and colours hanging from the rack, together with some cotton and wool scarves; they looked as if they belonged there, whereas the baseball cap with a 'US Open' logo on it, did not. He knew that he had to be careful not to touch anything but worried about his shoes contaminating the scene, and what Commander Morris would say about him even being there, never mind entering the house. However, he felt that he had no alternative but to do just that.

He took out his phone and started to record a video. Surprisingly, he was not at all shocked when he reached the kitchen and saw the two men seated at the table. One had his back to him, the other, Dr Smith was to one side. Had he already seen sufficient to alert the authorities? No doubt

Commander Morris would think that he had seen more than enough to leave the house and do so, but Krill's instincts took over. He sidestepped the large shopping bag which he assumed the woman had dropped in her hurry to get out, and slowly walked around the edge of the room. It was obvious to him that the second man was David's twin brother. He wondered whether David had lied about not seeing him for several decades? That would certainly explain why the two of them were there now together. Or had David invited his estranged brother to his house for some urgent meeting, perhaps to talk about their mutual acquaintance Peter Crow, and the questions that Moss had been asking?

That was when Krill saw the envelope which had his name printed on it, and for one second he was tempted to pick it up.

He recognised the clothing on the chair and the propped up walking stick. Could Christopher Smith be the man who had accosted him? It was clearly what he was expected to believe. What else? Doubtless the syringes and small bottles were the cause of both men's demise. Krill completed his circuit of the room and reached the conclusion that it was either a murder suicide or possibly a suicide pact, which was on display.

He walked back to the car and found his former colleague still comforting the woman. He signalled to Moss to join him at the roadside.

"Who is she?" he asked.

"Dr Smith's cleaning lady. What's happened? I still can't get anything much out of her beyond her name, which is

Lillian, the fact that she cleans for him every Friday, and that something terrible has occurred," Moss said.

"It's Dr Smith and his twin brother. Both dead; probably due to some kind of drug overdose as there's a syringe and bottles on the kitchen table in front of them. There's clothing which matches those worn by the man at the hospital, and a baseball cap in the hall which is the same as in the video I received. He's also left a letter for me."

"Bloody hell, Boss!"

"Don't worry Moss, I didn't touch anything."

"It's not that, Commander Morris is going to go apeshit when she knows you've come here and found them. Maybe I could say that it was me who entered the house and keep you out of it?"

"That won't work, not unless we can convince Lillian here to lie to the police. I'll just have to accept the consequences."

"No, it might still be OK. You take over here Killer, and chat to her, and I'll go and take a look myself before ringing it in. With any luck they'll just assume that it was me who found them."

"You can try, but that's one bet even I won't accept. How will you explain us being here at all? Anyway, it'll be good to get your views of what's happened in there before the forensics team arrives and all hell breaks loose. Have you got the number of that car from the multi handy? The one parked by Christopher Smith?"

"I can soon get it."

"Check the BMW parked at the front will you? I'm assuming it's his."

CHAPTER 33

As he waited on the Thames Embankment, Moss wondered why Krill had suggested meeting there, at that precise spot in Millbank, close to Vauxhall Bridge. Then he smiled because it dawned on him: just opposite, in plain view, was the futuristic structure which housed SIS, the Secret Intelligence Service or MI6. It was typical of Krill to be defiant, to want to 'cock a snook' at those who were attempting to undermine the investigation. He was saying - 'look at me, here I am, and I won't be stopped!' When Krill joined him, they walked and conversed, although it was Krill who did most of the talking.

"It's far too neat Moss, just like the Canal Killings. He's handing it to us once more on a plate, and this time he's put the Yorkshire pudding and bloody gravy on it too!"

"But the evidence is overwhelming Killer. It's indisputable."

"Exactly. That's exactly what I'm saying. But why Moss? Why would Christopher Smith become a serial killer, either on his own or in collusion with his twin? What's his motive? And why would he avoid capture all these years only to end his life now in such a quiet, unobtrusive way? It just doesn't work for me; not at all."

"Maybe he realised that we were onto him, or they both did? Let me list all the evidence…"

"You can list it all you like Moss but it still doesn't add up."

Moss went on undeterred:

"First there's his link to Crow - you always said that the killer knew him well."

"So too did Robin Butcher," countered Krill.

"There's the matching hat and cane we found in the house. Identical to the person you met at the hospital."

"Left there by the real killer, Moss."

"But there are witnesses who say that it's the way Christopher Smith usually dressed, and that the cane is definitely his. Plus there's DNA evidence which shows that they're actually the clothes he wore."

"What about the baseball hat left in the hall? Any witnesses to say that the doctor or his twin ever wore it? Any DNA evidence for that particular item of clothing?"

"No," Moss admitted.

"So what was it doing there? I can't see either of the twins wearing one, can you? It's a gesture from the real killer, who would know it would most likely be ignored by the police as irrelevant. It's two fingers, put there to taunt me. The killer obviously acquired similar clothes to the twin and found a replica walking stick. Can't you see Moss that he did the very same thing with poor Crow, by using the distinctive crash helmet?"

"There's also the syringe and drugs found on the kitchen table which match what we found in you and the other recent victims."

"Of course they match, because he brought those there with him, to kill the twins."

Moss wasn't easily put off by Krill's counterarguments, he was like a dog with a very juicy bone.

"They also found DNA in Christopher Smith's car."

"What DNA?" asked Krill. This was news to him.

"It was on the driver's seatbelt. It matches Colin Marshall's. And don't forget that his car was parked in the multi on the day he was thrown off the roof."

"That's why he chose that multi, because he knew that Christopher would park there. And why would our serial killer, who's evaded justice for decades, suddenly be so stupid as to leave some DNA in his own car? What is the DNA evidence?"

"A tiny speck of blood and a single hair."

"So, very easy for someone to put it there. It's that damned cloth on the barge again Moss! Deja vu doesn't do it justice! How do they think that it got in the car?"

"They assume on Smith's hand or glove. It was so slight he probably didn't notice."

"I might believe it if they can find some of Colin's DNA on his clothing or anywhere else, but I'm betting they won't."

It would be a challenge for anyone to judge who was the most exasperated of the two men as they strolled along in the sunshine. They'd both seen the same crime scene but were coming at the facts from completely opposite angles. Moss stopped, took hold of Krill's arm, looked at his old colleague, and asked the obvious question:

"So who do you think has done it, Killer, if it wasn't Christopher Smith?"

"The person who we've not been allowed to investigate of course. I just know that he was there too that day in the multi. Don't forget about him, as our friends across the river would like us to. If he had nothing to do with it why won't they release the CCTV footage? Why won't they let us at least talk to him, 'in camera' if need be. I don't want to know his name, if it's not Robin Butcher, or what he did when he worked for Special Branch or MI5 or 6, or even what he looks like. I just want to hear his voice, Goddammit! And they still haven't let me see the letter left on the table at Dr Smith's house or even told me what was in it. It was addressed to me, Moss. To me!"

"I'll ask them again about it."

"Sorry Moss, none of this is your fault. Look, if we hadn't worked on the Canal case and seen how the real killer framed Crow, then I might, just might, have accepted the evidence myself. I agree that it seems overwhelming. If it looks like a cat and meows, then it's a bloody cat! I can almost hear Commander Morris saying it. I know no one else except you and I have had that experience, so in a way it's understandable that they believe what the real killer wants them to believe. But not us, because we've been through it all before, and I'm damned if I'm going to let that bastard trick me again!"

"You need to be careful, Boss, about stirring things up. Commander Morris did speak about the possibility of charging you with obstructing the police by entering a known crime scene, and even attempting to pervert the course of justice."

"She was upset; it was just her anger talking. She has no case and she knows it. She didn't have to fire you though, that was petty. It's a good job that we both still have our own connections at the Met."

"I'm not sure how much longer anyone will be willing to speak to us Killer, especially if Morris lets it be known that we're persona non grata."

They stopped and both leaned on the parapet observing the London river scene in front of them.

"What we need is some conclusive evidence that neither of the Smiths could have committed at least one of the crimes. As you said earlier, one of them being out of the country doesn't preclude a double act during the Canal Killings, and it's too far back anyway to check those dates, but what about the times when he kept Richard prisoner, or the incident at the hospital? If we can show that both of them were definitely elsewhere for either of those occasions then the case against them begins to fall apart. Is Commander Morris checking that?"

"I don't think so; not that I've heard. She's going to be unwilling to commit further resources to it if she's certain that they already have enough evidence."

"But evidence against whom? Just Christopher Smith?"

"Presumably," said Moss apologetically.

"Could we speak to their families? What did he do before he retired?" asked Krill.

"He was a university lecturer."

Krill laughed. "So the proposition which we're being asked to accept is that either a university lecturer or a family doctor, or possibly both of them acting in collusion, were killers of dozens, possibly scores of people? That they also knew about surveillance techniques and bugged my cottage and tracked my car? That they had the wherewithal to evade capture for forty years? That no one suspected them; not their families or their colleagues? Come on Moss, it's totally ludicrous."

"I agree it's a stretch, but I'm not sure how we can counter the case which Morris and the others have against them."

"There must be a way, Moss, there must be a way. We just have to find it. Are there any recordings of Christopher Smith which Richard and I can listen to? If he was an academic then maybe some of his lectures are on Youtube? They can't stop us from talking to their families and associates in a few days time, can they? Or maybe we can go to their funerals when they release the bodies and we can get to know them that way?"

"In normal times we might, but not now, not with the restrictions on numbers. And I'm not sure why their families would agree to talk to us?"

"Because we're trying to prove that their father or brother or uncle or friend is innocent! That's why! Surely they would want that too?" Krill reasoned.

"Yes, you'd hope so. Maybe we can speak to them after the funeral, as they leave? We can wait in the car and then approach them?"

"Yes, let's do that, good thinking. Do you think Commander Morris will also be there, at the funerals?"

"No, I can't see her or any of the team going."

"So, with a modicum of luck we'll have a clear run."

"Just be careful, Killer. I know what you're like when you build up a head of steam."

"I will Moss, I will. Maybe I should also ring the mystery man from the Crem? I've got his number."

Moss shook his head. "Why? If anything he'll be happy that his stepbrother's claims of innocence have been vindicated and that the case is closed. I'm sure Special Branch is also delighted. Perhaps there's been pressure put on Commander Morris to wrap it all up as quickly and as tidily as possible."

"You're probably right about that; ending the search for a serial killer will no doubt please a lot of people. But don't forget that Crow's innocence will only be established if she says categorically that Christopher Smith also committed the Canal Killings, and I can't see her doing that because there's still no evidence....unless...?"

"Unless what, Boss?"

"Unless there's a match with Smith's DNA and that piece of cloth we found on the barge. That's right! Maybe the cloth is the answer after all! Maybe it's the one thing which the real killer has not taken into account, because he doesn't know we have his DNA. I'd bet a hundred pounds that there is no match with either of the Smiths, but that there is a match with our mystery spook. Can we get the test done?"

Moss looked very reluctant to commit to more unauthorised tests.

"It won't be easy. Morris certainly won't agree to it because she's understandably content with winding up the two live enquiries; especially now that Crow is dead. We'd also have to get hold of both Smith's DNA somehow. I can try."

"If need be I'll pay for the tests to be done privately, and we can possibly get a sample from a relative of the Smith's if we can't get theirs."

Not far from where the two men were standing, another meeting was also taking place. It had taken some considerable time and effort for Jo to select the preferred location, and it certainly could not have been on the Embankment just opposite the SIS building! Safe houses were now anything but safe; so was just about every possible public place such as a gallery or museum, as none of these were open. In the end she'd cajoled an old acquaintance of hers who worked for the London Assembly to let them use her office, as she was working from home.

Jo was the first to arrive, in part because she wanted to check it out before texting 'all clear', and also to purloin some mugs from the communal kitchen and make a cafetière of coffee for the two of them; one mug displayed lots of hearts on a pink background, while the other was cream with an outline of the London skyline. She chose them because they were right at the very back of the shelf and looked as if they hadn't been used in quite a while. Even so she rinsed them under boiling water.

She thought that her former mentor appeared far too relaxed given the circumstances, as he sat down opposite her, and wondered whether there was more than a hint of outright pleasure with developments, or a degree of self-satisfaction reflected in his smile? She'd long ago given up any attempt to read Robin's mind or fathom his moods. They watched one another for a few moments in silence, like long separated friends who had had a falling out, but now wished to patch up their differences. She wasn't sure whether or not she wished that he would remove his sunglasses; like others who'd worked with him, she'd learned to get accustomed to the icy colourless irises.

"Whatever you're doing Jo, stop it. You'll only get yourself into deep shit, and besides I don't need you to look out for me. You watch your own back, I'm perfectly capable of watching out for mine."

"Do you really want to go to prison Robin?"

He nearly choked on his coffee, he was so amused by the idea that he would ever be tried for his crimes.

"We both know that will never happen. Worse case scenario is that I disappear, but as I'm planning to do that anyway, why would they bother? Unless you've already slipped something into my mug while I was in the loo?"

She looked aghast that he would ever think her capable of doing such a thing, because she couldn't, not even if she was ordered to, not even if her own life depended on it.

"Poor Jo! Don't look so shocked - I'm joking! I know that you're the one person that I can completely depend on and trust."

"So this is goodbye?"

"Yes, I'm afraid it is. I can't let even you know where I'm going because Michael and his minions would find out somehow. Meeting you here was risky enough, even though I knew that their very best wouldn't be able to follow you. But I had to say goodbye face to face, mug to mug."

They clinked their two mugs together as an unspoken toast to their friendship and shared exploits. Jo had needed to use all her tradecraft, much of it taught by the man seated opposite her, to elude at least four watchers, who she presumed Michael had put on her tail.

"How long have you known?" he asked.

"Known, as in definitively, with any degree of certainty - only a few weeks. Suspected that you had a dark secret? For a long time. There's been a few telltale signs: places you've been where things have happened, times you've disappeared off the radar; things you've asked me to do; too many coincidences, and even hints here and there from you yourself."

"But you're in the clear. There's nothing to link you to my little hobby."

She shook her head at his misuse of the term.

"I won't ask you why you've done what you've done, assuming it's all true."

"Oh it's true Jo, all of it, believe me. And what they know, or think they know, is just the tip of a very large, very deep, very dark, iceberg. If you did ask then I'm not sure that I could explain it to you, because perhaps even I don't know the reason. Maybe it's very simple; maybe it's just the fact that I could. Perhaps it's complex, that I have a need to do it, that I'm driven to do it. Maybe I'm insane or maybe I'm saner than everyone else? Maybe it's because I think I failed in my chosen career and that my talents were not recognised, so I had something to prove to myself if not to others."

"You never had to prove anything to me."

"I know that Jo, and I've valued your friendship and loyalty so very much, but it's time now to let go, time to let me go, and time to leave Krill and Moss alone to do whatever they need to do."

"Can't I help? I could remove Krill and Moss permanently from the equation. Without them this would all go away."

"No!" he shouted, alarming her and making people in nearby offices look in their direction. For the first time she was actually frightened of him, and understood just what he could be capable of doing. He closed his unseen eyes, breathed out volubly, and calmed himself.

"I don't want Krill harmed, Jo, not by you or by me, and ideally not by any of my erstwhile friends and acquaintances. I want him left alone, left in peace, and given time to understand and reflect on it all. If you hurt him then you injure me. Think of it as if he's my voodoo doll and if you stab him then I feel the pain."

He could see that she was confused but didn't know how better to explain the bond he felt between himself and Krill.

What she said next surprised him:

"Actually, it was some of the things which you said in the past about Krill which first made me wonder about you, and what you might have done. I couldn't understand why you were so interested in a policeman and what he was up to."

"Was it that obvious?"

"Less so at the time, but now I can see that you were obsessed with him. Every time he appeared in the newspapers or on TV you would have that look on your face, like you and he shared some secret, and you'd always make some disparaging comment - like he's not as clever as he thinks he is. I started to wonder if you and he had some sort of a history?"

"I'm impressed Jo! There's only two people who have had the power to change my life radically and detrimentally - my father when he killed himself, and Krill when he almost had me in his sights. No one else comes even close. Anyway, as I say, leave him alone, and Moss too, you've already done more than enough to distract him. But don't be sad, I predict a great future for you. Now is the time to stop worrying about me and think about your own career. When Michael retires in a few years time you should aim to replace him. You'll do a far better job than he ever could because you're like me and understand how the world really works."

Was she like him? She hoped that she'd manage to take only the best that he offered, the obvious strengths, and not the hidden flaws. But there were some worrying parallels between the two of them. She knew, because he'd told her, that one of the reasons he'd singled her out for special attention was because of her own difficult childhood, when she'd been placed in a succession of foster homes and care facilities, after both her parents had been killed in a car crash.

He looked quizzically at her, now that it was all out in the open and no longer any secrets between them, a little uncertain of her.

"I can trust you, can't I Jo? You're not going to help them? I don't mean Krill, I mean Micky and the others. I know you're the only one who could ever find me if you put your mind to it, and possibly I would let you, if I knew that you were looking."

The delay in reassuring him was not because she would ever betray him, but because she felt that she might one day need to seek him out for her own benefit, to ask him to help her, as he had done so many times in the past.

"I wouldn't ever help them Robin, you know that. But they're bound to know that I've spoken to you, especially after today when I slipped out of sight. What should I tell them when they ask me?"

Robin smiled. "Be honest; well at least partially truthful. You know that a lie based as far as possible on the facts is always the best approach, because I taught you that little nugget many years ago when training you to deal with interrogation. So, admit that we did meet today and that I confessed everything to you - the abduction, the murder of that petty civil servant, accosting Krill at the hospital, the twin killings in Bracknell, and a host of other crimes spanning the past forty years. Tell them that you tried to persuade me to give myself up, and you were shocked and dismayed when I laughed in your face! Also let them know that I'm planning to leave the UK for good, so they can stop worrying about me getting up to anything else here. And if they ask you where you think I might have gone, suggest Amsterdam or Venice, because they have lots of canals don't they? I've always liked canals."

CHAPTER 34

A few days later, Moss contacted Krill again with the results. He'd used up all of his credit and more besides, to get samples from the mortuary where the twin's bodies were being held, and then have their DNA compared with that on the cloth.

They both were sitting on a bench next to lock gates on the canal near to Krill's cottage.

"You were right, Killer, there isn't a match for either twin. I also asked them to check it against Crow's DNA again just in case there'd been an error the first time, and guess what they've now found?"

"That it's not Crow's DNA but a relative of his?"

"Exactly! However, I've been giving it some thought before I came, and I'm not sure how it helps us; if anything it could point the finger once more at Crow."

"How so, Moss?"

"Because it provides a link between him and the cloth found on the barge, indirectly if not directly. If he was alive he would no longer be able to claim that it has nothing to do with him, would he? Maybe it was his mother's cloth and Crow always used gloves whenever he took it out of the drawer to carry the syringe."

"So you're saying that it was from some garment used by his mother or another relative, which he cut up and took in and out of the drawer numerous times, and never once got his own DNA on it?"

"Put like that no, you're right it's extremely unlikely. So you think the DNA is from Robin?"

"I have no doubt about it, Moss. Let's look at the evidence for it being our mystery man: the odds are that it's his DNA on that cloth because Crow's aunt married a Butcher, and that puts him directly in the frame for the Canal Killings. Let's make two further assumptions: that, like the man at the crematorium, Robin has some connection with the security services, hence all the fuss by Special Branch when his name came up. And if he has those connections then he would likely have knowledge of and access to surveillance equipment, and most crucially, he would also be very adept at avoiding any hint of suspicion falling on himself. It explains why we had no hope of arresting him in 1978, and why he's evaded justice ever since."

"That's a lot of assumptions, Killer."

"Yes I agree, but it does explain everything."

"And if you're right, then, given those connections, he's likely to evade capture again, because how can we prove any of that without getting access to Robin Butcher's DNA, and other evidence such as details of his movements on the days in question? Also where was he in 1978? Everything about him is likely to be as well guarded and protected as the Crown Jewels. They'd probably arrest us just for mentioning his name and asking for more information. Not that they need to answer any questions anyway now, because we have no official standing."

"I didn't say it was going to be easy. It could all be resolved by a five minute interview with him, with me blindfolded. I'll even sign the Official Secrets Act again, in triplicate!"

"How would that work, Killer? They could bring anyone in who resembles the suspect and say he was Robin Butcher."

"True. I hadn't thought of that."

All the talk about secrets and possible spies worried Moss. He stood up, pretending to light a cigarette, and looked around - along the towpath in one direction towards the road and level crossing, and the other way towards a bridge. There were a couple of people walking a dog and four moored barges. He checked behind them, where there was a signal box and a dozen or so parking spaces, mostly filled, including a white van.

"It's probably too late, but I think we should be careful what we say here, or anywhere else, about you know who."

"Becoming paranoid again, Moss? But OK, if you say so. Is it safe to talk about Youtube?"

"Probably. What did you find?"

"Well, searching for Christopher Smith yielded a lot of videos, but 'Christopher Smith lecturer' was better. I watched a presentation which he gave at the RSA several years ago."

"What's that?" asked Moss.

"Royal Society of Arts. I'm a member, believe it or not. Anyway I watched his talk and I'm ninety nine percent certain

309

that he was not the man in the video, or the man at the hospital. I know it's not conclusive evidence, but it lends weight to my theory about 'he who cannot be named'."

Moss was still troubled. "Let's walk to your cottage. I have something to show you. Well a couple of things actually."

"What are they?"

"Wait until we get there."

Twenty minutes later they were comfortably seated in Krill's garden. All was quiet next door and down the lane. The calm serenity reminded Krill that he still hadn't been to see his neighbour. The surroundings may have been tranquil, but he could tell that Moss remained twitchy.

"First things first, Killer - I got us both new mobile phones. Here's yours."

"A 'burner', isn't that what they're called? I've always wanted one."

Both men shook their heads but for different reasons.

"I definitely had a funny feeling about the van that was parked near us at the canal, plus there's everything that's been happening to me lately. Let's keep our phone conversations as brief as possible Killer, especially regarding anything to do with 'him'. The second present I have for you is a copy of the contents of the envelope found at the house where the twins died. I'm hoping that they will mean something to you because they made no sense to anyone at the Met. Dr K hasn't had a chance to see them yet but I bet that even she will be baffled."

"Speaking of Sharon, she would have been the ideal person to go to, with my theories, but I suppose that now even she will not agree to see me, either in an official or unofficial capacity."

"No, I'd be very surprised if she will, much as she admires your skills as a detective. Anyway, tell me what you think about these."

Moss took five folded sheets of A4 out of his coat pocket and handed them to Krill. Four of them were obituaries: one was for a man who died after a short illness - donations to Cancer Research, three others were for men who had died in tragic circumstances; and the fifth was a report of a missing person.

"I looked them up beforehand for you," said Moss, checking his notes. "Paul Watkins aged 35, computer programmer, died in 1986 after a short battle with cancer. The interesting thing about him is that he's from Crow's hometown. Duncan Collins aged 45, drowned in a canal in Warwickshire in 1974. Kevin Barnes 48 was hit by a train near Cambridge in 1991, verdict was suicide but as you can see the obituary describes it as a tragic accident. Henry Bright 51 was killed in a house fire in Camden in 2001, verdict was accidental death. Adam Heaton, aged fifty two, left his home in York in 1980 to go on a walk in the Pennines and was never seen again. The initial view was that they might all be past victims of the serial killer, except that it doesn't quite add up because of the one who died of cancer."

"Can you Google that one again for me now Moss. See if there are any entries other than his obituary."

Krill waited while Moss searched through several pages on his phone.

"Here's something interesting and also it's recent: 'Widow Marie Watkins, whose husband died in 1986, is appealing for the return of her husband's ashes!" He stared at Krill. "She noticed that they were missing when on Saturday she went to visit the Columbarium where they'd been kept for 34 years. A spokesperson for the facility said that it was totally inexplicable how someone could do such a thing, and similarly asked for them to be returned, assuring the heartless thief that 'no questions would be asked' when they did so'."

"It's Paul who's in our urn, I'm one hundred percent certain of it. He's the one that the killer wanted to murder but couldn't because he'd already died of natural causes. He's the one described in the email sent to Crow. Paul and Marie - it fits. He fancied Paul's girlfriend and contemplated killing him; would have carried it out if another girl hadn't come along to distract him."

"What about the others?" asked Moss.

"With those I believe he's boasting. 1974 is probably his first kill - maybe like lovers you always remember your first. The other three show the extent and range of his expertise, both geographically and technically. He can strike all across the Country and make it look like an accident, or a suicide, or apparently just make someone vanish. All were murdered but no one even suspected it. It's calculating, coldblooded, and chilling. I bet he attended their funerals, watched the families as they mourned, maybe kept an eye on them for months or even years afterwards, enjoying the pain and heartache he'd caused."

Moss thought for a moment. "Does that mean we should check out Colin's funeral in Perth? See if our man attends? I could suggest it to Commander Morris but I doubt she'll be prepared to even contact the police in Scotland. Me and the lads could go of course."

"Yes, someone should go, if for no other reason than to pay our respects. But he won't be there. He didn't kill Colin to see how it would affect his family. He killed him because of Margaret and her links to me. You're right, this information could help us - the email and the note could provide another link to the killer. I know it's a long shot, but can you get Jim or one of the other lads to return the ashes, assuming Commander Morris no longer needs them as evidence, and ask this Marie whether she remembers ever knowing our man when she was a teenager and dating Paul?"

That evening Krill was chopping vegetables when he received a call from an unknown number on his new phone.

"Killer, it's me. Just to say I've spoken to both Commander Morris and to Jim, and he'll collect the ashes and deliver them to the widow tomorrow or the day after."

"That was quick."

"Well, the quicker we sort this out the better as far as she's concerned. What will you do if Marie confirms that she or her late husband did know chummy?"

"I'm not sure. It adds more weight to my argument. At the very least we should check the other four deaths which the killer seems to be owning up to, and find out if we can whether either of the twins were around on the days in question. With a bit of luck they may both have been abroad for at least one of them. The university may have details of conferences Christopher attended or lecture tours he went on."

"But even if she can do that and more suspicion starts to fall elsewhere, we'll still be up against a brick wall won't we, assuming he's a spook of some kind? I mean that's your line of thinking isn't it?"

"Yes it is. I suppose I will definitely have to speak to the man I met at Crow's funeral again. I don't know how he, or the organisation he works for, would react if they knew that one of their employees was a serial killer. However, he did come across as someone decent, who might want to do the right thing."

"Even so, they wouldn't want a trial."

"On balance, that's my thinking too Moss."

"So aren't we really wasting our time?"

"Finding out the truth is never a waste of time. We may not get justice for the families of the men he killed, but I'll rest easier in my bed knowing that we did all we could, and at the very least stopped him from killing anyone else."

"I suppose if the families think it was an accident, or a

suicide, or that their loved one is still missing, then they won't be looking for justice anyway, will they?"

"True, but they might still want closure. What's Jim going to tell Marie about the urn?" Krill asked.

"Just that he found it. He'll also come up with some believable storyline about being local, and our suspect possibly being a mutual friend; you know Jim."

"Indeed I do, only too well! Better end the call Moss, or you'll say I'm being too chatty."

Krill had just put his dishes in the machine when there was a loud knock on the cottage door. That was a surprise as he didn't get many visitors, especially at night, even before the first lockdown. However, it was even more of a shock when he saw who his visitor was.

"Hello again Mr Krill. Can I come in? I've had a test recently so you're perfectly safe."

Krill thought that he might be safe from Covid, but that wasn't what he was most worried about at that exact moment. He checked outside but couldn't see any sign of George the minder.

"What a lovely cottage you have. Very homely. We could shake hands if you wish?" He whispered, "There's no one here to see it and shout at us."

They shook hands.

"Great. I wonder if we could also be on first name terms? Can I call you John? I'm Michael."

"OK Michael, how can I help you?"

"Perhaps we'll be more comfortable in your dining room?"

They went through and each took a seat at the table. Krill tried not to recollect the last occasion that there had been two men sitting at just such a table.

"I wonder if you would be so kind as to put both your mobile phones on the table, John, so I can see that they're switched off? I trust you implicitly, but you see my suspicious colleagues will ask me the question and I don't like to lie."

Krill did as he was asked, wondering how Michael had found out so quickly about his new phone? Michael put his gloves back on to check them, but somehow it didn't seem like a sinister act.

His guest smiled.

"Now we can talk frankly and in confidence I hope."

"I was thinking of contacting you myself Michael."

"Yes, I know, but I thought that I would save you the bother; the mountain going to the prophet so to speak, rather than vice versa. Anyway, maybe we can start with why you wanted to see me?"

Krill spent a moment marshalling his thoughts.

"To cut to the chase, I wanted to ask you whether you had any suspicions that your cousin might be a serial killer?"

"Straight to the point, John, I like that. The answer is no, I have had no suspicions about him in any regard, none whatsoever. Can I ask why you think he is one?"

"I think you already know why, but in the spirit of friendship and cooperation I will summarise: the crucial evidence in the Canal Killings was a cloth found on Peter Crow's barge which had traces of the drug used on the victims. We assumed that he had wrapped a syringe in that cloth. Without it I don't think Peter would have been convicted."

"Go on."

"We recently tested that cloth for DNA and found that it didn't match Peter's but was linked to a close relative. You told me yourself that Robin is related to the two of you."

"Yes I did."

"Point two - I believe Robin was at the car park on the day Colin Marshall was murdered."

"But you have no evidence for that."

"No, because your lot have removed the CCTV!"

"You do however have evidence that Christopher Smith's car was in the multi, and you also have DNA linking him to Colin Marshall. I would have thought those facts were quite conclusive. Commander Morris thinks so. There is also the method used for the apparent murder suicide found at his twin's house - the syringes and a bottle which contain a tranquilliser identical to the one used to sedate you, Mr Marshall, and your neighbour."

"You said bottle, but there were three on the table, what did the others contain?" Krill asked.

"Morphine. It appears that Christopher Smith first anaesthetised his brother and then injected him with a lethal dose of morphine before doing the same to himself. Do you have any other evidence, and please don't mention the urn."

"OK, I won't. As you know the killer spoke to me while I was visiting Peter at the hospital. I've listened to both twins speaking and can categorically state, if necessary in a court of law, that neither of them was the man I met at the hospital. So if we rule them out as the killer, then it must be the case that someone else planted the evidence in the BMW and at the house, just as they did in 1978 on Peter's barge. Also as far as I'm aware neither of them is related to Peter Crow."

"Let's assume for argument's sake that the same person who incriminated my stepbrother also tried to point the finger at the twins, and that this person is the man who accosted you at the hospital. Also, that he is what he said he is, namely a serial killer who has killed dozens, possibly scores, of people. What do you want me to do about it?"

"Check the DNA on the cloth against your cousin's and let me listen to his voice."

"I guess that evidence would be fairly conclusive one way or another. Of the two, the test would be far easier. And suppose I came back to you in a few days time and said that it didn't match, would you believe me?"

"I wouldn't believe you or disbelieve you, I would think that you were following instructions. I would also hope that you would do something about him if there was a match."

"By 'something' you mean what?"

"I know there would never be a trial, but I would hope that you, or someone connected to you, would somehow ensure that he couldn't harm anyone else."

318

"I see. That's interesting. If I do arrange for the test to be carried out then I want you to do something for me."

"What?"

"Well, you see there are some people, not me you understand, who have concerns, quite serious concerns really, that you might intend at some point in the future to have these theories of yours explored more openly in the Media. They feel that if you did do so then it would cause a lot of damage to certain reputations, not least to your own. They feel that while there is not much chance of the press or anyone else giving credence to your views, they do not willingly want to take the risk."

"Is that a threat?"

"Certainly not John. It is about developing mutual support and cooperation, and about trusting one another. They wouldn't wish to agree to any DNA matching without your categorical assurance that you will not seek any publicity for your views about my cousin. I personally don't see any point in asking you to sign the Official Secrets Acts again, as you already know that you're subject to them. However, you need to be aware that in these particular circumstances, if there was a breach, there would most definitely be a prosecution, and the maximum sentence would be sought. So I would like you to give a firm commitment to me now, that you will not go public regarding anything connected to my cousin."

"Before I do give you that assurance I have a few more questions."

"Fine."

"First of all, what happens to Peter Crow?" Krill asked.

"If the DNA matches my cousin's, then Peter will be posthumously and very quietly pardoned."

"That seems just. What about Colin Marshall?"

"I believe the Inquest will find it an 'unlawful killing by a person or persons unknown'. That won't help the family very much; they'll continue to wonder what he was doing at that car park and who killed him, but it can't be helped. However, his wife will soon discover that, unbeknownst to her, he took out a rather large insurance policy."

"My neighbour has also suffered greatly. He deserves compensation."

"Absolutely, and as a victim of crime he will be, very handsomely. Probably it will be sufficient for them to move out of their rented property and buy somewhere. There will also be therapy of course, and help with his trauma and blindness. Someone has already talked to his father and explained that the police now believe he was probably kidnapped by a person who had a grievance against you, someone unbalanced, a fantasist, and we're checking everyone who has recently been released from prison. I'm sure Richard and his family will want to move on as best they can with their lives."

"If for no other reason than to get away from me!"

Michael smiled.

"And the twins?"

"Accidental deaths or suicide, we haven't decided yet."

Krill was impressed so far with how Michael was intending to deal with matters.

"What about Media speculation that a serial killer is still on the loose?"

"That will quickly become old news, especially as the murders happened so long ago. The Press have no concrete evidence that any similar crimes have been carried out since 1978 by a serial killer. Also, there is no obvious link between those murders decades ago and the kidnapping of your neighbour and Colin's murder, apart that is from you, and fortunately the press have not discovered that you and Margaret are an item. No, as I've already said, the logical conclusion is that recent events are linked to someone recently released from prison who has a grudge against you, and wanted to damage your reputation."

Krill nodded. "OK, based on what you've said, I'm prepared to promise you that I will not attempt to breach the Official Secrets Acts."

"Excellent, and thank you John for your cooperation. I'll phone you in a few days with the result of the DNA analysis. We already have the DNA from the cloth so don't bother to send it."

"Well we know what the result will be, don't we? Can I really trust you Michael?"

"You can John, most certainly. I give you my word as a Knight of the Realm that I will deal with every eventuality thoroughly, and exactly as you would wish it to be dealt with. I regret what you've been through these past weeks; it can't have been easy for you, and in a way you're also a victim. I would offer you some recompense but I know that you would feel insulted were I to do so. But I will try to find a way to keep you up to speed with developments if I possibly can. Regrettably, it all may take a while, so ring me if you have any concerns in the meantime. You still have my number?"

"Yes, and knowing that you will do what's right is all the recompense I need. Nothing more, nothing less."

As soon as he was alone Krill poured himself a very large whisky and sat on the sofa in a bit of a daze. He wanted to tell Moss everything, but knew that he couldn't, not yet, maybe never. He did, however, need to clarify one thing quite urgently. He rang Jim:

"Killer. Long time no see? How's Margaret? I hope you're taking good care of that lovely lady?"

"I am Jim. Tell me, have you spoken to Moss recently?"

"Yes, earlier this evening. Why what's up?"

"A change of plan Jim. Can you return the urn but don't ask Mrs Watkins any questions, just say you found it and leave it at that. I'm sure she'll be very grateful. And forget that name which Moss mentioned to you. That's very important. You've never ever heard of them. Understand?"

"Absolutely Boss. Loud and clear."

Michael used his phone while waiting for a train to pass and the level crossing to open.

"How did it go, Michael?"

"Exactly as I hoped it would."

"You're convinced that he will do as you asked and not go to the Press?"

"Yes, I am."

"What are the chances of finding Robin?"

"Now? Virtually nil. He had too long to plan for his disappearance, and we trained him very well. So unless we get incredibly lucky or he slips up, then I'm afraid we won't find him."

"The DNA analysis was clearcut?"

"Yes it was, unfortunately. It was definitely Robin who committed those murders in the 1970's and framed my stepbrother. He also carried out the recent crimes. We can only guess at what else he's done in the intervening years; we'll never know how many victims there are."

"How can he have done this, Michael? One of our own? I just don't understand it. I mean we've had incidents before, even quite major ones, but this? It's an unmitigated disaster, even borderline armageddon! Our enemies are just waiting for an excuse to castrate us. If this gets out, then everyone whose family member committed suicide and failed to leave a note, or who died in an accident, whether or not it was along a canal, will point their fingers at us!!"

"Maybe if we ever find Robin we can ask him why. What I do know is that he was very unhappy in the last few years before we retired him. My belief is that he actually wants

Krill to go to the Press and expose him in order to denigrate the Service. He knows that if he leaked the information himself then the Media wouldn't believe it, but if Krill went to them it would be an entirely different matter."

"Krill will no doubt get impatient for it to be resolved, so can't we find a convenient body in the meantime? Prove to him that Robin is dead? End of."

"It won't wash I'm afraid, because Robin would be sure to find out and contact Krill again, so we'd lose whatever trust he has in me, and then we'd be 'paddle less' and up the shittiest shit creek. I'll keep Krill sweet somehow in the meantime."

"I only hope you can, Michael. We have the 'DSMA-Notices' ready to serve on the Media, but a lot of good they'll do if he does break ranks. You've definitely ruled out all other options? What about Jo's idea of discrediting Krill, so that if he did say anything to the media, or to anyone else, it could quickly be hidden in a much juicier story? A sex scandal of some kind - the press always like a bit of sleaze. Perhaps if some Category A images were found on his computer going back many years?"

Michael winced at the very thought; how could anyone, even Jo, suggest such a thing?

"I have, yes. It's not what we do, even in extremis. Also Krill doesn't deserve it, not after his years of exemplary service at the Met. And I think he's suffered far too much already because of Robin. What happened to his colleague Moss was bad enough."

"That was Josephine?"

"Yes, out of her misguided loyalty to Robin."

"You know best, Michael. Obviously you'll be keeping a very close watch on everything."

SIX MONTHS LATER

CHAPTER 35

"It's not too bad; probably the best that we could have hoped for really."

"Funny, I thought it would be me saying that to you Boss. I thought I would be the one trying to convince you that it was now time to draw a line under events."

The two men were sitting on a bench not far from Combe Gibbet in Berkshire. Krill had thought it highly appropriate that they should have their conversation out of earshot of anyone, and within sight of the ancient gallows, or at least a more recent replica. When he saw the structure for the first time standing proud on the brow of the hill, Moss found it easy to imagine Robin Butcher strung up and swinging in the breeze, whereas Krill thought it resembled a giant T proclaiming some message to the world - T for Truth? T for Traitor? Possibly T for Terminated?

"So he's definitely dead?" asked Moss.

"Yes Moss, I'm ninety nine percent sure, having seen what I took to be his body in the New York morgue. It was very surreal, just like you see on CSI. The attendant rolled out the gurney and checked the tag, then unzipped the black body bag, and I looked at his face for the first time. I couldn't positively identify him of course because I'd only seen him wearing a mask, but there was no reason to believe it wasn't him. They confirmed to me afterwards that it was definitely him and showed me evidence: fingerprints and DNA. I felt like a celebrity on my trip. I think my companion from the Embassy had been told not to spare any expense - not only the private plane to JFK and being rushed through border control, but the best New York hotel, sumptuous meals - the full treatment. They'd have got tickets for a top Broadway show if the theatres had been open. I suppose they knew that if I'd just seen photos then I might not have been convinced. If it was a hoax then it was a remarkably expensive and elaborate one."

"Well it was the least they could do given all that their ex-employee had put you through."

"Maybe."

"How did you feel when you looked at him?" asked Moss.

"Strangely, I felt a little sad. I suppose it's how you feel whenever you see a dead person, unless you're a psychopath yourself, without emotions or any empathy, like he was. Maybe sorry as well that we wouldn't have our day in court, but we knew that wasn't going to happen anyway."

"But how did he look?"

Krill thought for a moment, recalling the scene.

"Old, ill, pale, very dead. There wasn't the Devil's sign on his forehead, if that's what you're imagining. He didn't look wicked. Any evil which he might have had inside him seemed to have dissipated. He looked very ordinary and just like thousands of older people you meet on the streets every day."

"What did he die of?"

"Officially Covid, but the medical report said that he also had stage 4 cancer, and wasn't expected to live for more than a few weeks in any event. Evidently, one of the reasons for him being in America was to try some new treatments."

"He knew he was dying?" asked Moss.

"Must have done, and for some time according to the doctors. I think it explains why he decided to break cover. At the very least he wanted me to realise that I'd got the wrong man all those years ago. He wanted someone to know what he was and what he'd done."

"So we can definitely close the case?"

Krill laughed, a little bitterly. "Yes we can categorically state that after only 42 years we have without doubt solved the Canal Killings!" He gazed into the far distance. "He sent me one last text, you know. His final words were: ''Twas Murder by Degrees. Goodbye Krill'. Initially I thought it might be the title of an Agatha Christie novel, but then I discovered that it was a line from a poem by Emily Dickinson; one that I wasn't familiar with."

He went on to explain that it was about death, the subject of several of her poems.

"It's not surprising that Emily was interested in death because it was all around her throughout her life: not just her friends and family dying of typhoid or in childbirth, but the thousands killed and maimed in the American Civil War. Her own health was not good so she probably believed that she would die young. As we know the killer was also apparently obsessed with death, which I think is why he liked the poem.

She also wrote several about cats, seeing them as dark animals bringing death to birds and other creatures, and in this one there's a cat playing with a mouse before finally killing it. I wondered if he maybe saw himself as the quiet assassin, and, like a cat, he would catch his victims off guard, and toy with them whenever he had the chance."

"Makes me shiver just thinking about it! We should just be pleased that he's no longer a threat to anyone, however he died."

Moss had brought two bottles of beer, together with glasses knowing that Krill hated to drink out of a bottle. He opened one and poured them each a half measure; the foam rose to the lip before sinking back down again. They took in the magnificent scenery in silence for a while. The only discernible movements were the clouds drifting slowly across the sky, and some blackbirds attempting to see off a hawk.

"It's quite a view from here isn't it? You can see for miles. Probably a strange place to be brought after your execution; to be left hanging there as an example to others, and for the crows to peck."

"Who did they hang from the gibbet?" asked Moss.

"Only two people were ever hanged here, in 1676: a man and a woman who were lovers. They killed the man's wife and son not far from where we're sitting. Believe it or not the first film ever made by John Schlesinger was about their crime and the subsequent trial - it was called 'Black Legend' and made in 1948."

"You've looked it up for my benefit."

"Of course I did, this morning just before you arrived to collect me. I've been trying to improve your education for nearly fifty years now."

"And I've been trying to improve your fishing skills!"

"Touché Moss. Touché!"

CHAPTER 36

Jo felt that she'd had no choice but to tell Michael about the postcards and the parcel which she received during the weeks following her final meeting with Robin. She knew that he would have assumed that she would be forced to do so, so it didn't feel disloyal.

The first postcard was from Peru, the second from Tonga, the third from Moscow, and the fourth from Tibet. She'd been impressed by the unlikely geographical spread of Robin's supposed travels, and had assumed that he'd wanted the others, but not her, to think that he'd first tried to defect to the Russians, and then having failed to get a lucrative enough deal, had eventually crossed the border into China. She knew that Robin was guilty of many things but was not a traitor.

The messages had been unsigned, brief and somewhat inane: 'missing me?', 'weather wonderful', 'food fantastic', and 'hope you're happy'. She thought that even these brief communications would have been examined very carefully for any codes or hidden meanings, and also that embassies and agencies across several continents had no doubt been contacted, airport records checked, and CCTV pored over where it was in place and available.

The parcel had been posted in London and contained a book on Greek Mythology. That had also started a lot of hares running, not only because of the passages which were underlined, and the various comments made by Robin in the margins, but also to ascertain whether there was any possible link between it and the postcards. Did the messages point to particular pages, lines, or words? Even the significance of the alliterations would have been considered: M for missing me, W for weather and wonderful, F for fantastic food, and H for hope and happy. Especially the numbers the letters of the alphabet might refer to, in every possible combination - 13, 23, 6 and 8. All of which no doubt took up hours, even days, of several people's time. Jo knew that if Robin did ever use a code then it would be one that would be virtually impossible to crack, and that it was an insult to him to think that he would utilise anything as simple. It took her a while to realise that MW were Michael's initials, and that FH was probably Robin saying 'Fuck Him!'

They'd not told her any details about his death, only that his body would be returned from New York and interred without ceremony somewhere in the UK. She was reasonably confident that she would eventually find out where he'd been buried and be able to visit his grave. Did she actually believe that he was dead? No, not one hundred percent. They'd been so close that she'd assumed that she would feel something if and when it happened - a sudden shudder or sense of loss. But nothing like that had occurred, which made her wonder. Had

Robin somehow fooled them or had they performed some well rehearsed charade in order to fool Krill? Of the two possibilities, the latter one seemed the more likely.

The well thumbed book was eventually returned to her, and she had quickly read it from cover to cover, but of course concentrated on the pages turned down by Robin and the numerous highlighted paragraphs. He'd obviously been very interested in Greek gods, especially the Fates - the Moirae or Moirai. She'd not known the details about them beforehand, even that there were three: Clotho who spun the thread of life, Lachesis who measured it and allotted time to someone, and Atropos who cut the thread and ended a person's life. In the margin Robin had neatly annotated in tiny writing: 'logically I am like Atropos because I kill, but then I also determine how long someone lives, so possible aspects of Lachesis?' He'd carried on with his thoughts at the bottom of the page: 'More important than the Fates? They influence one life at a time, whereas my killings affect many simultaneously. Also they didn't weave themselves permanently into someone's life and death.' A colleague had subsequently written in red ink next to that comment: 'signs of megalomania/God complex?' Jo in turn had found an old, still usable bottle of Tipp-Ex and obliterated the offending remark.

She still had sufficient influential friends both inside the organisation and externally to guarantee that her links to Robin would not permanently damage her career, and after all, Michael and other senior members of staff, right up to the very top, had trusted Robin and believed in him for virtually his entire career and in some cases beyond it. And she was pretty certain they would have continued to do so had not Robin himself, for some unfathomable reason, wanted the cat let out of the bag. Perhaps the intrepid and unrelenting sleuth might have some answers, but would Krill agree to meet her? Maybe one day she would see?

Perhaps if she did eventually replace Michael, as Robin had believed, she could do some more digging for the truth herself? It was not wise to do so just yet. She was very patient; it was something else that Robin had taught her.

Enough reminiscing, she thought. Jo took the last piece of pizza from the box at her feet and resumed her watch of the London street below. Everything seemed normal. Nothing to report, as the previous occupant of the chair had told her, and the others before him. But she sensed that something was about to happen.

After he returned from his trip to the US, Krill had also begun to wonder about events, especially whether Robin had actually succumbed to the virus, or whether it and the cancer diagnosis could be false trails? Might he have been 'played' one final time? Again it seemed almost too neat, too perfect, too good to be true, that the serial killer had succumbed to Covid19. While almost certain that his nemesis was actually dead, he remained highly suspicious about the circumstances. Was his cover blown while he was being treated for cancer in a New York hospital? Had Margaret been right all those months ago, when she'd speculated about the pandemic being the optimum time to slip a body through the system, with few questions being asked? But maybe he'd read one too many spy novels!

He knew that he could never express any thoughts or concerns he might have about Robin's death to any living soul, never mind start asking questions. Michael's advice to him when he was being dropped off from the airport, was, as he put it: 'a word to the wise John, best forget everything you know or think you know about my cousin. Probably not a good idea to even speak his name out loud, never mind talk about him to anyone else. I'm going to pretend that he was never born, and I would encourage you to do the same.'

Krill suspected that he remained on some Whitehall list of people who presented a risk to National Security. He also knew that he had to take great care with all future searches on the Internet. He'd so far resisted the temptation to try to find out about the people listed in the obituaries which Robin had left for him at the twin's murder scene. They were the only other potential victims that he knew of, and he wished that he could at least speak to the relatives and check the police reports, even though doing so would no doubt be a complete waste of time. It was like a terrible itch which he could never scratch.

He hadn't heard back from the researcher at the BBC, and had been tempted to ring her to find out if they had decided whether or not to make a programme about the Canal Killings. Once he'd even started to dial the number, then he'd thought some more about it and how it might be perceived as crossing a line? Anyway, how could anyone make a programme about those murders without exposing the real truth? At the very least there would be speculation about who the killer might have been if Crow was innocent, and they would want to interview him and ask his opinion. It would be a media minefield. Lately, he'd even begun to suspect that the BBC had never rung him, and that it had been another of Robin's ploys to stimulate a reaction from him. If so it had worked.

Krill opened his phone and read again the lengthy missive Robin had sent him, he assumed from the US shortly before his death:

'In my darkest moments I wonder if any of it was worthwhile? The killings, the subterfuge, even meeting you? The pandemic has made me question whether my exploits had any real meaning? How can any serial killer, even one as successful and prolific as myself, ever hope to compete with the virus's randomness and extreme pervasiveness? I could kill hundreds now and no one would notice; especially not here in the US, where middle-aged men are dropping like flies! There wouldn't be any obvious impact from my actions. It would be like tossing a stone into the raging sea!

Unlike the Canal Killings all those years ago, Krill. Those murders had ripples which went on and on, perhaps even until the present, didn't they? One thing you may not have realised, is that you forced me to change tack. I had to abandon my MO of killing one or two a year on the canals of Old England,

337

because you'd caught the killer, hadn't you, so they had to stop. I had to try other methods, and actually became excited at the prospect of branching out. So much so, that I doubled, redoubled, quadrupled even quintupled my efforts! Think about all those extra people I killed Krill, because of you 'solving' the Canal Killings! Funny that isn't it! But maybe you can't see the funny side? I always did worry about your sense of humour.

Yes, the pandemic is a bit of a disaster in more ways than one. But hey ho, nil desperandum as they say! Perhaps when things return to normal I'll take on an apprentice, someone who can carry on my work when the time comes? That's a very intriguing idea, isn't it! I bet you hadn't thought about that had you? A follower, an acolyte? Just when people start to believe that their fathers, uncles, and older brothers are safe, something untoward and unexplained might happen to them? Perhaps, completely out of the blue, they commit suicide? However, I shouldn't be presumptive. Maybe he or she who follows in my footsteps will wish to focus on an entirely different client group to the one I chose? Hopefully not prostitutes or children, those wells have already been tainted, but maybe the Millennials or Generation Z should take a turn? I don't want to be dogmatic, let's hear what they have to say! However, on reflection, could a female follower do what I have done? Doesn't it require a strength which few possess? Not just of will and determination, but also a physical strength? We shall see.

I have to say Krill, that I am more than a little disappointed in you! Not in your efforts as a policeman - your

338

skills in detection are superb. Nor is it your intelligence or powers of deduction - you were a very worthy opponent, almost my equal, and I knew you wouldn't be fooled by my little theatrical efforts with the twins. They and the others were just 'dramatis personae', whereas you Krill were never a pawn or a piece of the jigsaw. You were always similar to myself - the puppeteer pulling strings, the author deciding the fate of his characters, the overseer of events, the artistic director of a drama.

It's in the role I gave you as whistleblower where you have failed me; not met my expectations. I suppose it was inevitable that you would be silenced. But never forget those I chose to kill Krill, and hopefully, when the dust has settled, when Michael and the others have long since departed this earth, there might be an opportunity to tell the truth? Finish those memoirs Krill! Tell it exactly as it was. Leave the manuscript somewhere safe for the next generation. It's those who follow in our footsteps who really matter, those who are left behind when we are gone, isn't it? Think about that Krill; focus on those people.

Here's some final thoughts about a title for your memoirs: 'Silent Killer' may be apt because there were no screams, no crunching of bones, no gunshots, not even a last whimper from my victims, or a loud splash as I popped them into the canal! But perhaps Silent Killer sounds too much like the virus sweeping the globe? 'Canal Killer' is too limiting, restrictive; it doesn't do either of us justice, because those murders were only the start of our very long and varied careers. 'Secret Killer' - now I think that title has its merits, *especially as 'secret' can apply in more ways than one, can't it? Or perhaps 'Murder by Degrees'? Is that too ostentatious, erudite, or enigmatic for your readers? I'll leave you to choose.*

Goodbye Krill, or is it au revoir once more?'

Krill hoped that Robin had died well before he got the chance to train a successor. During his thirty five years in the police force he'd visited many gruesome crime scenes and interviewed the very dregs of society, but those experiences had not adequately prepared him for this last, and hopefully final, tussle with evil. On several occasions as a policeman he'd been offered counselling, but had always refused it, believing that he could cope quite well on his own. But this time felt different, probably because it had also been very personal, so that he felt that he might need to seek some help.

Robin was both a puzzle and a puzzler. Even dead, the man was creating his ripples, as he called them. Was he insane? He was almost certainly a psychopath, and as Dr Knox had said, probably obsessed with death in all its forms. He was no doubt deeply affected as a teenager by his father's suicide, but, thought Krill, many children who lose a parent in equally tragic circumstances go on to have very worthwhile lives, as do lots of those who are brought up in care.

He knew that he would never get even close to understanding how Robin's mind had worked, particularly the various contradictions. On the one hand he had seemed driven by a desire to outwit Krill time and time again, in order to prove that he was the better man. While at the same time,

Robin also wanted him to see through the deceit, discover the truth, and expose him and the people he thought were complicit in his crimes. Similarly, he had wanted to stay hidden and out of sight but also needed proper recognition of his skill as a murderer. Lastly, while he showed no remorse or empathy for his victims and their families, he always wanted it to be a painless death. Could it have been a form of split personality? Were there two or more Robins competing for attention? One totally evil and the other still having some vestiges of humanity? One a ruthless professional killer; the other an insecure individual trapped in his adolescent past, and still seeking a lost father's love? Krill did not know enough about such things to be able to make a judgement or reach any firm conclusions.

He'd finally got up the courage to go to see his neighbour and had been very surprised by what he'd found. Not only were there embarrassing elements of hero worship and effusive thanks for what he'd done, the family seemed somehow to be in a better place than previously. Richard explained that he'd always hated his job but had gone into financial management to please his father. He now had the perfect excuse to stop and try something else. There also seemed to be a great deal of affection between the couple - lots of smiles, soothing words, and hand holding. Maybe it had always been there and Krill had never seen it, or maybe Richard's wife was enjoying her new role as carer and person in charge? They were very excited at the prospect of buying a house near to her parents, so obviously Michael appeared to have kept his side of the bargain.

Richard had told him some more about the conversations he'd had with his captor, and specifically about what Robin had said regarding Peter Crow - how his life might have been both prolonged and made more rewarding because he'd spent it locked up. Krill was shocked by the idea that he and Robin had somehow done the innocent man a favour. He believed very much in freewill, and that Crow had been denied the right to choose his own destiny. Maybe he would have died an early death, maybe not. Maybe he'd have continued to live a relatively destructive life, maybe not. Or maybe he would have somehow found a way out of his predicament, stopped drinking, and got a rewarding job? And maybe he might still have become a Buddhist? No one would ever know. It was all idle speculation, but in any event Krill still found himself saddened more than anything by what had happened to the poor man, and couldn't entirely shift the guilt that he felt about it from his shoulders.

However, it was as he was leaving that he got the biggest surprise of all, because at the door 'Mrs Honey' had stopped him, and said that she hoped he wouldn't mind but they'd finally got round to registering the baby's name, and had decided to call him 'Johnnie', in recognition of him saving her husband's life. She'd explained that of course Arch still called the baby William, but eventually he would get used to Johnnie's new name. Krill had been gobsmacked and quickly escaped before he could be asked to be the child's Godfather!

Robin was right, in many ways telling the whole truth would be both cathartic and make his memoirs more readable; possibly even a bestseller. Perhaps it would be OK to write them if he was very careful, and made sure that no one else, not even Moss, could read them until the time was right? After all, only he had signed the Official Secrets Act, not his children or grandchildren, and they couldn't threaten him with prosecution forever, could they? Was it a risk he was prepared to take? Absolutely!

He was so engrossed in his thoughts that he didn't hear Margaret come up behind him, and the first that he knew she was there was when she kissed him on the back of his neck and put her arms around him.

"Darling, please stop looking at your silly phone and computer, and come through to the other room." She nibbled his ear. "I am so lonely there all by myself, and Strictly Come Dancing is about to begin."

He stifled a sigh and stood up. Being with her, having a normal life together, doing simple things like watching TV, were all no doubt helping him to cope with his own demons, and for that he was very grateful. He tried never to think that Robin had also been instrumental in bringing them back together.

They'd recently agreed on several compromises. She would watch Inspector Montalbano with him and he would watch Strictly with her, and they would each separately watch their recordings of Call the Midwife and Scandinavian crime dramas. She would do the cooking in her own house and he would prepare all the meals for them at the cottage. They would go to Poland once a year, and have a second holiday somewhere else where they'd both never been before. She had wanted them to be together all the time whereas he preferred some of the time, so they'd settled on 'most of the time', which meant seven or eight days a month apart when they could see family and do other things, including the occasional fishing trip.

He knew that she still hankered after them getting married and he supposed that if there was little or no choice, then he might, if it was that or lose her, possibly sometime in the future, when it seemed right, agree to a short civil ceremony without any fuss or family present. He could almost hear Moss chuckling away to himself in the distance.

It was during the 'dance off' that Krill had his epiphany. His throat went dry, a shiver ran down the length of his spine, and a cold sweat sprang from his forehead. How could he have been so stupid! Even a rookie cop straight out of police college would have realised that it didn't add up. Stupid! Stupid! Stupid! It shouldn't have taken the killer's words to make him realise; it should have been obvious even to an old addled fool like him. He forced himself to wait until the programme ended before checking the message again to see if he was right; he didn't want to alarm Margaret.

"Just need the toilet, darling."

As soon as he'd locked the bathroom door he scrolled through the text again. It was all there in black and white - the key words, they jumped out at him! Especially not having the physical strength, that was the trigger, that's what he should

344

have questioned! How could an old man, and one suffering from cancer, have the strength, the ability, the wherewithal, to overpower a fit young cyclist on a public street in broad daylight, manhandle him into and out of a van, and then lift him over a four foot parapet at the car park? Also how would he be able on his own to kidnap his neighbour and take him to some secret location while he was unconscious and a dead weight? Then, carry him again comatose to a barge? There were enough clues even without Robin's repeated entreaties to him: *'think about my crimes', 'think about them Krill', 'not have the physical strength'.* Also: *'those we leave behind, they're the ones who really matter, aren't they Krill?'.* The ones we leave behind - it was so obvious when he did think about it.

And if it was practically impossible for Robin to have carried out these latest crimes on his own, who had helped him, and where were they now? Was it a man or a woman? Had Robin deliberately ruled out a woman as an acolyte in order to throw him off the scent? It was probably true that a woman would struggle on her own to commit the murders. It was also evident that the person who'd accosted Colin on his bike that day had certainly been a man. But acting together, Butcher and a woman, lifting Colin up and throwing him off the multi, carrying their victims to the cellar and to the barge, that would certainly work. Krill had another horrible thought: could there have been more than one accomplice?

Had the text also been a warning for Krill to be on his guard, because there was another killer or killers out there, left behind? Persons unknown who were no doubt younger, fitter, stronger, and possibly even more dangerous than Robin had been? No, it didn't bear thinking about, but that was exactly what he had to do, and fast!

The really unforgivable thing was that he'd thought about an accomplice before hadn't he? When he'd wondered how Robin had known about his trip to the hospital that day to see poor Crow. He'd thought that perhaps the killer had had someone there watching and waiting for him to visit the dying man. He'd let his preconceptions take over, because he'd always assumed that the Canal Killer had acted alone. He'd always seen Crow, and latterly Robin, as a lone wolf. He shook his head and swore under his breath, even more angry with himself. He rang Moss.

"What's up Killer?"

"We need to talk. Can you get here as soon as possible? Bring an overnight bag. I'll make some excuse to Margaret about your flat being repaired. No, we've used that one before. I'll think of something."

Moss was surprised because his old Boss sounded quite flustered, and that wasn't like him.

"OK, will do. But what about Covid? Doesn't it break the rules?"

"Bugger the rules Moss! We need to get our thinking hats on! There's no time to lose. I can't tell you any more on the phone, just get here as soon as you can! Oh and bring that revolver of yours, we may need it."

That last remark really got Moss worrying. He started throwing things into a holdall in a panic.

CHAPTER 37

He'd been told in no uncertain terms that Krill was 'off limits', not to be touched. Never, ever. Krill belonged to Robin, and only to him, he'd made that very clear. He would have to be satisfied with the disgrace and ruination of Krill's career, that's what Robin had said, and the fact that he could no longer take any credit for what had happened all those years ago, for solving the canal murders. That should be sufficient. 'I need him, battered and bruised but still fighting fit. He's a key part of my plans. So it's his reputation or nothing' was the way Robin had put it. He'd gone further and said that no one close to Krill could be targeted. Certainly not that smirky faced ex-sergeant, or the foreign whore!

But ridicule and loss of public esteem were not enough; nowhere near enough - he wanted much more. He wanted Krill to wish that he'd never stepped foot in Hampshire, never become a policeman, in fact never been born!

He'd been scared of Robin right from the first moment they'd met. It wasn't just his weird eyes, pale almost transparent like those of a predator; it was his whole demeanour - his aura was all wrong as his mum would say. He leaked malice and poison like a broken sewer pipe.

But Robin was no longer around, was he? He hadn't heard anything from him now for months. He'd said he was going away, but not told him where. He'd said that they would probably never see one another again, and that had come as both a surprise and an immense relief. He'd known of course that Robin was ill, seriously ill. He tried to hide it but it was obvious. His mother would have said that he had the smell of death about him, and not only because of his many victims. His mother had a lot of sayings. Never say never was another one. Which was the stronger emotion - his hatred of Krill or his fear of Robin? He had to admit that it was definitely the latter. If only he could be sure that Robin was dead.

The problem was that Krill wasn't just any member of the general public was he? And so if something did happen to him - if he disappeared or died - it would be reported in the media, and almost certainly Robin would find out. Even an 'accidental' death would bring down Robin's wrath; a suicide even more so. Even if he had nothing at all to do with Krill's demise he risked a maniacal Robin bearing down on him and demanding answers!

Unless Robin was dead, then he would be safe. Probably. But perhaps Robin had some sort of contingency in place for even that eventuality? Could there be others watching over Krill? He couldn't completely ignore that possibility. So that even from beyond the grave he might find some way, someone, to punish him if he stepped out of line? The only good thing was that if that happened then at least his last vision on earth wouldn't be of those terrible eyes!

Perhaps he could try something which stopped short of the ultimate penalty, to see if Robin reacted? An accident which resulted in injury; not too serious but enough to put him in hospital? He warmed to the idea of a severe beating which he could administer himself, and visualised Krill with several cracked ribs, a damaged spleen, and a broken nose. That should get in the papers: 'Ex Chief Inspector Krill mugged!'; he could see the headlines. And if Robin did react, then it would probably only be with a 'like for like', wouldn't it? He wouldn't get someone to throw him off a multi would he? Probably not; and he would accept the risk of a broken arm or his car being torched, if it meant that he could finally get his revenge.

Testing the water first would be one way to do it, probably the safest in some ways but not others. What if he got arrested before he had the chance to finish it? He definitely didn't want to go back to prison. He had to end it once and for all, lance the boil which had grown and grown, and that meant not being caught by Robin or the police before he could finally do so.

The fact that he'd been caught committing a crime was one of so many differences between himself and Robin. He was pretty sure that he wouldn't have been Robin's first choice as an accomplice; that he wouldn't have been in his top ten or even his top one hundred. Robin didn't select him because of his skills or intelligence, or because he could see parallels between the two of them - a younger version, a rough diamond that he could cut and polish. None of that was true. Robin may have talked about him following in his footsteps but deep down they'd both known that it was all just words spoken to encourage him. No, Robin chose him because of who he was, not what he was or what he could become.

He knew that he wouldn't have passed many of the tests Robin might hypothetically have set for an apprentice: stealth, patience, evil intent, an ability to carefully plan and work out the finest details, a need to kill, intense cruelty, an enjoyment of the act itself, a desire to toy with the victims and their families. He possessed none of those attributes, or few of them in any great measure. He suspected that he also lacked the necessary intelligence; he wasn't thick but no one would ever describe him as clever or even 'bright'.

What did he have? Strength - yes, which Robin had needed because his own was failing. A huge chip on his shoulder - yes, that was one important thing they shared. A latent desire for vengeance which Robin had all too easily awakened - yes, the two of them definitely had that in common.

Perhaps if Robin had had the time to teach him, things might have been different. Perhaps if he could have spent months or ideally years watching and learning the craft of a serial killer, then he might possibly have been able to become a pale shadow of what Robin was. But time was in short supply; Robin had been in a rush.

The truth was that he didn't really have the stomach for it either. Fortunately he'd not been tested, because Robin had insisted on being the executioner. He wasn't sure what he would have done if Robin had told him to push that guy over the edge and watch him plummet to the ground. He might have been able to tip him over, but he would have had to close his eyes in the final seconds before he'd hit the pavement. He couldn't have leant over the parapet and enjoyed it, as Robin had done. The barge was a bit different; he could easily have placed the petrol soaked cloths on the worktop and lit the candle, had Robin let him.

Robin had said many things to him in the weeks they had collaborated - 'know your strengths and weaknesses' had been an important one. Perhaps that was an entreaty he could follow? He knew that because of his inabilities he would only ever get one chance to kill Krill, so he had to make it work. Maybe it could be done in a way that even surpassed Robin's achievements, after all he'd only killed them one at a time hadn't he? He'd never attempted several at once. And Robin had always been invisible, under the surface, unknown, and unseen. Whereas with Krill he could do so much better, make something really spectacular happen; something to grab the headlines; something to make Robin spin in his grave, if he was already there! And if he wasn't, if he was still alive, something which would also mean that Robin couldn't take his revenge on him for Krill's death? He smiled as the last remnants of doubt and uncertainty left him. He had a plan. He knew exactly what to do. He quickly packed a holdall of his own.

CHAPTER 38

Krill didn't believe in a sixth sense. He didn't really even believe in his gut's ability to know when something was right or wrong; and he didn't try to follow it, despite occasionally speaking as if it was some augury. He may have believed in instincts because they at least had some basis in science. What he believed in most was hard work and the power of intellect, not some magic or even luck.

So it wasn't a feeling which woke him; not that he was sleeping very soundly after his conversations with Moss. It wasn't even a noise. He'd become accustomed to the strange creaks, the cracking, the mechanical tick tocks, ingrained in the wood and paraphernalia of the old Victorian house. He'd eventually become used to the constant traffic from the busy road outside and the fairly frequent police sirens. His brain could now shut all those things out.

It was a smell.

At first he couldn't quite place it, couldn't identify it, but he knew that it was alien and shouldn't be present. Eventually, as he lay there next to Margaret, he came to associate it with

Moss. That was his deduction: it reminded him of Moss. It was just the hint of a cigarette, like the odour he could sense when Moss was near him and not even smoking. Could it be Moss? Unlikely, because he was in one of the guest bedrooms, one floor up, probably with his door shut, and most certainly not smoking inside the house, because he would never dare do that - not in Krill's cottage and definitely not at Margaret's!

It was so trivial and innocuous that Krill didn't even think about waking Margaret, or taking any precautions - not that he had any weapons to hand. As he was now awake he decided to have a pee, and on his way to the toilet he would see if he could make any sense of it. Maybe Moss was smoking in his room after all? He would go and check.

The smell was definitely stronger on the landing. He knew that Moss had a habit of smoking on the toilet, both at the station when they'd worked together, and most likely in his flat. He'd been unfortunate enough to have experienced the noxious combination of smoke and farts on more than one occasion after following Moss into a cubicle. But as he stood there, carefully taking aim, he could only smell talc and perfume. He didn't flush because it was the middle of the night.

When he climbed the stairs to the next floor, he saw that the door to the room which Moss was using was open and the light was on, but that didn't alarm him, in fact it made sense. 'Bloody hell Moss', he thought, as he crossed the threshold, 'why are you smoking in your room and being so blatant about it?'

He saw Moss sitting on the bed wearing boxers and a tee shirt. He wasn't smoking, yet the atmosphere in the room was heavy with the fug and stink of cigarettes.

"Come in Krill, and close the door behind you. Moss and I have been having a quiet chat. We were just about to get you. Why don't you join him on the bed? And please, no sudden movements."

Krill looked at the unknown man sitting in an armchair in the corner. He had a lit cigarette in one hand and a revolver with a silencer attached in the other. He couldn't be certain, but it looked like the gun Robin had used when he'd threatened him at the hospital. He wondered where Moss had put his own revolver? Maybe it was still in his bag in the wardrobe, or in the drawer of his bedside cabinet? But even if it was just a few inches away, under the pillow, he wouldn't be able to grab it, aim and fire, before being shot himself.

He did exactly as he was told.

One thing the stranger had learned from Robin was about games, and the importance of playing them with your victims when you had the opportunity, and this certainly was one. A degree of repartee was also nice:

"Perhaps if you can tell me who I am I won't kill you Krill. Or maybe I will only kill you and no one else? Perhaps I'll only kill the two of you and not your lady friend? Then again, maybe I'll still kill everyone even if you're clever enough to guess my identity?"

Both Krill and Moss had similar thoughts at the same time: this one's as crazy as Butcher!

"You're an associate of Robin Butcher."

"Yes I am Krill, or to be more precise - I was. But that's not what I meant. That's not sufficient, not by a long chalk. However, I'm a fair minded person, perhaps it's too much to expect you to know precisely who I am without a little help. What about if I give you some hints, but extract a price for each one? Say I put a bullet into Moss each time? Nowhere fatal, we don't want it to be too quick, do we? In his arms or legs? Do you want a hint or two Krill?"

"Why don't you stop the fucking mind games and just do what you've come here to do!!"

"Tut tut Moss! Temper temper!"

Krill looked pleadingly at Moss. He didn't think it was a good idea to make this lunatic any more fired up and angry than he already was. No, he definitely didn't want hints, not at that price, but was there another way?

"Rather than giving me hints, will you answer my questions without shooting Moss?"

The stranger thought about it as he stubbed out the cigarette on the arm of his chair. "OK. Ask."

"We've established that Robin chose you as his accomplice, the question is why?"

"Why indeed?"

"We believe that Robin worked for the security services, so it's possible that he knew you in that capacity, that you were a colleague?"

"Wrong."

"No, I didn't think so. Another possibility is that he chose you at random but that wouldn't fit his character; he always had a reason for doing everything."

"Go on."

"Quite often criminals meet one another in prison. Have you ever been to prison?"

"Yes."

"But that doesn't help because I doubt Robin ever had a criminal record. Of course, he could have met you via a third party, someone who knew him and had been in prison with you? Peter Crow was in prison, perhaps you knew him?"

"Wrong again. This is getting a little boring Krill, and rather futile. Even if we had met in prison, or I did know Crow, how would that help you? You don't have the time to check criminal records. I suggest you hurry up with your deductions before I decide to put one in Moss just to motivate you."

"OK, I'll be quick. You obviously have a connection to Robin, most likely linked to his past. And we can deduce from your presence here and the threats, that you have a grudge against myself, and possibly Moss. Also I don't believe that Robin sent you to kill me. That's not his style, to send someone else. And he had plenty of opportunity to kill me himself, had he wanted to. So this is about you, not about Robin. Perhaps you could be related to one of his victims, someone he killed because I failed to catch him all those years ago? Did he kill your father? Is that why he chose you?"

"No, but you're on the right track. My father is important."

Moss was once more impressed with Krill, both with his powers of deduction and with his calmness. How could he, or anyone, think in such a situation? He knew what he was doing: keeping the lunatic busy chatting and not shooting them was at least something. But it wasn't a hostage situation was it, where it might be useful to try to establish rapport, so he didn't know what good it would do? Perhaps Krill wanted to show one last time how clever he could be, or maybe he just wanted to know who the hell was threatening to kill them and why? Possibly he even believed this guy when he said he wouldn't kill Margaret? Moss was pretty sure that he definitely intended to kill Krill and himself, not least because they could identify him, but maybe they could save her? Moss looked carefully at their assailant: late forties or early fifties, unshaven, scruffy both in the way he was dressed and hairstyle, possible West Country accent, typical loser. He even looked familiar, had they met before? Then it came to him. It was probably his one and only chance to outdo Krill! It fitted. He even looked like his dad. But Krill still got there first.

"You're Peter Hopkin's son. Inspector Hopkins' son."

They could both tell from the look on the man's face that he was impressed and that they were right.

"Yes I am, and you killed him Krill! You were responsible for his death, just as much as you would have been if you'd driven his car off the road that day forty years ago."

Krill nodded; even smiled slightly. "That's why Butcher chose you, because your father had committed suicide just like his, and because he knew that he could use your anger and resentment to good effect, to get you to help him."

"OK, that's enough chat, let's go downstairs. Time to end this charade." He stood up. "Now we're going to do this very carefully and very slowly."

He threw two pairs of handcuffs onto the bed. He thought that of the two men, Moss was the stronger, more dangerous, more resourceful, and therefore more likely to try something.

"Hands behind your back Moss - Krill put them on him. Now put your own on. Good. Stand up, slowly now. You go first, Krill, and if you make a noise or try anything, then Moss gets it."

The procession descended the stairs. Krill couldn't help glancing into the bedroom as they passed it, hoping to catch a glimpse of Margaret, to check she was OK.

"Into the kitchen." He whispered. "Sit down at the table."

Moss saw a rucksack on the floor. The man took some restraints out of it and secured their legs and arms to the chairs. He couldn't see behind him, but knew that just for a moment he must have put the gun onto the floor. He was tempted to act but it was too little time and too risky. Then the man sat down opposite them, took a bottle of whisky out of the bag, drank greedily from it, and lit another cigarette.

"Isn't this cosy!" He laughed. "I would offer you a drink but you seem to be too tied up for a tipple!"

"Do you have your van nearby? I assume you have a van? If so, Moss and myself will willingly go with you, wherever you want. We won't struggle. Why not take us for a ride? Maybe back to Hampshire where all this started? Surely that's appropriate? Won't that be better for you? More just?"

"Are you up to something Krill? Hoping to get a chance to overpower me outside or on the road? Or are you just wanting to get me away from your girlfriend? If we did leave then surely we would have to take her with us? It would be so impolite not to. But no, we're not going anywhere. Here will do very nicely."

Moss flexed his back and leant forward, stretching the plastic tie attaching his wrists to the back of the chair, but it was too strong and tight. Would it break or would the wood snap if he pulled hard enough? He was pretty sure that he could smash the chair against the fridge or the cooker, given half a chance, and get himself free and able to at least stand up and move. He decided that it was their best hope if the madman went upstairs to get Margaret.

"Stop moving Moss. Don't worry, you won't be sitting there long enough to get cramps. A few more drinks and this fag, and we'll be done."

"You said you wouldn't harm Margaret."

"I only said I might not. I suppose there's a slim chance she might survive the explosion." He took another large drink. "But probably better for her if she doesn't."

That got Krill and Moss thinking. Did the guy have explosives in the bag?

"Which is best, Krill - for her to die quickly in her sleep, or be dragged from the rubble and die later? Or be so badly injured that her life is never the same? 'Life changing injuries' isn't that what they call it? Can you picture her in a wheelchair or as a paraplegic with twenty four hour care? It's quite appropriate really. My father's body was so badly smashed up by the crash and the explosion when his car hit the floor of the quarry, that there wasn't very much left for us to bury. And don't either of you dare to say it! That you're sooo sorry he died, because I know you weren't even sorry back then when it happened! I don't want to hear your bogus, trumped up apologies! Of course, you could try a little pleading? That would be music to my ears, and who knows, if you grovelled enough I might change my mind and let her go?"

By now the bottle was half empty, and the intruder was starting to slur his words. Moss looked at Krill, all the time calculating their chances. As if reading their minds, the man put the cork back in and stood up. Without another word he crossed to the cooker, turned on all the gas rings, and opened the oven door.

"I don't think natural gas is poisonous any more is it? But then again, maybe we will fall asleep before the house blows up? Maybe it will be a painless death after all, just like all of Robin's murders were. If so, it's far more than you deserve."

Moss could see the panic on Krill's face as the hiss seemed to get louder and louder. What would ignite it? Another cigarette or would something as mundane as the lightbulb burning overhead be sufficient? He became fuzzy headed and nauseous from the smell. It reminded him of trips to the dentist as a child when they had still used gas as an anaesthetic. The room began to spin, slowly at first, then faster and faster. He felt as if he was falling into a deep dark hole.

CHAPTER 39

Krill didn't want to open his eyes because of his blinding headache. The lights looked so bright through his closed lids, as if he was about to be interrogated, or was trapped inside one of those fiendish contraptions in a tanning studio! He felt like he had the flu. Everything ached. Even taking short breaths was painful. He knew he was lying down, but had no idea where he was. He could smell disinfectant. He opened his right eye a fraction. The room seemed very white. He could hear voices and something rattling and clattering nearby, coming closer.

"Good morning Mr Krill. How are you feeling?"

It was a woman's voice. He was pretty sure he'd not heard it before.

"You're a very lucky man and so is your colleague; he's in the room next door. Oh and your girlfriend is fine too. She's outside, waiting to see you, but I wanted a quick word first."

Krill wasn't sure he could speak; his throat felt like he'd been a lifelong smoker of forty a day. "Wa..water?"

The woman got up and fetched a beaker, before putting it to his lips.

"Is that better?"

He nodded very slightly. "Who…"

"Who am I? You can call me Jo."

"Wha…"

"What happened? Where are you? How did you get here? I suppose those are your next questions, followed by where is the person who assaulted you? Unfortunately he didn't make it. No loss to the world is he? Just be grateful that he won't ever bother you again. Now as for your other questions - apparently someone broke into your friend Margaret's house with the intention of blowing it up! Fortunately, I just happened to be passing, smelt gas, broke in, dragged you and Mr Moss out, and also woke Margaret and got her to safety. I then called an ambulance and the two of you were taken here, to the nearest hospital. Sorry to say that there was an explosion soon after, before I could alert the authorities, and her house is quite badly damaged. It will be some time, probably several months, before she can live there again."

"Thank…"

"No need to thank me, Mr Krill, I only did what any person would have done in the circumstances. No more questions or I think the nurses will be berating me. One thing the doctors did tell me though was that exposure to gas can lead to memory loss, so I wouldn't worry too much if you can't recall many details when the police eventually speak to you. Perhaps that's a blessing in disguise? I'm sure they will be very understanding in the circumstances if you fail to recall events. Shall I send Margaret in? She's very keen to see that you're OK and awake."

Krill nodded again, a little more obviously than before. The woman approached the bed and took his hand, but he was too weak to shake it. It felt ice-cold in his palm.

"Perhaps our paths will cross again one day. From what I've read about you in the papers, I think it would be very interesting if that were to happen."

Krill shivered, and it wasn't because he was cold.

As Jo walked quickly down the corridor, she wondered what Michael would think about her actions? She was certain that, like Robin, he would applaud the rescue, but would believe that her coming to the hospital was extravagant behaviour, unnecessary, a silly risk to take. But then he always had a tendency to be overcautious and sticking to the rules, which Robin had frequently complained about.

Michael would definitely not have sanctioned her final act after she'd got Krill and the other two out of the house. If he'd been there he would have raised his very singed eyebrows in disbelief at the foolhardy and blasé way she'd returned to the kitchen, picked up that tosser's own lighter, and then used it to throw a lit newspaper into the hallway from the street! It had been a very near thing - she'd been blown off her feet by the explosion. She smiled. That had been by far the most exhilarating aspect of the entire adventure! And it had other benefits too, not only removing Robin's troublesome helper, but also ensuring that, with a word here and a word there, he wouldn't be identified and everything would be kept very low profile. All in all, a good night's work. Shame though that Hopkins wasn't older, and had been just a child in the '70's when the Canal Killings happened. He would have been the perfect candidate for drawing a thick line under those murders, and once and for all ending the risk that Robin and the Service could ever be implicated.

Would Michael reprimand her? She thought not. She might even be rewarded if the right people became aware of her actions, because surely now Krill would realise that he owed them; not only her but those she worked for. Hadn't she made it less likely that Krill would want to harm the very organisation which had saved not only him and Moss, but also his lovely girlfriend?

That stupid Inspector's son hadn't been worthy of Robin's attention. She knew why he'd been chosen of course - because of his links to Krill, and also because he was expendable. Robin did so love his 'ripples' from the past affecting the present and the future! He had served his purpose in more ways than one.

She'd been unable to resist visiting Krill, even if he had been only semiconscious and not fully alert. She wanted to see for herself what all the fuss was about; why Robin had been so obsessed with the retired detective. Why he was important; why he mattered so much? And she'd wanted to make him aware of what had really happened, and personally deliver some unspoken messages. Not only - 'you and the public need us', but also 'look what I can do when necessary'. Eventually he would understand and take heed.

As she approached her sports car she hummed a tune, one of Robin's favourites, she recalled. It was 'Wouldn't it be nice?' by the Beach Boys.

CHAPTER 40

Several weeks later, Krill and Moss were sitting once more in the garden of his local pub, enjoying the peace, the sunshine, and the beer, although not necessarily in that order of importance.

"I see you're not smoking, Moss. Have you given up, yet again?"

"I have Killer. Somehow they don't taste right at the moment, not after what happened."

Moss looked at his old boss: the frown lines on his forehead seemed to have deepened significantly in the last few months.

"I know you're still blaming yourself, Killer, and you've probably now added Hopkins' son to the list of those you feel guilty about. You shouldn't. He decided to be led astray by Robin; he made up his mind to try to kill us, and don't forget that he was already a lost cause because it was always going to be a murder suicide. He was never going to walk away from the scene. No one forced him to do any of that."

"He clearly believed I was responsible for his father's death." Krill shook his head in a sad recollection. "We didn't go to Peter Hopkins' funeral, and I didn't enquire about his family. That guy who tried to kill us, his son, I don't even know his first name!"

"We were incredibly busy at the time to worry about any of that. If I remember correctly, we'd just arrested Crow."

"But even so, it shows a lack of respect to a dead colleague."

"You know what I think?" said Moss, "I believe that sooner or later his father would have driven his car off that cliff and into the quarry anyway. The guy was clearly unbalanced; a ticking time bomb. I knew he wasn't right the very first time I met him. I didn't say anything back then, but there were lots of rumours going around, about marital problems, gambling, serious debts, even corruption. You speaking your mind that day may have been what he wrote in his suicide note, but most people wouldn't top themselves because of a disagreement at work, or a clash of personalities, would they? He said what he did because he wanted to get you, not necessarily because even he believed it. I read the coroner's report, Killer. He didn't place any weight on that aspect of the suicide note, but stressed other things, such as the history of depression, not just regarding him, but other members of his family as well. The Chief Constable also said as much to you at the time, didn't he - 'don't blame yourself', or 'you're not to blame'. I was there, I heard him say it. And you know what, if anyone is to blame, it's not you, it's Robin Butcher, for committing those murders. If they hadn't occurred, if he hadn't murdered that man by the canal, then we wouldn't have stepped even one foot into Hampshire."

"All that's probably true, Moss."

"You're damned right it is!" Moss took a large swig of his beer. "You still don't know who that woman was who rescued us?"

"The mysterious Jo? No I don't, not for certain, but it's pretty obvious isn't it? What are the chances of an ordinary member of the public passing by at 4am, and not only smelling gas, but deciding to play the hero rather than just ringing 999, and then managing to break in and get us all out in time? No chance. She was expecting trouble, and was very well trained to deal with it when it happened. Also, the police were incredibly cursory with their enquiries weren't they, like it was a formality and they were just going through the motions. They didn't even ask if we knew the guy or had any idea why he broke in. Nothing was said about any guns found at the scene and why they were there. Very shoddy, unless they were following strict orders not to delve too deeply. She also said some very curious things to me at the hospital, about not remembering what happened, and about the police being very understanding. Joe public wouldn't have made those comments, but Jo Spy or Jo Special Branch would. And there was no mention of you or me by name in the media, only about an unidentified body."

"That's something to be grateful for though, isn't it? You'd already had enough hassle from the press. I'll tell you something else to be grateful for: you thought they might be keeping an eye on you, didn't you, Special Branch and the others? Well, it was a good job really, the way things turned out! By the way, do you think she deliberately left the guy in therc - closing off a loose end? He was someone else who knew what Robin had been up to." Moss had a further horrible thought. "In which case, if she had let matters run their course, just ignored the smell of gas and what was going on, it would have eliminated all the risks of something getting out and becoming public, wouldn't it? If you're right, then you'd think it would be the expedient thing to do, even if there was collateral damage in the shape of Margaret?"

"And you Moss, you would have been an innocent victim too. It was mainly me that they were so concerned about."

"Speaking of Margaret, was she interviewed by the police?"

"Yes, but obviously she couldn't remember anything except being unceremoniously woken up and frogmarched out of her house. She thinks it was a terrible accident, and wants to put all the recent events behind her. Evidently someone in the village who knows her, said that 'trouble usually comes in threes Margaret', and that she's now had her share, actually enough to last a lifetime - the death of her fiancé, then Colin's murder, and now her bloody house blowing up! I think she's looking forward to years and years of good fortune! I hope she never realises that two of the three are because she met me!"

"All my fingers are crossed about that one Boss! How is she settling into life with you in your cottage?"

"Fine. She's decided to completely mollycoddle me, I'm not allowed to lift a finger. Cups of tea in bed, lots of healthy stews, no fish, and steak three times a week!"

Moss laughed.

"The only good piece of news is that the structural survey of her property has come back, and it's not too bad. Lots of internal damage of course, caused by the explosion and fire, but everything can hopefully be fixed within a few months, once the insurance coughs up."

"Sounds like you'll miss her when she leaves."

Krill wasn't sure if that was a statement or a question. He'd already decided that he wouldn't tell Moss that he and Margaret were now unofficially engaged; not until absolutely forced to do so.

"Yes and no. LTA Moss, remember? That's the best arrangement at our age don't you think? By the way, talking about arrangements, she's told me that a friend of hers from the Polish Club wants to meet you."

"Meet me?" Moss looked alarmed.

"Just for a meal. The four of us."

"Couldn't Jim go instead? He loves Polish cuisine."

"No, she's pretty adamant it has to be you. Besides, Jim already has a partner. Evidently this friend of hers is very nice, inside and out, that's what she said. Oh, and Margaret also told me that this lady doesn't drink any alcohol and she's a vegetarian."

Krill enjoyed the look on Moss's face. It was absolutely priceless!

- THE END -

Printed in Great Britain
by Amazon

19153749R00210